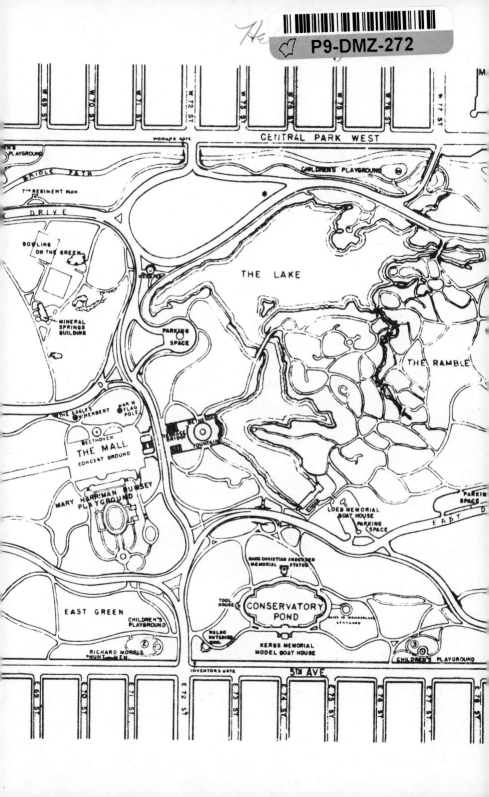

NIGHT OF THE JUGGLER

NIGHT
OF
THE JUGGLER

A NOVEL BY

William P. McGivern

G. P. PUTNAM'S SONS
New York

For Maureen

NIGHT OF THE JUGGLER

1

HIS name was Gus. He had another name, of course, a last name, but sometimes he forgot it. When this occurred, when he was swept by a dreadful and chilling loss of identity, the experience made him as tense as a threatened animal and deepened a redness in his mind that caused him to shake with fury.

When they teased him about this in the fruit and vegetable store he helped keep clean, when the Puerto Rican clerks would laugh at him and say, "Hey, Gus! You Gus who? Gus *who?*" he would avoid their eyes and try to control the trembling in his hands, while wondering in his dim, lacerated mind at their cruelty.

When this happened, when the insolent clerks with their soft eyes and glossy hair and slurred, liquid English grinned at him and teased him, Senor Perez, who owned this decrepit vegetable shop in the South Bronx, would give them angry, warning headshakes, and the clerks would stop smiling and some might even shrug in a gesture that suggested an indifferent contrition, and then they would all return to their work, ripping brown outer leaves from heads of lettuce, watering mounds of green onions and young cabbages,

9

waiting on the Puerto Ricans and occasional blacks who bought their meager orders of fruits and vegetables at Senor Perez's shop in this pocket of decay in New York City.

At these times Gus would go into the back room of the shop, and when no one was looking at him, he would hurry into the alley that ran through an area near 135th Street and St. Ann's Avenue. He was more at home in alleys and in darkness than he was in the shop or in daylight on crowded sidewalks. A tall, huge man, Gus went along the alley with the stalking strides of an animal, at home with the stink of garbage, the slithering sound of rats, and groups of Puerto Ricans in leather jackets bunched ominously at street corners; none of this fetid and potentially dangerous ambiance menaced him; it was not so much that he was confident in this environment, it was rather that he was simply unaware of it.

In the vestibule of the tenement where he lived with Mrs. Schultz in a small rented room, Gus would stare with an annealing sense of impending relief at the dirty oblong cards beneath the mailboxes. When he found Mrs. Schultz's name, he would drop his eyes an inch and there, penciled in below it, was his own name: Gus Soltik. He never received any mail; there was no one to write to him, but it gave him a sense of security to know that his name was written there under the mailbox. He couldn't read his name in a conventional sense, but he had memorized those particular letter shapes and knew the smudged pencil marks meant Gus Soltik.

While he could not make change and had only vague notions of the value of money, he was familiar with the concept of numbers and could easily make his way to the numerically designated streets in the various boroughs of New York City.

Gus Soltik's "thought processes" were unconventional, to put it as simply as possible. He did not "think" in consecutive patterns; it was as difficult for him to string ideas together as it would have been for a "normal" person to enumerate and define the physical objects of his environment without an alphabet. Thus, to "understand" concepts and emotions and things, Gus Soltik required a specific word, which appeared in his mind as clearly as if it were written in chalk on slate. Thus, the word "cage" was his reference for all animals. He had no name, however, for his physical needs. He had no way to get inside himself; he was conscious of his existence as an object, but there was no way he could assess or conceive of Gus Soltik in subjective terms.

He did not know that his odor was rank. He wasn't aware that people on the sidewalks frequently turned to stare after him. He did not understand why it made him feel so desolate and desperate when he forgot his name. It was one of many things he didn't understand, although it worried him the most. He didn't know that his physical strength was as great as the combined strength of several average men. He did not know, for another thing, that the small yellow leather hat he wore above his bulging forehead made him look ridiculous, as if he were a mongoloid child dressed by someone with a malicious sense of humor.

But Gus Soltik knew some things with the instincts of an animal. His eyesight was acute, and his sense of hearing was exceptional; he was always the first to be aware of approaching subway trains, for example, and in the old tenement where he lived, he could track Mrs.

Schultz all through the house by her footsteps, even though she wore soft felt slippers indoors. His sense of direction was impeccable; he could drift through any of the boroughs of New York at any time of the day or night, but when he wanted to return "home," some indicator in his mind pointed straight at the Triboro Bridge in the lower Bronx. He could walk for hour after hour, mile after mile, sometimes breaking into a clumsy, lumbering trot but never feeling tired, never breathing hard.

And one other thing, Gus Soltik knew. He knew that he was thirty years old. His mother had died when he was twenty-five, and after she died, he did something each year, and he had now done it four times. And he would do it again within the next twenty-four hours, a total of five times in all, which made him thirty.

He knew vaguely that it was disloyal to his mother to forget his name. All he had left of her now was one of her dresses, black and shapeless but with a pretty collar made of tiny seed pearls. That dress hung in the small back room he rented from Mrs. Schultz, and with the dress were the dried flowers and the card.

It was all he had left of his mother.

But Gus Soltik, with the instinct of a wild creature, could always sense the approaching anniversary of her death. It was the time of year when the days were darker and shorter and the winds against his bulging forehead and massive hands were streaked with a coldness which would intensify until snow was falling in the streets and the gutters were noisy with the sound of running slush and water. And when it became cold, he listened and watched Mrs. Schultz with the wariness of an animal because the old woman did something each year that told Gus Soltik the exact day his mother had been killed.

On each anniversary of his mother's death Mrs. Schultz paid the priests at the crumbling heap of St. Stanislaus to celebrate a requiem high mass to deliver his mother's soul from all evil and from the torments of hell. She had tried to explain all this to Gus, but he understood nothing but the horror of his mother screaming in some place that raged with fire.

Mrs. Schultz had taken him to the first mass. But he had never gone again; he had been frightened by the three black-clad priests on the altar, and the sound of the vengeful, wrathful music from the choir loft had so terrified him that his heart had thudded and pounded like an imprisoned animal within his massive rib cage. So he had never gone again. But Mrs. Schultz was proud and happy to save her dimes and quarters until she had enough to pay for that dead mass which commemorated the soul of Gus' mother.

When she told him about it, he knew the time was coming; when she waddled off to the church thick with sweaters under her old black coat, Gus Soltik knew for certain it was now time to mark the day of his mother's death.

On an afternoon in the middle of October, Gus Soltik sat in the sunlight of Central Park and looked at little girls playing in the children's zoo at Sixty-sixth Street and Fifth Avenue.

There were blacks and Puerto Ricans and white girls, some running in shrill packs, others accompanied by young mothers or nurses. The sun was warm on the backs of Gus Soltik's hands and warm on his face, and the iron bench he sat on was pleasantly warm, excitingly so, under his heavy, powerful thighs.

It was early afternoon, and the sunlight on this lovely fall day dropped through the tawny crowns of changing maples and elms and struck the worn brick walks and green lawns like a shower of copper pennies. And the sunlight fell on the bare and flashing arms of little girls, brown and white and black, caressing them with a shimmering radiance and transmuting all the various colors of their flesh into tones of glowing gold.

Gus heard the growling of the lions from the big zoo at Sixty-fifth Street. That told him the time. Two thirty. That's when they fed them. The growling that was like distant thunder made him think of Lanny Gruber. Lanny was his friend. Lanny talked slowly to him, and Gus could understand him.

Children were playing ball on the lawn near Gus, their voices a piping counterpoint to the guttural cacophony of the lions. Old men and women sat nearby feeding peanuts to squirrels. Some of them, with tired, sagging faces, stared with wistful hostility at the romping children.

Neatly groomed businessmen crossed back and forth on their way to Fifth Avenue or Central Park West. Gus was not afraid of them, but in some fashion they diminished him, with the arrogant swing of their briefcases, the fact that they seemed to know things. When Gus thought of them sitting in offices and phoning from one city to another (as he believed was possible) to tell people things, it made him feel small and vulnerable. Still, he wasn't afraid of them because he knew they wouldn't hurt him.

Then Gus noticed something that made his big body

14

go tense with fear; a patrolman in a blue uniform was watching him. Policemen would hurt you, he knew. It was his worst fear; not so much being hurt, but knowing no way to make them stop it.

He vividly remembered one of his mother's anniversaries, and a basement with someone his mother had warned him about, teaching her a lesson, feeling strong and excited, when a door was kicked in and they came at him like raging animals, one big with orange-red hair, the other dark with a terrible scar on his cheek, and Gus had seen all this in splintered bars of light coming through the door they had smashed in. They had shouted at him, fury straining their voices, and had fired at him with guns, but with a strength made boundless by terror, Gus had knocked them down and fled from from the basement. Yes, they would hurt you and never stop it, he thought, staring sullenly and fearfully, but from the corners of his eyes, at the young cop in the blue uniform.

Patrolman Max Prima, who stood rocking on his stout boots while watching Gus Soltik, summed up his first impressions of that hulking figure in one word: "weirdo." (Patrolman Max Prima had been named after his great-great-grandfather, Massimo Prima, who had lived in Florence and had been distantly related to one of the ancillary branches of the Medici family; Max Prima had become a welterweight finalist in the Golden Gloves as a result of a thousand fistfights connected with that unwelcome bequest from his great-great-grandfather, which his tough, alley-smart peers in Brooklyn had converted into various adaptations such as "Assimo" or "Masturbatio." After his triumphs in the

Golden Gloves he had had no more fights, but he had become sick of the name Massimo, and despite his mother's tearful remonstrances, he had legally shortened it to Max.)

Patrolman Max Prima was twenty-four years of age. He had become a cop because he admired his uncle, Ernesto, who had been a police officer in the borough of Manhattan and had filled him with stories of historic exploits (largely crap, Max Prima later decided); but there was a primal truth in them which had stirred a romantic streak in his nature, and he had never regretted for an instant buying illusion for reality and putting in for the police department.

Other words were occurring to him as he continued to study Gus Soltik. Hype? No, probably not. Whipdick? Probably. But in the main it was Prima's instinct that told him Gus Soltik was bad news. A wrongo. It was the way he was looking at those little girls in the children's zoo. The fact was, this big, hulking man in the brown turtleneck sweater and silly yellow cap was pretending *not* to look at them. That was what had alerted Max Prima's interest. He was learning to trust his instincts, as Uncle Ernesto had told him to. It was a thing, a fact, a vector, that veteran cops depended on with an almost implicit faith but that few of them could describe with any accuracy. Uncle Ernesto would say, "You see a woman sitting in a window all week. All month. One day the window is closed. Better check it out. . . . A family without children taking four quarts of milk a day . . . the price of hash dropping . . . you keep your eyes open, you see and hear things like that, you check 'em out, or buck the information up where action can be taken on it."

16

Patrolman Prima sauntered toward the bench on which Gus Soltik was sitting, but while he was still twenty yards away, the big man looked at him closely with glazing, narrowing eyes, then stood and walked with heavy, lumbering strides along the curving pathway that would bring him out to Fifth Avenue in the upper Sixties.

Max Prima stopped. So what could he do? Collar him for what? Read him his rights? Slate him at the 22d Precinct on Transverse Three? On what charge? Because I got a funny feeling in my gut that he's trouble? Because he looks sick? He could imagine what the sergeant would say to that.

But because Max Prima was an excellent young cop and would one day be an even better one, he took a pencil and notebook from an inner pocket of his tunic and wrote a careful description of the big man in the brown turtleneck sweater. He wrote:

"Subject: Caucasian, early thirties, six-three, two-twenty or more, moves like he's fast and strong. Thick blond hair, grows ragged down his neck. Low, round forehead, bulging. Eyes set wide apart. Small nose and mouth, big chin, thick neck. At about 2:30 P.M., October 14, subject was wearing a brown sweater, denim work pants, and Wellington boots with stacked heels. Small yellow leather cap. No cause to interrogate or arrest. But subject was staring at young girls in the children's zoo in a manner that looked suspicious and unhealthy. Seemed to have nothing else to do with his time, but took off when I started walking toward him."

Max Prima decided that the best thing he could do was to get this report over to Lieutenant Vincent Tonnelli's Special Unit, which had been set up a couple of months ago, with headquarters at the 19th Precinct on East Sixty-seventh Street. (Rumor had it that Gypsy Tonnelli's assignment came not only from the chief of detectives and the commissioner, but from the man in Gracie Mansion himself. But only after the Gypsy had fought for it.)

The Gypsy would know what to do with it. If anybody could stop the Juggler from making it five in a row, it was that legendary Sicilian cop, Lieutenant Vincent "Gypsy" Tonnelli.

As he circled back toward the arsenal and the lion house, the words blazing like fire in Gus Soltik's mind was "walls." This word was Gus Soltik's mnemonic unit to embrace concepts of fear and uncertainty and unfairness. It warned him that he was being threatened or that a trap was waiting to spring shut on him. The cop frightened him. But it wasn't fair. The cop was wrong. Gus wasn't planning to teach a lesson to any of those girls. He knew the one he would teach a lesson to. And it was too early. Not until three. He thought of her in a pair of separate references, which at times blended confusingly into a single baffling semantic unit. The words she caused to form in his mind were alternately "green skirt" or "white legs." But when the words on occasion mingled together in a mysterious fashion, they stood out in his mind as "greenropes."

Chimes sounded from the Delacorte clock. Two thirty. Now the cages were feeding. The clock, on a high arch above the peristyle linking the monkey house with the lion house, was surrounded by a cortege of humorously sculpted animals, all of which "played" a merry musical accompaniment to the clock's chimes.

18

As always, Gus Soltik watched with fascination and a sense of awe as the smiling beasts circled the base of the clock, providing a tinkling, bell-like concert for the appreciative audience that had grouped itself in the courtyard between the peristyle and the pond of sea lions. The chubby gray metal animals caught in prancing dance steps filled the air with sweet and innocent music.

The hippo bowed a violin, the kangaroo blew a horn, the bear shook a tambourine while the elephant played an accordion and the goat tinkled his pipes and the penguin pounded a pair of drums.

Lanny. This was where he had met him. The day he had brought the food. Gus liked standing here with the name "Lanny" forming in his mind. There were big people here, too, watching the show. Not just children. That made it all right for him to be here. While he enjoyed the prancing animals and occasionally clapped his big hands together in an attempt to show approval for their antics, the music disturbed him; it was frightening because he didn't understand it.

Gus went into the animal house where Charlie, the tiger, was feeding and the big lion, Garland, was pacing behind his bars with the regularity of a metronome, obviously having savaged and pulped and devoured his twenty pounds of raw meat, for his eyes were sleepy and there was blood on his whiskers and the floor of the cage.

Gus felt at home with the cages. He liked the smell of the animals, acrid and fetid, and despite the tang of ammonia in the air, the smell was wild and exciting.

Without realizing it in any way at all, Gus Soltik was also given a sense of annealment and strength by the

19

behavior of many of the people in the lion house. They were afraid, and they held their children up to be frightened by the sudden, erratic roaring of the big cats. And for reasons he was forever helpless to define, Gus Soltik took some pathetic comfort from this spectacle.

He stood looking at the big lion called Garland because it was too soon for "greenropes."

Garland was eight years old, a black-maned African male, a gift to the city of New York from Jomo Kenyatta, President of Kenya. He had been named by the schoolchildren of New York in a contest conducted by the *Daily News*. The name which had, in fact, topped all others had been Bert Lahr, but this had been disallowed (privately) on the assumption that the children's votes had been influenced by adults who remembered the great comedian from *The Wizard of Oz*. The contest officials decided to name the little cat Judy, which they thought would satisfy all age groups, but Jomo's gift had turned out to be a male, and so they had decided on the lovely but epicene Garland, a name which had not received a single vote in the contest.

He could not tell time, but he could estimate it with reasonable accuracy. And now he knew it was time to look at "greenropes."

The growling of the lions waiting to be fed had fixed the time for Gus Soltik. Soon, very soon now, he thought, as he hurried toward a place of concealment he had already chosen, thick privet underbrush just behind the wall bordering the eastern side of Central Park at Fifth Avenue in the upper Sixties—soon, he was thinking with a surge of agitation, because he mustn't be late. The bus would be stopping at the intersection, and she would get off and stand talking with her friend, the winds blowing their green skirts about their white legs, and it was very important that he see her now, because tomorrow was the anniversary of his mother's death.

Shortly after three o'clock a yellow bus with black trim from Miss Prewitt's Classes stopped at Fifth Avenue in the upper Sixties of Manhattan. When the front doors opened with a gentle pneumatic hiss, a pair of chattering youngsters climbed down the steps and stood at the intersection waving good-bye to friends, who waved back to them from behind the windows of the bus which was accelerating, heading toward the southern boundaries of Central Park at Fifty-ninth Street.

The names of the two girls were Kate (Katherine Jackson) Boyd and Tish (Patricia) Tennyson, and they were eleven years of age and wore identical uniforms, which consisted of smartly cut black blazers, short green flannel skirts, green berets, white socks, and black moccasins. The girls lived in adjoining apartment buildings whose drawing-room windows faced the verdant and dramatic views of Central Park.

Kate Boyd had shining blond hair which she wore in a ponytail, secured by a green ribbon, and a pale, unblemished complexion from which her cherry-dark eyes blazed with an almost comical intensity. It was apparent from even a superficial view of these youngsters that the confident excitement and aggressiveness in Kate's manner completely dominated her friend, Tish Tennyson, whose skin tended to be sallow and whose chubby hips and rounded stomach had scored permanent diagonal creases in her green flannel skirt.

As the crisp gusting winds whipped their hair about

21

their foreheads and cheeks, the two girls hugged their book bags to their chests and chattered at each other with ferocious intensity. Their present preoccupation and stimulation stemmed from a mix of heady ingredients: boys, older boys at that, practically men, and the girls' shabby betrayal by these adult and arrogant males.

Kate and Tish had scored a coup for their fifth-grade class. They had worked up their nerve to approach Bob Elliott, who was seventeen and the leader of a rock group called The Purple Dreams, with an offer to play the Prewitt School's "sweet young thing" afternoon tea dance. To their surprise and delight, Bob Elliott had accepted; The Purple Dreams were cool and "in," thus an impressive catch indeed for a fifth-grade tea dance. Even though the fee was high, one hundred dollars for a three-hour gig, plus fifteen dollars for the transportation of their electronic gear, Kate Boyd had committed the class funds to the project without reservations, knowing that whatever the price, it was a triumph and worth it.

But this morning their excitement and dreams had collapsed, after Bob Elliott had called to tell them the gig was off because two of The Purple Dreams were down with the flu. This, while wretchedly disappointing, was something they could live with, but at lunch in a pizzeria near Miss Prewitt's, Kate had learned a bitter, unacceptable truth: Bob Elliott had simply dropped them to play a more prestigious date at Darwin Prep's senior dinner dance.

Kate Boyd, who was flamingly outraged by any and all degrees of injustice, had cabbed across town to Bob Elliott's apartment immediately on learning of his betrayal.

"He just laughed at me," Kate said for about the fifteenth time to Tish. "Laughed at me. He said we were just kids and wouldn't understand his music anyway."

"Did you really say it to him?" Tish said with a thread of excitement in her voice. "What you told me?"

Kate sighed. "No, I didn't."

"But you said you said it."

"Well, I wanted to. I wanted to say, 'I'd like to kick you' "—Kate lowered her voice theatrically—" 'right in your jewels, Bob Elliott.' "

"But you didn't."

"Don't be stupid. I wanted to, it's the same thing."

"No, it isn't, Kate."

"You don't even know what it means," Kate said.

Tish looked anxiously at Kate. She could stand neither Kate's dismissal nor Kate's displeasure. "Maybe I don't," she said. "Where'd you hear it?"

"They were in bed and she was laughing," Kate said, and then added the logical prologue to the sentence as almost an afterthought: "I heard my mother say it to my father."

"When's your mother coming back, Kate?"

"Well, we're not sure. She calls every day, of course, but she's got to take care of her aunt."

"What's the matter with her aunt?"

Kate shrugged in what she meant to suggest was a gesture of casual dismissal, but she felt the sting of tears in her eyes and looked quickly away from Tish, tilting her face against the cold, freshening breezes.

"She's got some kind of flu, from Brazil or from Greece or wherever it's coming from this year."

Again Tish felt a pang of anxiety; she shouldn't have asked about Kate's mother.

"Can I call you later, Kate?" Tish asked, with a

fruitless effort to make the question sound casual. "I mean, after homework?"

"If you want to," Kate said, and hurried off into the lobby of her building where old Mr. Brennan, the uniformed doorman, greeted her with a genuine smile and walked the length of the foyer with her to the elevators.

At about six o'clock that night, Luther Boyd let himself into the Fifth Avenue apartment which he had rented for three months from a theatrical producer who was staging a show in London, a production (he had explained to Boyd's complete disinterest) which would feature Sir Laurence Olivier as an albino Othello, surrounded by an otherwise all-black cast, save for Desdemona, who would be played by the Oriental actress Yoko Tani, whose role—as opposed to the others—would be comprised of operatic recitative and arias. Luther Boyd had wished him well but without excessive conviction since the last play he himself had seen had been a production of *Camelot* after Julie Andrews had left the company.

The walls of the large apartment were covered with memorabilia of the theater: faded playbills, first-night telegrams, the glossy photographs of actresses and actors with intimate greetings and signatures. None of this held much interest for Luther Boyd, although he knew that some of the glamorous faces awed and fascinated Kate.

Luther Boyd thought there was something sentimental and childish about the lavish salutations and congratulations on the photographs and in the telegrams. And he thought there was something tacky and

24

unsporting in the defensive effusions which obviously stemmed from box-office flops. But he could live with all this. He had rented the apartment, not for its furnishings, but for the dramatic and sustaining views of Central Park afforded him from the formal drawing room and his book-lined study. The shining crowns of Chinese elms and black alders that he could observe from these fifth-floor windows gave him cheerful memories of the six hundred open acres which surrounded his dairy farm in southern Pennsylvania. Also, he enjoyed walking in the park in the evening, and since flora and fauna and terrain were as much his profession as his pleasure, his investigations satisfied him as both a soldier and a naturalist.

On his leisurely strollings from the southern end of the Mall (his customary starting point) north past the cruciform esplanade of the band shell and then farther north to the boathouse and lake, he had observed dozens of domestic and exotic trees and shrubs; in his east-west crisscrossings along this north-south route (he had been advised to avoid the Ramble), he had found what amounted to a naturalist's laboratory. In these few weeks Boyd had seen and studied, sometimes to his astonishment, towering cork trees, monumental magnolias with leaves like polished green leather, English and peach-leafed hawthorns, cucumber trees, bald cypresses, red and silver maples, and oaks of all varieties, black and English, red and willow and scarlet.

As he closed the door of the apartment, Luther Boyd was greeted by a furious excitement by Kate's Scottie, Harry Lauder, and by what he judged to be a gratified insolence from their housekeeper, Carrie Snow, a stout middle-aged black lady, who stood waiting for him in the long drawing room with her hat on and a brown-paper market bag in her arms.

"You'll have to clean up after your ownselves tonight, Mr. Boyd." Her white teeth flashed in a smile of relish against the gloom of the long room, which at this hour was lighted only with a pair of table lamps. "Food's in the oven, and the plates are out, so you'll have to serve yourself, too."

"Very well, Carrie," Luther Boyd said. "And Kate?"

"She's in the bathtub, but first she did some homework before she used up all that was left of that pheasant in a sandwich."

"We've still got six or eight brace in the freezer, Carrie."

"I know, but it seems strange."

Whatever Carrie's point was, Luther Boyd thought with a certain weary humor, she was certainly determined to make it.

"What's strange about it?" he asked her, trapped by their relationship—which was blended of what: sympathy, courtesy, guilt?—into asking a question when he didn't give one goddamn about the answer.

Barbara had never appreciated his frequent need to get back to barracks and training camps. In those simple environments, one could cut through just such knots of superogatory sensitivities. One told a captain what to do, and the captain did it. Or he'd better have a goddamned good reason for not doing it. But here Luther Boyd stood pleasantly tired after six hours in an office and two hours on a squash racquets' court, fencing with a gloomy black lady's hurt feelings,

26

judging without interest what finesse might incline this tiny, boring conflict toward a sensible and, he hoped, speedy conclusion.

"Well, the strange thing is, Mr. Boyd, is a young girl, I mean, a baby child, sitting around in the afternoon watching TV and eating pheasant sandwiches."

There it was, the rebuke. Now presumably Carrie Snow felt better, having got that off her chest. Luther Boyd glanced at his watch.

"I'm afraid you'll have to hurry, Mrs. Snow, if you're going to make that bus."

This was a nice, tactical stroke, but it made Luther Boyd feel irritated with himself, because that had been his rebuke to her, a dismissal, with all that meant to her crotchety but basically kindly sensitivities.

Luther Boyd disliked insolence, not because it rankled him in any personal sense, but because he correctly assayed it as a surrogate for anger, an emotion he respected, particularly if it resulted in positive and constructive action. Yet stern as he was in his judgments on everyone around him, including himself, he was fair enough to understand that anger was a luxury that certain blacks and other misbegotten creatures of the world could savor only in the silence of their souls.

Mrs. Snow looked uneasily past him toward the kitchen.

"I could catch the next bus, Mr. Boyd—it don't matter that much—and put away the things after dinner."

He saw the white flags of surrender in her fluttering eyes. ("Thank you kindly, General Lee. It's a privilege to accept such a magnificent example of the swordmaker's art.") What else could he do but accept her offer of service? He paid her well, and he and Barbara and Kate treated her well; but if they denied her a sense of usefulness, what did the rest of it mean?

"That's very kind of you, Mrs. Snow," Luther Boyd said.

And so, his tactical energies expended in trivia, Luther Boyd went toward his study, while Mrs. Snow, her dignity flying like plumes, strode importantly into the kitchen.

Kate Boyd, who like to think of herself as a curious observer rather than as a busybody, made it a habit to take her bath with the door open a crack so that she missed nothing that went on in the apartment, and when she heard her father's footsteps going toward his study, she sang out, "Daddy, is that you?"

"Yes, honey. I'll see you after your bath. . . ."

"But I've got some absolutely dreadful news."

He opened the door of the bathroom and looked in on her. The air was steamy and warm and fragrant. Kate was up to her chin in bubbles, and whorls of thick, creamy shampoo had tranferred her hair into what looked like a great white Afro.

"What's the trouble?" he asked her.

"It's about Bob Elliott."

"After your bath," he said, and smiled at her and closed the bathroom door.

On this particular night, Luther Boyd would have preferred that Carrie Snow had gone home on schedule and that Kate was sleeping over with Tish or one of her other new friends. Luther Boyd did not mind taking care of himself, in fact, he preferred it; one look at him would have confirmed this in in the eyes of anyone who understood the physical disciplines of thoroughbreds. He was tall and rangily built and, at the age of forty-two, still played hours of squash racquets every day, lifted weights, and worked out regularly with a judo expert, who was proficient enough to give him an active, though ultimately inconclusive, match. They played only for exercise, which put Luther Boyd at a disadvantage, for—if they had played to a conclusion—it would be no contest for him.

As a result, his stomach was as hard as something fashioned from whalebone, and as recently as six months previously, he had scored a remarkable ninety-seven over the Rangers' obstacle training course at Fort Benning, Georgia.

His clothes camouflaged the power of his body because he preferred gabardines and coverts, fabrics which streamlined the width and strength of his shoulders with chiseled economy.

Walking into this study, Luther Boyd was frowning and rubbing his jaw with the thumb and forefinger of his left hand, one of his few physical gestures which revealed an inner anxiety. He would have preferred to be alone tonight because he was trying to solve two problems, one simple and the other very complex, and the frowning concern in his expression now made him look oddly youthful and vulnerable. This oddness stemmed from the fact that everything about Luther Boyd, from his closely cut black hair, sharply angled features, and cold gray eyes, suggested a confidence and authority of such an impregnable essence that it was difficult to imagine a problem he couldn't solve with simply a snap of his fingers.

The first problem centered on Major General Scott

Carmichael's putatively authoritative three-volume work on the strategy and tactics of what the general described as "Phoenix Confrontation" by which he meant "guerrilla warfare."

That was problem number one. And that was why Luther Boyd was in New York in an apartment which he had rented for three months: to check the proof of the general's three-volume exegesis of guerrilla warfare, to verify facts, dates, and place-names and, more exasperatingly, to reshape what seemed to him a variety of warped conclusions in Carmichael's treatise.

That was the simple problem. Since retiring from the Army in the early seventies with the rank of bird colonel, Luther Boyd had augmented the income from various substantial trust funds by free-lancing as a military consultant to publishing firms, motion-picture companies, foreign governments and, on more than one occasion, the United States Army.

Luther Boyd's special area of expertise was guerrilla warfare. He had served five years in Vietnam with Ranger units and had volunteered to serve an additional five years as a special consultant and instructor at the Rangers' permanent facility at Fort Benning, Georgia.

But presently, he couldn't concentrate on the first problem because of the second, which was the fact that his wife, Barbara, whom he loved and needed desperately, had walked out on him after fourteen years of marriage. And there seemed to be no way to get her back. He couldn't beg, couldn't explain himself to people. Colonel Boyd had given orders so long that he was almost physically uncomfortable in relationships which required a democratic exchange of viewpoints and opinions.

Pacing restlessly, Luther Boyd glanced about the large study, looking for solace and solutions from his own personal effects, the hunting prints that had belonged to his father, the deep chairs of antelope hide, the small-scale maps whose battlefields he knew from personal experience, and the portable campaign desk on which was a tray of bottles, glasses, and bucket of ice cubes. And his books and charts and maps, of course.

Luther Boyd had asked the producer, his landlord, to clear all the shelves of leather-bound collections of scripts and press clippings, and now a portion of Boyd's personal library stood in their place: military histories, biographies, and the battle orders of classic conflicts from Hamilcar Barca to Grant and Patton.

Still massaging his hard, angular jaw in a gesture of reflexive anxiety, Boyd stood at the windows and looked down at the pedestrian and automobile traffic on Fifth Avenue and the sidewalk running parallel to Central Park. He noted something then, absently, without interest, his reaction a simple professional reflex; in the pedestrian traffic moving along the eastern side of the park, one man stood as motionless as a rock in a stream, a big man, Luther Boyd could judge, even from this height, who was simply standing there, streams of pedestrians eddying around him, and his head, topped by what seemed to be a yellow cap, was tilted back as if he were staring up at the windows of Boyd's apartment.

Good soldiers, like good cops, trust their instincts. They try to understand an unnatural silence on a battlefield; they try, and frequently succeed, to define

31

the cannon or tank beneath nets of camouflage; and with a combination of experience and instinctual perceptions, they sense the movements of troops, know well in advance the vectors of attack and the possible collapse of flanks. And if these martial nuances were correct, the reserves would be committed in time and those flanks would hold like solid walls of iron and will.

And because Luther Boyd was an expert in military tactics and strategy, he was wondering idly, but without real interest (in truth, distracting himself from thinking of Barbara), why this big man was standing motionless in the rush hour when everyone was hurrying for trains and buses and home.

Kate ran into the room, and Luther Boyd swung his daughter up in his arms and sat down with her in one of the deep suede chairs. She had changed into plaid slacks and a light-blue cashmere sweater whose color flattered her blue eyes and shining blond hair. Straight from her bath, she was as fragrant as a bar of fresh soap.

"Now what's all this about Bob Elliott?" he said, after she had given him a hug and a kiss.

Kate told him about their betrayal with flashing eyes and ferocious zest, but when she finished, her mood changed, and she sighed and said, "I really felt a little bit sorry for him afterward, because he knew that *I* knew he was lying."

"I wouldn't waste any sympathy on him," Boyd said. "He broke his word to you and he lied to you because he didn't have the guts to tell you the truth."

Kate looked into her father's eyes, then looked away from him and with the tip of a finger drew a slow, small

32

circle around the buttonhole in the lapel of his gabardine jacket.

"Daddy, if Mommy's never coming home, shouldn't we talk about it?"

He searched vainly for words to answer her question, and the silence between them became awkward and embarrassing. At last he said, "Very well, we'll talk about it."

They heard Harry Lauder barking with excitement and anticipation at the front door of the living room.

"I'd better take him out for a walk first," she said. "He knows it's time."

"All right," Luther Boyd said. "Then we'll have our talk. But remember the ground rules, Kate. Make sure Mr. Brennan is on the sidewalk where he can see you, and stay on this side of the avenue."

Kate untangled herself from his arms and lap and walked to the door, where she stopped with her back toward him, a suggestion of tension in her little shoulders. She looked back at her father, and he realized from the sad maturity in her expression that she had guessed at the core of the abrasive estrangement between himself and Barbara.

"Does she blame you because Buddy got killed?"

He had no ready answer for this question, and feeling helpless, he stared in silence at the backs of his big, powerful hands. Then he glanced about the room as if seeking some escape from Kate's troubled eyes, noting irrelevantly how the last of the daylight had coated the surfaces of the furniture and carpeting with a fine veneer of rose and lemon reflections. At last Luther Boyd did the thing he feared to do (which was something his father had always commanded him to do without hesitation), and that was simply to turn away from the familiar, sustaining volumes of his military library and to look steadily into his young daughter's troubled and faintly accusing eyes. "Yes, it's got something to do with Buddy's death," he said.

"But it wasn't your fault that Buddy got killed."

"I'll try to explain it to you, although I'm not sure I can," he said.

"But it wasn't your fault," she said, and there was a tone of stubborn loyalty in her voice. "How could it be?"

"That's one of the questions I'm not sure I can answer," he said wearily.

After she had gone off with her Scottie, Luther Boyd stood and paced the floor restlessly, rubbing his jaw with the wedge formed by his thumb and forefinger. He tried not to think of Barbara. To distract himself, he thought of General Carmichael, whose problems at least presented a fair and reasonable challenge. One of the general's most serious flaws stemmed from a paradoxical stylistic ingenuity; he was, in fact, an excellent persuasive writer, but this was a talent best served in the breach in the writing of military manuals. War was not a debate, with issues to be decided by closely reasoned arguments. The object was not to win on paper and lose in combat, or to study maps and ignore the battlefield. He took a volume at random from a shelf and flipped through the pages until he came to this quotation: "The enemy is badly beaten, greatly demoralized and exhausted of ammunition. The road to Vicksburg is open. All we want now are men, ammunition and hard bread. . . ."

That was the kind of writing soldiers understood, clear and unequivocal, General Grant to Sherman.

From another volume he read: "It is 132 miles to the Rhine from here, and if this army will attack with venom and desperate energy, it is more than probable that the war will end before we get to the Rhine. Therefore, when we attack, we go like hell." General Patton to the 95th Division in October, 1944.

And from yet another volume he read wise words from a statesman who was not only a military but a political strategist: "The problems of victory are more agreeable than the problems of defeat, but they are no less difficult." That was the British bulldog with the cigar, Sir Winston Churchill.

But as he replaced the volume on the shelf, Luther Boyd realized he was committing a mistake which he would not permit in any officer in his command; he was postponing the decision of what and how much to tell his daughter, Kate, and that was an unforgivable and cowardly indulgence.

John "Buddy" Boyd had been Barbara Boyd's son by a first marriage to a man who had been killed in an automobile accident on the New Jersey Turnpike when Buddy (then Buddy Shaw) had been four years of age. When Luther Boyd married Barbara Shaw, he had adopted Buddy, and when the boy was old enough to discuss the matter, they had mutually agreed to change his name legally from Shaw to Boyd.

Luther Boyd had loved Buddy as he would have a natural son and had gloried in his triumphs and suffered with his defeats, caring for him as wisely and completely as he cared for their daughter, Kate.

35

Buddy Boyd had enlisted in the Army four years before, despite a perforated eardrum, which would have automatically exempted him from service, and despite a high draft number, which mathematically excluded him from any chance of conscription.

But Buddy Boyd had ignored his mother's injunctions to stay in college and had died unspectacularly but with great finality in a two-truck collision during his boot training at Fort Riley, Kansas. At first, Barbara had been a rock of determination and strength. She had packed off Buddy's clothes and cameras and butterfly collections to Army hospitals, and she had converted his two rooms, which were directly above Luther Boyd's library, into a ballet suite for Kate and her friends, complete with mirrors and bars and Degas prints. But after the first year, something insidious and virulent eroded her resolution and confidence. She began to question her son's death and then her husband's life. She questioned his decisions, his values, his code of honor, which was the very core of Luther Boyd's existence. She had come to believe that Boyd's feverish preoccupation (her phrase) with weapons and falconry and hunting and killing had created an atmosphere that was like a stench of death in their home, and in this noisome air her son had sickened and died. How could the son of Colonel Luther Boyd decide *not* to go to war? Hating it, despising it, fearing it, loathing the guns and the killing, Buddy had nonetheless embraced it with his young life rather than risk Colonel Luther Boyd's disapproval.

It wasn't that way, Boyd thought bitterly. He simply was what he was, and there was no way to change that. Barbara could change, but he couldn't. She could slip into the oblivion of drinks at dusk, she could exercise her grief in these spasms of neurotic indulgence, but there were no such anodynes or escape for Colonel Luther Boyd. He had been bred to take it, to clamp his teeth against any cry of pain or loss, leaving the possibly annealing tears to women and children and cowards.

The front doorbell echoed through the silent apartment. Luther Boyd walked through the corridor and living room and opened the door. Mr. Brennan, the uniformed lobby attendant, stood in the outer hallway. Behind him the elevator doors were open.

"This just came in special delivery, Mr. Boyd," Mr. Brennan said, handing Boyd a neatly wrapped package about the size of a deck of playing cards. Luther Boyd took the package but didn't glance at it; his eyes were fixed hard and straight at Mr. Brennan.

"Did Kate go outside with Harry Lauder?"

"You'd better believe she *didn't*, Mr. Boyd," Mr. Brennan said. "She's waiting right in the lobby for me to come down and keep an eye on her."

As a young man Mr. Brennan had been a welterweight contender with the ring name of Kid Irish, and at sixty-four he was still in excellent physical condition and would have dearly relished the opportunity to deck any bastard who'd lay a finger on Kate Boyd.

"Well, fine," Luther Boyd said. "And thanks."

He closed the door and unwrapped the package. His fingers were a bit clumsy because he recognized Barbara's handwriting on the heavy brown paper. The package contained a slim cartridge of electronic tape and a note from Barbara.

The note read:

I can't ever explain anything to you, because I know you're waiting for me to finish so you can point out in your logical, precise manner how wrong I am. But you do deserve an explanation. And so does poor, dear Kate. I've put down some of my feelings on this tape. Whether they "explain" anything, I'm not sure. But please believe that I have tried to be honest.

There was no signature. Luther Boyd stood uncertainly for a moment or so in the dimly lighted living room, tossing the slender cartridge up and down gently in the palm of his hand. At last he came to a decision which gave him very little pleasure. He sighed and walked back to the den, where a tape recorder rested on his desk alongside a neat stack of unanswered correspondence.

Luther Boyd made himself a mild scotch with soda and packed a pipe from a soft leather tobacco pouch. Then he set the tape in its spool, snapped the switch, and watched it begin to spin, his expression hard and thoughtful.

2

THE New York police department was not unaware of Gus Soltik. Nor was it unaware of the "lessons" which he had adminstered to four young girls on four successive years, precisely in the middle of the month of October.

Four in a row, Lieutenant Vincent "Gypsy" Tonnelli was thinking, and this is October, and tomorrow is the fifteenth, and would they nail the psycho bastard then, or would the Juggler make it *five* in a row? . . .

They didn't know Gus Soltik's name, and they had only a vague description of him, but they knew certain areas of his MO very well indeed.

The murderer who in the past four years had abducted, mutilated, raped, and then slashed the throats of four young girls in the borough of Manhattan was known to the police as the Juggler because that was the final dreadful gesture in his pattern, a knife ripped across tender jugular veins.

These thoughts were in Lieutenant Tonnelli's mind as he strode along the corridor of a precinct in the upper Sixties of Manhattan.

This was headquarters of the task force which had been assigned to Lieutenant Tonnelli two months earlier by Assistant Chief of Detectives Walter Greene, a graying veteran with a rasping voice and a head shaped like an artillery projectile. Tonnelli's second unit was stationed at the 13th Precinct on the East Side and was under the command of Detective Sergeant Michael "Rusty" Boyle.

In each unit of Lieutenant Tonnelli's task force were two switchboard operators and four detectives, second grade. At headquarters, which was located in the 19th Precinct on East Sixty-seventh Street, were Detectives Clem Scott, Jim Taylor, August Brohan, and Carmine Garbalotto. On the switchboards were Patrolmen Jules Mackay and August Sokolsky. Collating and indexing the steadily mounting piles of paperwork were two uniformed policewomen, Doris Polk and Rachel Skinner.

In Detective Sergeant Rusty Boyle's command in the 13th Precinct on East Twenty-first Street were Detectives Miles Tebbet, Jason Corbell, Roger Fee, and Ray Karp. On the switchboard were Patrolmen Joe Knapp and Ed Maurer, and the flow of files and reports was in the competent hands of Patrolwomen Alice Halzer and Melissa Foreberg.

Lieutenant Gypsy Tonnelli was short and stocky, with a huge chest and heavily muscled arms so thick that he couldn't wear jackets or sports coats from a rack, but had to have them fashioned by a tailor. Since he was forced to spend considerable money on his clothes, he had over the years cultivated a certain sartorial elegance; in fact, the lieutenant looked like a prosperous broker with a subdued but excellent sense of fashion rather than a very tough and, in this particular city, a nearly legendary cop.

A bachelor, Lieutenant Tonnelli lived in a modest apartment in the East Thirties and indulged himself in very few extravagances beyond his taste for well-made clothing. His father and mother were dead, and his only living relative was his sister, Adela, who was married to a Greek used-car dealer in Baltimore. She had some kids, he knew, but they didn't see each other anymore, didn't even exchange Christmas cards.

Gypsy Tonnelli's features were usually composed in a deceptively pleasant smile. His eyes were dark brown, and his lips were full and red. A scar coursed from his left temple to the point of his jaw, a vivid cicatrice which he had acquired while subduing a carload of unruly blacks during one of the riots in the late sixties. Lieutenant Tonnelli had once been so ashamed of the scar that he had grown a beard to conceal it. But to his consternation the beard, unlike his coal-black hair, had emerged in an embarrassing pepper-and-salt mixture. Preferring the scar to a prematurely graying beard, Tonnelli had shaved off the stubble and later had become quite proud of the villainous-looking crease that ran down the left side of his face, for it had become a cherished memento of the citation he had received, a benchmark on the legend that was Gypsy Tonnelli.

And why "Gypsy"? The nickname had been hung on him when he was still in uniform and stemmed from the fact that he was a Sicilian, hence was nurtured by a tradition that believed in evil eyes, believed that good and bad luck could be divined by cloud masses and falling stars, and believed that dogs howling in the night were often predicting their masters' deaths and that silver bullets and strings of garlic were specifics against vampires and werewolves.

41

In a word, the Gypsy was superstitious, but he did possess an uncanny ability for predicting the variety of crimes lurking in store for his city, which he knew as a wise old mother knows her children. Some mysterious sixth sense sould warn him that in the weeks ahead they could expect a rise in arson and a decline in murders, a dip in muggings, a surge of bank robberies.

At first, his superior officers didn't take the Gypsy's predictions all that seriously, but they couldn't explain his high percentage of accurate guesses by luck or coincidence. The Gypsy was dead right so often that at last everyone on the force began to respect his Sicilian intuitions.

However, despite the Gypsy's track record, he hadn't been able to convince his superiors that more than coincidence was involved in the murders of Encarna Garcia and Bonnie Jean Howell, whose bodies had been tortured and violated and whose throats had been slashed on successive years under the sign of Libra on the nights of October 15.

The following year, again on Libra 15, Trixie Atkins had been murdered after suffering the same sadistic refinements that had been inflicted on the bodies of Encarna Garcia and Bonnie Jean Howell.

Gypsy Tonnelli, in the next year, starting on October 1, had prowled the streets of Manhattan on his off-hours, praying that by luck or coincidence he might get his hands on the Juggler. And after Trixie Atkins' murder he had demanded and been reluctantly granted a meeting with Deputy Chief of Detectives Walter Greene in the chief's office at 240 Centre Street.

What Tonnelli wanted was a task force of experienced detectives to prepare a defense against what he was convinced would be a fourth ritual murder in the coming year.

The chief had said, "Sure, there's going to be a homicide next October 15. Probably a half dozen or more. We had forty-one a couple years back during that hot spell in July and August. I hear you been putting in overtime without pay on this job, Gypsy. Right?"

Tonnelli wasn't surprised at the chief's on-the-mark question; the word of any erratic conduct by a cop (particularly one with Tonnelli's rank) would inevitably spread through all echelons of the department.

"I worked my shift, Chief," Tonnelli said with the trace of an edge to his voice. "Then I hit the streets on my own time. Just hoping to get lucky."

The chief had sighed and stared with a certain weary irritation at the ceiling of his office. "Gypsy I don't like my cops running around off duty with this Dick Tracy hero bullshit. You want to moonlight, fine. Do something useful. Drive a hack, or ride shotgun for a numbers runner. Being realistic, Gypsy, the people who pay our salaries, the public, they don't like dedicated cops either." The chief's voice had been threaded with sarcasm. "They think a cop putting in extra time on his own is just looking for a chance to whip some more heads. When my cops are off duty, I want them at ball games or at the beach with their kids so they can come back to the precinct feeling a little bit human. "

But Lieutenant Tonnelli had stubbornly continued to press for manpower and resources to prevent the

Juggler from making it four in a row. The raping and mutilation of those tender young bodies had become a consuming obsession with the Gypsy.

At first he hadn't understood this compulsion. Couldn't understand why he was knocking on official doors, aggravating his superiors, indulging an almost always fatal professional flaw which was, in effect, a distrust of the department and the corollary conviction that he was the only man who could get the job done, Gypsy Tonnelli in a *mano a mano* against the Juggler, not the city's thirty thousand cops acting in impersonal concert to trap a killer.

Later he understood his compulsion, but that served only to make it more bitter and relentless.

On one occasion Tonnelli had recklessly driven to Camden, New Jersey, to seek out the New York commissioner of police, who was in that city to speak to a group of the nation's top law enforcement officers. (The commissioner's topic was kinky and typical of him: He advocated that bachelors, not having the responsibility of wives and families, should be drafted as reserve police officers certain given hours per month.)

Tonnelli had found the commissioner in his hotel room and had pleaded with him for a special force to stop the Juggler. The commissioner had been impressed by the Gypsy's zeal but mildly exasperated by the interruption, since at the time he had been putting the finishing touches on his speech. The commissioner's "mild exasperation" had picked up velocity and strength as it raced back down the channels of the department, and this had ultimately struck Tonnelli like a gale force tornado.

He hadn't been suspended but had been threatened with that action.

Then Jenny Goldman had been murdered on October 15. And Tonnelli picked up an ally strong enough to break the power of any police department in the free world, said ally being the aroused, challenging, accusing national and international press. And since Tonnelli now had a physical make of sorts on the Juggler, Deputy Chief of Detectives Greene had called the Gypsy into his office on sweltering afternoon in August. "Bunch of goddamn vultures," the chief had said. "Headlines calling us incompetent because we can't find a needle in a haystack."

"You could turn that around, Chief," the Gypsy had said. "Problem is, we've got a million needles in our particular haystack. The job is finding the right one."

"So what do you want?"

"Two units. One under Rusty Boyle's command. The other under mine."

"What kind of troops you talking about?"

"Sixteen second- or third-grade detectives."

"I'll give you eight. What else?"

"Reserves of uniformed troops I won't commit unless we go to a Red Alert. Dispatchers, a few bird cops to handle the paper."

The chief made notes. "And?"

"On October 8, I want helicopters standing by, attack-trained dogs, light trucks, and a team of marksmen."

"For Christ's sake, Gypsy, you sound like you're going to start a goddamn war."

"I hope I'm gonna end one."

45

Lieutenant Tonnelli and Detective Sergeant Rusty Boyle had selected their staff with extreme care, dipping into precincts in all five boroughs of the city to find the men they needed. What they had to do in the lead time represented by August and September was to redevelop complete biographies of the four dead girls, with a renewed attempt to determine whether or not the victims had traits or flaws in common which appealed to the Juggler's sadistic needs.

This all had been done before, of course, but by detectives normally and routinely assigned to the task by the department's table of organization. Now all that mass of official reports would be reworked by a special unit honed and chiseled in advance to stop the Juggler.

Thus, the men Tonnelli and Boyle had selected were chosen for their tact and understanding, in addition to their rigorous efficiency as investigative officers. They must interview once again the parents and relatives of the four dead girls. And this must be done without unduly lacerating the emotions of grieving fathers and mothers. This was not only basic, decent humanity, but it would also help create an almost confessional climate that would allow the parents to re-create the activities and patterns of their children's lives as accurately as possible.

Detective Second Grade Miles Tebbet in Sergeant Rusty Boyle's unit had studied for the priesthood until he realized his vocation was not a true one, and at this time he had joined the New York police department. He was twenty-eight, a slender blond who usually wore jeans and a poncho, and was about the best man on the force to talk down a jumper.

Second Grade Detective Clem Scott in Tonnelli's unit

had a bachelor's degree in urban affairs from Fordham University. Scott was married, with two children, and spent one day a month at a VA hospital typing personal letters for disabled veterans.

The remainder of the units were men of similar bents and endowments. While some were more educated than the others, they shared one thing in common. They were, in Tonnelli's view, a group that represented the toughest and most dedicated traditions and skills of the department. They were expert marksmen, and Tonnelli knew from their records that they had guts; damned fine men to be at your side if you were going into an alley after a killer.

Carmine Garbalotto, in Tonnelli's unit, was a veteran of eighteen years on the force, who lived in Brooklyn with a wife and nine children. He was an expert in the areas of perversion and child molestation; he could check a crowded playground at a glance and determine whether it was "clean" or not. Garbalotto's specialty was movie theaters; his big hand had fallen heavily on the shoulders of hundreds of men he had observed attempting to molest young boys or girls, whose attention was so riveted by what John Wayne or Doris Day might be doing up on the big screen that they were hardly aware of the fingertips probing toward their loins.

Tonnelli and Boyle's units had processed every sex crime committed in all five boroughs of the city during the past five years, using these profiles as the base of their investigative mosaic. But none matched the Juggler's MO.

In September, Tonnelli had dispatched Detectives Tebbet and Scott to the morgue of the New York *Times* to check news stories on October 15 on the years before the murders had commenced their crimson flow through the borough of Manhattan. They were looking for stories which might have triggered a need for revenge: massive lawsuits, bitter, expensive divorces, medical malpractice suits, tragic accidents, suicides, something bizarre or catastrophic that could send someone around the bend, misfortune driving a victim toward a series of paranoid slaughters. Tebbet and Scott had indeed found catalogues of disaster in every edition of the *Times* published on October 15 in the five years before the Libra murders: rapes, drownings, explosions, hit-run victims, murders by ice pick and fine nylon stockings. But the sheer number and variety of tragedies had been so massively complex and unrelated that the precious hours given to the project had ultimately been unproductive, a sheer waste of time.

Libra—September 24 to October 23. All the murders had occurred on Libra 15. Something dark and hidden and mystical in the mysterious signs of the zodiac, like the movement of a leviathan in fathomless waters, appealed powerfully to the Gypsy's Sicilian intuitions. But none of the victims had been Libras. Encarna Garcia, Gemini. Trixie Atkins, Aquarius. Bonnie Jean Howell, Capricorn, and Jenny Goldman, Scorpio.

Gypsy Tonnelli wondered at the possible significance of the symbol of Libra, the classic golden scales. Did that suggest a perverted sense of justice or retribution? Or the sinister balance between himself and the man they called the Juggler. . . . But so far, with all their research, with all the potentials they had explored, with so much talent and dedication going for them,

Tonnelli's task force had come up dry, had drawn blanks.

Yet Gypsy Tonnelli knew in the depths of his Sicilian heart that the Juggler was ready to make his move; he could feel that presentiment in the marrow of his bones, in a cold, painful clench in his guts. The Juggler was out there in the city, living maybe like a stinking animal in somebody's basement, making his plans, preparing to snatch some young girl and enjoy his sadistic fun with her before slashing her throat. Well, Tonnelli thought, this time he wouldn't make it. They'd catch him and trash him. The Gypsy felt that, too, in his bones. And there wouldn't be any bleeding-heart psychiatric apologies for the Juggler. No pleas of temporary insanity, no judicial wrist slap followed by six or seven years in some cozy funny farm. No, when they caught the Juggler, they'd waste him as they would a mad dog. . . .

Lieutenant Tonnelli walked into the large offices he had been assigned in the upper floors of the 19th Precinct on East Sixty-seventh Street. Carmine Garbalotto, huge and balding, with a face like a kind bloodhound, was on the phone reassuring a young mother that she hadn't caused them any unnecessary trouble.

"Look," he was saying in his slow, patient voice. "Your daughter comes home from school and uses the back door and falls asleep in her room and you don't see her. So you're worried. So you call us. That's what we're here for. We sent a couple of cars over to the school, checked the neighborhood. Don't you worry about us. Any time your kid is missing, irregardless of the hows or whys of it, you give us a holler."

Gypsy Tonnelli nodded to Sokolsky and Jules Mackay

at the switchboards. Detective Clem Scott got up from his desk and joined Tonnelli, who had stopped to stare with bitter eyes at the four large glossy photographs of the girls the Juggler had tortured and murdered. Scott, whose lined and weathered face made him look older than his twenty-nine years, gave Tonnelli a sheaf of reports. The two policewomen clerks were typing in the adjoining office. August Brohan and Jim Taylor were not at their desks.

"Taylor and Augie went up to a school in Harlem." Scott checked his watch. "Around eight P.M. somebody reported a character bothering black kids playing basketball. Augie just phoned in. It was a fruitcake with a beard down to his balls and a wooden leg. He was passing out Tootsie Rolls to the colored kids because it was his birthday. His daughter made the scene at the same time as our guys and threw a net over him."

Tonnelli continued to glance through the reports. Drunks for the most part, vagrants, seventeen in all, three or four with records. B&E. GT Auto.

"Sergeant Boyle called in from the Thirteenth," Scott said. "Rape squeal around Thirty-fifth Street and Eighth Avenue. He and Tebbet went out on it." In response to Tonnelli's sharp, questioning look, Scott shook his head. "It's not our stud, Lieutenant. The lady's in her forties. She's alive and well and probably won't be drinking martinis with a stranger until the next time."

Lieutenant Tonnelli glanced through Max Prima's report of the hulking figure the patrolman had noted in Central Park earlier that day.

"Max Prima," Tonnelli said to Scott. "You know him?"

50

"I think his uncle used to work out of the Fourth Division over on Eighty-second Street," Scott said. "He made first-grade before he put in his papers. But no, I don't know Max Prima."

Tonnelli continued to study Max Prima's report. "He's got a good pair of eyes," Tonnelli said. "And his instincts are right."

Gypsy Tonnelli frowned and rubbed a hand in a tentative gesture along his scarred cheek. The gesture suggested that he remembered the agony of a cold knife slicing through his flesh; his fingertips were gentle on the old wound, as if loath to stir memories of pain.

He read Prima's report again, aware of the deliberate beat of his heart. Subject, Caucasian, early thirties, six-three, two-twenty, fast and strong . . . thick blond hair . . . bulging forehead . . . brown sweater, denims, Wellingtons . . . yellow leather cap. Staring at the young girls in the children's zoo. Weirdo. . . .

Again Gypsy Tonnelli felt the slow stroke of his heart. Some instinct, a premonition, a dark complex of Sicilian superstitions, or simple gut cop instinct, warned Tonnelli that he was close to the Juggler now, so close that he could almost see him and hear him and smell him; he could never explain these almost mystical convictions or calibrate them in any fashion remotely approaching scientific accuracy. But he believed (or wanted to believe) they had been given a sudden glimpse of their quarry, and as that belief grew firm and solid, he could almost feel the Juggler's thick, corded neck within the grasp of his own big hands.

Gypsy Tonnelli glanced from Max Prima's neatly written report to the large photographs of the Juggler's young victims, whose fresh and innocent faces were

51

graced with hope and excitement and bore no shadow of the fates in store for them.

Encarna Garcia. Fourteen, black hair, sparkling eyes, smiling confidently, innocently at the camera. Obviously proud of her frilly new dress, which had been a birthday gift from her father. Reported missing five P.M., October 15, five years ago. Found nine P.M. the same day in a condemned two-story dwelling near Eighty-seventh Street and Broadway. Rope burns on wrists and ankles. Four fingers of the left hand broken. Sexually assaulted, throat slashed.

Bonnie Jean Howell. Thirteen, black. Pigtails, wide grin, white, healthy teeth. Father a Pullman porter. Mother a dentist's receptionist in Harlem. Bonnie Jean was found in a tool shed on a school playground near 129th Street and Lenox Avenue. Bonnie Jean had been reported missing at six thirty P.M., October 15, four years ago. The coroner's report was pure Grand Guignol. Both arms broken, left kneecap shattered, burns on abdomen and small of back. Two of those fine healthy teeth broken. Sexually assaulted. Throat slashed.

Trixie Atkins. Fourteen. White. Lived with her mother, a hooker, in an apartment on West Forty-seventh Street. Trixie was blond, with lively eyes and a big grin for the world. Her mother had gone off with a customer to Detroit, and Trixie wasn't reported missing until a week after she had failed to show up for school. Then the police got a call on October 22 complaining of an odor stemming from an empty loft in a Greenwich Village apartment building. That's where they found Trixie Atkins. Rope burns on her thighs, three fingers on her right hand broken, the blood dried and hardened on the gaping wound in her throat.

Jenny Goldman. Thirteen. Pale, red-haired, solemn as a mouse in her eighth-grade graduation picture. Father a doctor, mother a commercial model. Sexually assaulted, throat slashed, October 15 one year ago.

Looking at Jenny Goldman's grave little face, with her oddly wise and wistful eyes, hurt Tonnelli so much that it almost made him physically ill, because he and Rusty Boyle had come within minutes of saving Jenny Goldman's life.

Last year they had almost nailed the Juggler. . . .

They had been cruising on Thirty-ninth between Lexington and Third when a pair of excited kids waved their squad down. "He got Jenny, took her into the basement," a frightened little Irisher had yelled at them.

Tonnelli and Boyle had stormed into the basement of a brownstone but had arrived too late to save Jenny Goldman her interval of monstrous anguish. She had suffered and died minutes before they had kicked open a bolted door that led to a furnace room thick and blurred with shadows.

In the darkness, they had had only an impression of motion, of fetid air stirring, and then the heavy, powerful figure of a man had smashed them aside, charging with an animallike speed toward the open door. Tonnelli had fired twice from the floor, but the bullets had struck the sagging door, and the Juggler was gone. . . .

Acting on Tonnelli's report, Assistant Chief Inspector Taylor "Chip" Larkin, Borough Commander South, had flooded a twelve-square block area (its epicenter at Twenty-ninth and Lexington) with hundreds of uniformed patrolmen and detectives, fleets of motorcycle cops and cruising squads, but this massive and rolling stakeout had been counterproductive, attracting crowds into the area, creating rumors and "tips" that jammed Central's switchboards. In the confusion of this spasmodic police action, the Juggler had managed to slip through their lines.

The only description they had ever got of the man had come from that excited little Irisher whose name was Joey Harpe and who had directed the detectives to the basement where "the big dirty giant," in Joey Harpe's phrase, had taken Jenny Goldman. But patient questioning had developed a few more facts. The man was white, he had a rank odor about him, and he'd been wearing some kind of leather cap. Also, his clothes looked poor. . . .

What had frustrated them from the start of their investigation was that they had found no revealing pattern in the Juggler's murders. There were no racial or ethnic clues to guide them. He had killed a black girl, a Jewish girl, a Puerto Rican, and a hooker's daughter who attended a Catholic grammar school. Young females, tortured, raped, and murdered on the fifteenth day of October in widely scattered areas of the borough. That was all they had to go on, but now the description of the little Irisher and the sharp eyes of Max Prima had given them what might be the first lead to their quarry.

If he was right, and it was about a thousand to one he wasn't, what about him? Big, strong, denims, Wellington boots. Some kind of laborer. Probably poor, probably little education. That was guesswork, but he had to start somewhere. You could figure he'd used loan sharks, Tonnelli thought, and that was something they could check out.

Milky Tichnor in the Village. Ted Chapman on the docks south of Forty-fourth Street, Solly Castro north to the Seventies, Maybelle Cooper with the blacks, and the Puerto Ricans in their barrios in Spanish Harlem. And what was the big spade shylock calling herself these days? Somebody had told the Gypsy. Yes. Samantha Spade. That was it. He shook his head. Just like her.

Tonnelli handed Max Prima's report to Scott. "Let's find this dude, Scotty. Start by calling in Max Prima."

As Scott gave this message to Sokolsky, who would put it through Central to the patrolman's home or precinct, Lieutenant Tonnelli, in an automatic but unnecessary reflex, mentally checked the strength and disposition of the extra units which had been assigned to this task force by the assistant chief of Patrols Office.

Standing by in Manhattan's twenty-odd precincts, and its divisions one through six, were details of uniformed patrolmen who could be alerted and transported to any area of the city within minutes on orders from Tonnelli. Extra squad cars, big and little "trucks," emergency lighting equipment, two ambulances, and medical orderlies were stationed about the city in patterns which would allow Lieutenant Tonnelli as narrow a lead time as possible to commit those units to a given neighborhood, street, park, or playground.

Attack-trained Dobermans, schooled and handled by Patrolmen Hogan, Platt, and Branch, could also be brought to any area of the city within a matter of minutes.

Three police helicopters, Bell 106-B's, had been on an alert status for the past week, their pilots and crews awaiting Tonnelli's orders at Floyd Bennett Field in Brooklyn. The choppers were equipped with Apollo nets and powerful floodlights in the bellies of their fuselages, any one of which could at night create a noontime brilliance in a square city block.

In addition to this physical muscle and sophisticated equipment, there were the four-star chief inspectors, and below them the four so-called superchiefs and their assistants and deputies and inspectors, down through captains and lieutenants and sergeants and patrolmen, all of this concerned human and mechanical potential at the ready now to spring the trap on the Juggler.

But, Lieutenant Tonnelli thought, it was usually just this way, with all this personnel, all this preparation and equipment, the first break and perhaps the most significant one usually came from some alert, observant cop walking his beat. . . .

Certainly not, however, from Commissioner Joseph Harding, who was presently in Stockholm at an international convention of lawyers and statesmen whose agenda included a discussion of the feasibility of criminal surveillance maintained on special platforms in outer space.

3

DETECTIVE Sergeant Michael "Rusty" Boyle had personally checked out the alleged rape which the putative victim was willing to swear on her mother's Bible had occurred in this closed parking lot on West Thirty-fifth. He and Detective Miles Tebbet had made the scene with sirens and red lights because through some confusion (either at Central or from the anonymous tipster) Hilda Smedley's age had first been reported as sixteen, which had alerted them to the possibility of the Juggler.

Every formation standing in New York for the past ten days, in all divisions and precincts, had been ordered to report any suspicious characters loitering around playgrounds, comfort stations, or public parks; any molestation, rapes, or missing child reports were to be funneled directly to Tonnelli and Boyle's units. The evaluation of the information was Lieutenant Tonnelli's responsibility, and he had the authority from both the assistant chief of patrol and the assistant chief of detectives to raise his task force to a Red Alert status if he believed it necessary.

Detective Sergeant Boyle had checked the rape in

person and fast and had already reported to Lieutenant Tonnelli through Detective Scott.

This wasn't the Juggler at work.

The woman's name was Hilda Smedley, and she had given her age as thirty-four to the patrolmen from the Midtown Precinct, whose squad cars with dome lights revolving were parked at the curb behind Sergeant Boyle's unmarked car.

Sergeant Rusty Boyle was in his early thirties, tall and wide-shouldered, with the speed and strength of a professional athlete. He had thick red hair, angular features, and a preference for kinky sartorial gear; he favored flared slacks, boots, macho belts, and black leather jackets. Rusty Boyle secretly admired the spade pimps he used to collar around the Times Square area and would have enjoyed wearing huge wide-brimmed hats, boots with silver heels, and ankle-length overcoats.

Regulations frowned on such high-profile outfits unless they were needed as covers. But the real reason was Joyce. She thought they were tacky, and what Joyce thought was the bottom line, the Bible, for Rusty Boyle.

"I told you, he didn't give me no name," Hilda was shouting at one of the uniformed officers. She was a mess, Rusty Boyle thought, but with grudging compassion. Tears streaking her makeup, the front of her dress ripped apart to expose pendulous breasts, closer to forty than thirty, Hilda Smedley was a thickening old harpy, who smelled of gin and who would have fallen flat on her face if she hadn't had a squad car to lean against. There was no tragedy in her violation, Rusty Boyle thought, and realized that that was the tragedy of it.

"We just got talking, the way people will in bars," she

had told Detective Miles Tebbet, who had listened to her with the sympathy and compassion of a man who had once studied for the priesthood. "He was polite and everything, and he looked kind of Jewish. Maybe he was, but I never had that kind of trouble from a Jewish guy before. Like I told you, he offered to drive me home. Instead he parks in here and goes at me like King Kong."

While Tebbet listened gravely, Sergeant Rusty Boyle put his hands on his hips and stared at a group of what he judged to be whip-dick hippies bunched together on the sidewalk. They wore ponchos and dirty jeans and were grinning at Hilda Smedley, obviously savoring her flushed, swollen face, ripped blouse, and hysterical tears.

A third-grade detective from the 10th Precinct arrived, Dennis St. John, a bulky man in his forties who was wearing a windbreaker and a beret. St. John double-parked his car alongside Boyle's unmarked vehicle, blocking traffic and touching off a fusillade of blasting horns.

Christ, Rusy Boyle thought, with swiftly mounting exasperation and anger. Chaos was part of a police officer's life, Detective Sergeant Rusty Boyle knew full well; death in its most violent forms, from gunshots, fires and drownings, from knives, razors, the strangling hands of maniacs, these were the items stacked up on the shelves of every policeman's shop. But Rusty Boyle hated the merchandise he dealt with and traded in and thus tried with all his skill and strength to prevent its occurrence or at least to camouflage it with some semblance of form and discipline. And that was why the present scene so offended him, with its noisy untidiness,

59

its disheveled and violated Hilda Smedley, the gawking street freaks, and the other pedestrians stopping to stare with insulting intensity at the ravaged woman and even, he thought furiously, goddamn dumb Denny St. John from the 10th, puffing officiously onto the scene and contributing to the turmoil by double-parking his car and blocking traffic all the way back to Sixth Avenue.

Rusty Boyle began shouting orders, beginning with the hippies, and scaring them half out of their wits by bellowing at them in a voice that was like a clap of thunder.

"Get moving, you kinks. Go find some school to drop out of, or I'll kick your butts up between your shoulders."

As they backed away from him, covering their embarrassment with awkward grins, Sergeant Boyle turned and stared with cold eyes at the other pedestrians who had stopped to witness Hilda Smedley's pathetic anguish.

"Everything snap-ass in your homes? Kids all straight-A students? Nobody banging his secretary or sneaking a few belts of whiskey before breakfast? Take care of your own lives. You heard me. Move!"

Dennis St. John tapped Sergeant Boyle on the arm and nodded with an air of gravity and importance toward Hilda Smedley.

"What we got here, Rusty?"

"What the fuck you think we've got?" Rusty Boyle said. "I'll tell you what we got here. We got a fucking traffic jam here. Will you get your car off the street? Pull it into the parking lot."

There was no reason to shout at him, Sergeant Boyle

realized; St. John would probably handle this case, but the detective's dumbness, which was annoyingly coupled to a manner of pompous self-importance, gave Boyle a pain in the ass.

"I'll move it," St. John said. "But I thought something was breaking. That you guys might need some muscle."

Sergeant Boyle stared in disgust at the backed-up lines of honking automobiles. "What's breaking are my damned eardrums," he said.

"Come on, cool it, Sergeant," St. John said in a petulant voice, and waddled back to his car.

Rusty Boyle noticed then that one man still stood on the sidewalk at the entrance to the parking lot. The man was forty or forty-five, Rusty Boyle judged, wearing slacks and a sweater over a sports shirt. His hair was thinning and gray, and his features were nondescript; a worthy burgher, a taxpaying Mr. Straight, Boyle thought, except there was something haunted in his eyes which were large and clear behind bifocals. He didn't look the type, Boyle thought, to be getting his jollies at the sight of a sobbing, battered woman, but Boyle had stopped judging people by appearances ever since he collared an altar boy who had hacked a janitor into bloody pieces and then had set fire to him and, in addition to which, had seemed largely pleased by the charred wreckage he had made out of what had once been a human being.

Boyle walked over to the man and said, "Look, the lady's been through a rough time of it. You're not helping staring at her."

"I want to talk to you, Officer," the man said. "My name is Ransom, John Ransom." He pointed at the second-story windows of an apartment which over-looked the parking lot. "I heard her scream. I looked out my window just as she was pushed out of the car."

"You see the guy?"

"Just a glimpse. I couldn't identify him."

Well, that figured, Boyle thought with weary exasperation. No way would he get involved. Saw a girl being raped, took his sweet time to come down and lend a hand.

"Was he black or white?" Boyle asked him.

"I'm pretty sure he was white."

"Any guess on his age?"

"I really couldn't say," Ransom said. He fished into the pocket of his slacks, removed a slip of paper with numbers on it, and handed the paper to Sergeant Boyle. "But I got the license number of his car."

"Well, what were you planning to do? Save it for Christmas?"

"I wasn't dressed, you see. I just had a robe on. So I had to get on some clothes. That's why it took me so long to get down here." Ransom's tone was defensive and apologetic. "I got here as soon as I could."

"You did fine, you did just fine, sir."

Why the hell am I chewing everybody out? Sergeant Boyle was thinking, in one of his rare but honest moments of self-criticism. First St. John and now this nice John Doe of a citizen.

"Look, sir," he said by way of making amends. "If everybody in the city did as good as you did tonight, we could close down half our precincts."

Sergeant Boyle gave the license number to St. John, saying in a pleasant and conciliatory tone, "I'd suggest you get Miss Smedley checked out at the hospital and bust that stud quick."

"Thanks, Sergeant," St. John said, staring with grave intensity at the license number. "I'll call Motors and get a make on this plate."

Dumb. What was the use? Where else but Motors? The dog pound? The morgue? Macy's basement?

"Thanks again, Sergeant," St. John said. "I'll get this lady checked out at the hospital and bust the stud quick. I'll see you around."

Let's hope not. . . .

Sergeant Boyle started for his car but stopped when he noticed that Ransom was standing on the sidewalk outside the parking lot, staring at him with those haunted, pain-bright eyes.

Still feeling a bit repentant, Sergeant Boyle walked back and gave him a pat on the shoulder.

"I'll say it again, you did beautiful tonight," he said.

"I've got cancer," Ransom then said, but so simply and unexpectedly that the words struck Sergeant Boyle like blows under his heart.

Thanks, he thought wearily, thanks a lot. I don't get enough death and shit on this job, bodies in the river, bodies hanging from ropes, heads blown apart by crazies, but I got to have more of it handed to me by a civilian who probably thinks that's what he pays his taxes for.

"My wife doesn't know about it," Ransom said, and smiled uneasily as if to indicate this was a casual oversight on his part. "I sell upholstery fabric for B. Altman, it's part of their at-home decorator service, but a couple of months back the weight of the fabric case got too much for me. My arm and chest were hurting. I haven't been working at all for the last three weeks, but I haven't told my wife that either." Ransom smiled again, and this time the nervous flicker across his lips suggested that he and the sergeant might be sharing a mild joke at Mrs. Ransom's expense.

"Jesus," Sergeant Boyle said, "when are you going to tell her?"

"I just don't know," Mr. Ransom said, with another dismissing smile. "I didn't believe the first doctor, I guess nobody does. But the second one said the same thing. I still go out every morning like I used to, and when I get home at night, I have to make up stories for her. That's the worst part of it. I'm not much good at making things up."

"What do you mean? Why do you have to make up stories?"

"Well, I tell her about my calls. Our daughter's away at school, she's in premed, so there's just the two of us. So I tell my wife what fabrics people like and any little stories I can dream up, like some lady matching a sofa to her poodle or maybe a redheaded grandchild. Then I sit at my desk and write up orders on sales that I pretend I made during the day." He sighed, but his smile and manner remained oddly apologetic. "I just don't know how to tell her," he said. "It will be so hard on her. There's no money for my daughter to finish college, to go on to med school. I really don't know what to say to her either. My daughter, I mean."

Police work had not made Detective Sergeant Boyle a fatalist; on the contrary, despite massive evidence which failed to support his view, Rusty Boyle remained an optimistic and charitable human beng who detested

64

what seemed to him a manifest unfairness in life. Here was a prime example of it.

Sergeant Boyle's father had died when Rusty was four years old, and this had seemed a gross unfairness to him, and he had never truly got over it. But the scales had been balanced by his mother, a marvelous person, who had believed that man had no business trying to get up to the moon, but had also quoted Micheas, Chapter Six, Verse Eight, to her son, saying in her musical Irish voice, "What more does the Lord require of you, but to do just, to love mercy, and to walk humbly with your God?"

He had had all that. And he had Joyce, whose love for him and his for her was much deeper and even more significant than the riotous physical pleasure they took in each other. And he had the Gypsy to work for, while this poor bastard had a body laced and woven with pain and was staring death in the eyes and couldn't even tell his wife about it. And on top of that, forced to write fake orders and tell her funny stories while his guts were dying inside him.

"Jesus," Rusty Boyle said again. Then an idea occurred to him. A splendid idea. And when such thoughts occurred to this large emotional Irishman, they struck him with a force of natural laws. He put a big arm around Ransom's shoulders and gave him a conspiratorial smile.

"Look, where's your wife now?"

"She's out shopping."

"All right. Let's you and me go across the street and have a couple of beers. A time like this, a guy should have somebody to talk to. So how about it?"

"I'd like that very much," Ransom said quietly, and

then looked off down the street, but not before Rusty
Boyle saw the glint of tears in his eyes.

Detective Sergeant Boyle told Tebbet to notify
Lieutenant Tonnelli that he'd be out of the office for a
half hour or so, but if the Gypsy needed him for
anything, he'd be across the street at the Grange Bar.

At approximately the same time that Rusty Boyle and
Mr. Ransom entered the Grange, Gus Soltik was
prowling the jungles of Manhattan looking for a cat.

The Juggler walked slowly and quietly through a
refuse-littered alley in the vicinity of Eleventh Avenue
and Fifty-sixth Street, his shadow falling massive and
tall beyond him, his black silhouette topped by the
leather cap with its metal button. They liked cats, he
knew, anything small and soft and warm. Like they
were. . . . He heard a faint purring sound and stopped
in his tracks, looking about tensely, but finally realized it
was only the hum of high winds in the power lines above
his head. Something bothered Gus Soltik. He felt a stir
of panic. It wasn't forgetting his name. He knew that all
right. "Gus Soltik," he said, speaking the two words
softly into the winds of the night. It was something else.
It wasn't a cat he wanted. It was something else. He
sighed with relief, remembering what it was. A kitten,
Not a cat. A kitten. He stood then, turning his head
slowly, forcing himself to listen, straining to hear the
sound of sirens and fire engines. That's where kittens
were. At fires. He had seen the cats carrying the kittens
in their mouths, running from fires and streams of
water and the sounds of men's voices echoing hideously
from horns. He must find a fire. And then a kitten, Gus

66

Soltik thought. He bobbed his head quickly at these conclusions, pleased that he had forgotten nothing. The knife, the ropes, nothing. . . . All for what he thought of as "white legs" or "greenropes."

4

"I MUST have understood you when we were younger. Or maybe I just accepted you and was too stupid to ask any questions. At any rate, bein' a young and dutiful Southern belle"—the voices dropped suddenly into a mocking, mushmouth Southern accent—"Ah just didn't feel Ah had the right to ask my little ole hubby any questions at all 'cept did he want anything from me before he went off to beddie-bye and sweet old dreams."

Luther Boyd sat in his study listening to his wife's voice as it came to him from the slowly spinning reels of the tape recorder. He sat forward on the edge of the chair, his hands locked tightly together, his elbows resting on his knees. His face was creased in a line of bitter frustration. On the table beside him was an untasted whiskey and soda and pouch and pipe, which he had put aside after listening to his wife's first words to him: "I expect you've got your pipe lighted and a drink in your hand and are prepared to listen with that goddamn respectful and skeptical smile of yours to all my sad stories."

Luther Boyd had played the tape several times and almost knew it by heart. He punched a button stopping the tape and let it spin forward to her last few paragraphs, which contained the crucial substance of her accusations. Pressing the play button, Boyd settled back in his chair and picked up the drink in which the ice had long ago dissolved, his mood a curious and uncharacteristic blend of defeat and confusion. He had picked up his wife in mid-sentence. " . . . oh, damn it, I missed my point." There was silence. Then he heard the clink of ice in a glass, the liquid splash of what he assumed to be vodka, since that was her preference in increasing quantities since Buddy had died. "Yes, I'm having a tall, cold one, Colonel. Well, what was my point? Oh, just this. I could understand a young boy hunting down every animal that moved just so he could kill it. And when you couldn't do the job personally, you trained dogs and falcons to do it. After all, young boys don't know any better. And I can understand a youngster going off to the wars. That, except for that shameful pig-sticking in Vietnam, was the patriotic thing to do. But I can't understand a grown man devoting decades not just to killing animals and men but to teaching others to do the same thing and publishing books with diagrams to make the slaughter ugly and efficient and scientific. That's what Buddy couldn't understand either." Barbara's voice was rising emotionally. "He went into the Army and got himself killed. Not because he loved and respected you. But because he needed *your* love and respect. And that was the only goddamn way he thought he could get them."

Luther Boyd heard his daughter Kate's bedroom door open, followed instantly by a blast of music from her hi-fi set. He winced while quickly punching off the

70

tape recorder. Goddamn it, he thought resentfully—and he was thinking now of both Kate's music and Barbara's attitudes—he *was* a square, and he hated that cacophony of raucous noise called rock music, and he *was* a patriot and he loved his country and had fought for it, so why should he be put on trial for his attitudes and convictions?

When Kate ran into the study wearing a quilted red robe and matching slippers, his resentment ebbed at the sight of her rosy, pretty features and her long blond hair which, released from its ponytail, fell smoothly down to her shoulders. While she came over and sat on his knee, he smiled appraisingly at her, judging her points, the soft line of her developing bosom, the good, square shoulders and coltishly slim legs, as he might assess the qualities of a thoroughbred filly. "Well, Miss Katherine Jackson Boyd, let's see you hollow out your back," he said.

She smiled at him and sucked in her stomach, squared her shoulders, and put her hands together on the pommel of an imaginary horse. "How's this, Daddy?"

"Blue ribbon," he said, and she relaxed and snuggled herself into his arms.

"Could we talk about Buddy now?" she asked him.

"Do you remember your grandfather, Kate?"

"Just that he was tall and had white hair. And he told me to lean forward and grab my pony's mane to help him when we were going up a hill."

Boyd smiled faintly. "Anything else?"

"Well, he always smelled of Pears soap and tobacco."

"I admired him because, above all, he was fair," Boyd

71

said. "And I've tried to be like him. So I believe we should talk about Buddy sometime when your mother is here. That's the fairest way to make you understand."

She sighed and snuggled into his arms.

"But I don't think she's being fair," she said.

"Hush now," he said and patted her shoulder gently.

And Katherine Jackson Boyd rested in her father's arms, physically safe and secure and privileged in their electronically guarded apartment building high above the mean streets and alleys where Gus Soltik was looking for a kitten.

5

SAMANTHA SPADE stood looking out a tenement window in Spanish Harlem, while a pair of her enforcers—black professional muscle, Biggie Lewis and Coke Roosevelt—were systematically and unemotionally smothering a young Puerto Rican boy, Manolo Ramos, who was delinquent by six hundred and ninety dollars in his payments to Samantha, a statuesque black Shylock, whose turf embraced much of Harlem from river to river and south of 125th Street. Samantha was tall, five eleven in white leather boots, with classically chiseled features and wide, luminous eyes, which she enlarged in a startling and almost comic fashion with heavy black liner and silver-white eye shadow. She wore a high-crowned dome-shaped red velvet hat and a flared leather coat over a black denim pants suit, which glittered with sequins forming clusters of patriotic designs, stars and eagles and shoulder patches from the old glory outfits, the 182d Airborne Division, and the Fourth Infantry, the Ivy Division.

The room was small and filthy and smelled of drains.

Coke Roosevelt and Biggie Lewis were large, powerful young men who amused themselves by dressing with piratical flourishes; they wore silver earrings, Aussie digger hats, tight leather suits with brilliant scarlet kerchiefs wound around their powerfully muscled throats.

With effortless ease, they held young Manolo's writhing figure on a narrow bed, twisting his slim brown arms high up between his shoulder blades and pressing his curly head and pretty brown face deeply into a soiled and matted pillow.

"All right! That's enough!" Samantha Spade said abruptly, and Coke Roosevelt and Biggie Lewis immediately released the boy, reacting like well-trained guard dogs to the thread of irritation in Samantha's voice.

"Mother, Mother, don't let them hurt me!" Manolo screamed at Samantha.

All this Samantha found degrading. You started with something clean, and while the interest was ball-breaking, they couldn't go to banks, so they came to her. When they got behind and started hiding, you had to use muscle, or your work and reputation went down the drain.

"We didn't advertise for you, Manolo."

"It's my brother," Manolo said, barely whispering the words, while watching Samantha's cold black face as if it were hostile terrain he must try to cross to find sanctuary.

She knew about his brother, a junkie with a big habit, whose whining and desperate appeals for help lay across Manolo's spirit like a draining poultice. Manolo, at twenty, was two years older than his sick brother and had been told countless thousands of times by their dead mother to take good care of his little brother and

74

hold his hand crossing the streets. All the streets of life. . . .

"But you and me made a nice business deal, and it didn't have anything to do with your brother," she said.

"He makes me cry, and I can't stand it."

Oh, Jesus, Samantha thought. Coke and Biggie flipped Manolo over onto his back, locking his arms behind his head with their huge black hands. Manolo was naked except for a pair of clean white sweat socks, and the overhead lights coated his slim body and small but shapely private parts with shimmering silver reflections.

He's really something, Samantha thought, staring with frank interest at his vulnerable body. What a super trip she could make with him, toying with him like an elegant little doll. Manolo had curly brown hair, the dimpled face of a cherub, and skin as soft and finely textured as pure silk. But none of this sweet stuff was for the ladies. Manolo was strictly for cockbirds.

Samantha—who had been christened Maybelle Cooper in Mobile, Alabama, and educated in New York—sat down on the bed beside Manolo and let her fingertips stray across the velvetlike skin of his stomach.

Manolo shivered unpleasantly; the touch of her flesh against his revolted him; it was a perverse, unclean feeling, like flowers acrid with rot.

Coke Roosevelt lighted a big cigar and blew smoke into Manolo's face.

"Staff of life, faggykins," Coke said in a soft but rumbling voice.

"He means, like bread," Biggie Lewis said. Manolo was not afraid of Biggie. He knew Biggie wanted him, but if Biggie hurt him, he'd lose any chance of getting him to go down on him. But Coke Roosevelt didn't want him and might enjoy hurting him to prove it. Samantha wanted him, too, but there was no leverage there for Manolo.

"What's the most you tricked in one night, Manolo?"

"Eight, maybe ten times."

Samantha looked at him thoughtfully."This may set Women's Lib back a ton, but I'm giving you a break. You got two nights to get that six hundred and ninety dollars. Don't make us look for you."

"Thanks for shit nothing," Manolo said sullenly.

"You talk nice to Samantha," Coke Roosevelt said to him. "If you don't, I'll twist off that little spic cock of yours. But knowing where you like to put it, I'd do the job with a pliers."

"Go fuck yourself," Manolo shouted, and spat in Coke Roosevelt's face.

"Stop it!" Samantha said.

Manolo spat at Coke Roosevelt again, and then he screamed in pain; Samantha had tugged sharply at his pubic hair, a gesture more reflexive than sadistic, expressing the casual tyranny of all ghettos, pain and violence employed as impersonal proof of power.

"When I tell you to stop it, you stop it," Samantha said to Manolo.

Samantha, her manner absent and distracted, drew her fingernails across Manolo's stomach; his reaction was spasmodic and helpless, a shuddering contraction of the muscles in his loins.

"Manolo, there's a convention of florists at the Plaza this week, and a lot of them cats are only a couple of degrees from flaming fags. Pick yourself some pansies.

76

Maybe work Central Park the next couple of nights, find yourself some passion fruits."

Her fingertips continued to stray across the velvet surface of his stomach. She was amused but irritated at his deliberate refusal to respond to her efforts to arouse him.

He knew what she was trying to do to him, but he was angrily determined to frustrate her. Manolo lay perfectly still and turned his face away from her. He made no attempt to struggle against the massive black arms and hands that held him like a rack on the narrow bed. Manolo enjoyed the feel of that warm male muscle against his body, and he savored his helplessness, the bondage and restraint imposed on him, and so he made no move to struggle against those powerful hands because that would only excite him and make Samantha's victory inevitable.

Manolo thought of his mother and the little white sugar cakes she had made for him. Sometimes she filled them with pinola nuts, sometimes with yellow raisins. He and his brother ate them watching TV after school. They watched old movies. Game shows. Fuck Samantha, he thought, his mood vicious and triumphant, surfacing to the present. But that was a dangerous indulgence. Dick Clark's *Bandstand.* His thoughts went back to his childhood, where there was safety and where his mother was alive and where his brother was sweet and weak and not as yet in trouble.

But to his shame and horror, he felt his flesh betraying him. Helplessly responding to Samantha's sensual ministrations, his stomach muscles contracted convulsively and sent seismic currents of ecstasy into the very root of his sexual organ, and slowly the base of his spine began to dissolve in delicious agony.

"Stop it! Stop it, you shit bitch!" he screamed into her face.

Biggie and Coke chuckled at the signs of rut on Manolo's slim, smooth body.

But Samantha was disgusted and angry with herself. She stood abruptly and walked to the door.

"Save it for somebody who'll pay for it," she said.

"Samantha," he said, barely whispering her name.

But her heart wasn't easy, and she didn't know why. It was always that goddamn Emma and Missoura thing. Walk through the mud, you dumb niggers. But she was touched and moved by Manolo's physical response to her. She wondered if it would be amusing to help him, to take care of him. Her own life was so full of dreck and pain, so tinted with the lavender of resignation that she was desperate for any emotional diversion.

"Take care of business," she said to no one in particular, and walked out of the room.

On the street in front of Manolo's building, Samantha's chauffeur stood beside her Cadillac and scowled irritably at six or eight young Puerto Ricans who were admiring the loaded green Coupe de Ville. When Samantha came down the steps to the sidewalk, her chauffeur, whose name was Doc Logan, opened the rear door of the car, and said to her, "Got a call while you were upstairs, Samantha. Chuck from the poolroom. Gypsy Tonnelli is looking for you."

"Chuck say why?"

"Yeah. Something about that psycho's been wasting them little chicks. The Gypsy knows what he looks like, and he's thinking maybe one of our sharks could maybe make the cat."

"Screw the Gypsy," Samantha said, and slid her lithe, elegant body into the interior of the luxuriously leathered and perfumed Coupe de Ville.

Seconds later Coke Roosevelt crowded in beside her and Biggie Lewis climbed into the passenger seat alongside Doc.

There was a musing smile on Samantha's lips. "Yeah, screw the Gypsy," she said, and crossed her long, slimly booted legs. "You know, I went to the same school with him. Right here in Spanish Harlem, when there were a lot of ginzos around. He was way ahead of me, but I kind of hung out with his sister, Adela. I used to help her with her arithmetic." Samantha laughed, displaying splendid white teeth. "Lordy, was she dumb." She tapped her forehead. "Solid bone, solid. We called the Gypsy the Pope then, because he never scored as far as we knew."

The green Coupe de Ville moved smoothly and arrogantly into an intersection on the yellow, cruised on slowly and insolently against the red.

In a squad car a young uniformed cop spotted the infraction and reached for the ignition key, but his partner, a seasoned old bull, looked at him and shook his head. "No way. That spook's off limits to you and me."

The Harlem night was blue with a smog reflecting brilliant neon lights in dancing patterns, and in the cruising green Cadillac, Samantha's mood was as blue as the night itself, a mix of emotions that turned her thoughts toward her childhood and her drunken giant of a father, rotting with syphilis, his own eyes turned inward in bitter recollections of old angers, dead illusions.

Samantha's father used to say to her, "The game ain't worth the shame, honey. You win, you just shippin' some tired shit. Lose, you turn it around. You the tired shit gettin' whipped."

It was Gypsy Tonnelli who was darkening her thoughts, she knew, because the only reason Tonnelli would call her was that he needed help, but helping Whitey was the thing that gave Samantha those migraines. . . .

Manolo Ramos dressed hastily in his most provocative gear, a pale-gray silk shirt open to his navel, a short white fur jacket, stacked blue leather boots, and midnight-blue suede pants that fitted his rounded buttocks like a second layer of skin. He patted a sweet cologne on his cheeks and hair, which he had already teased into a halo of brown curls. Flashing a brilliant professional smile at himself in the mirror above his hand sink, Manolo let himself from his room and ran down dirty, uncarpeted stairs to catch the crosstown bus to Central Park.

Six hundred ninety dollars, he was thinking. Shit, I'm a bargain. . . .

At eleven thirteen P.M. on the fourteenth of October, engine and ladder companies were dispatched to a fire in a shabby tenement west of Ninth Avenue in the middle Fifties of the borough of Manhattan. Firemen contained the blaze that was smoldering in a mattress in the first-floor bedroom and that had been started by an

80

elderly wino who had fallen asleep smoking a twisted stogie.

The hissing of water under compression, the sound of shouted orders, the thud of firemen's boots, had alerted and terrified a nursing alley cat nesting in the basement of the tenement with four lively kittens. The big tabby bitch, in panic, began evacuating her young, carrying them in her teeth with a soft but firm grip on the backs of their necks, running with them through an open window to the safety of an unoccupied garage in another area of the block. She made three such trips, but when she returned for her fourth and last kitten, she couldn't find it. She circled restlessly, whining in distress and anxiety, but receiving no answer at all to her plaintive, demanding calls, she leaped a last time through the open window and ran off into the darkness.

The lobby of the Plaza Hotel at Fifth-ninth Street near Fifth Avenue was in brilliant contrast with the slum district where firemen had doused the flames in a mattress and chewed the ass out of a dumb Puerto Rican wino who had fallen asleep smoking a cheap black stogie—and where in the dim brain of a nursing tabby gleamed the distant, receding memory of some part of her forever lost.

Crescent Holloway was making a harried, distracted entrance into the lobby of the Plaza, blinking with jet-lag weariness and irritation at the exploding flashlights of a phalanx of news photographers. In Miss Holloway's van and wake streamed protective and supportive members of her personal entourage, forces beefed up by baggage-laden bellhops, a brace of assistant managers, and several executives from National Films, whose firm had become a financial phenomenon among the majors by distributing back-to-back smash hits displaying the explosive sexual pyrotechnics of Miss Holloway, who had become known in the trade papers as the Stacked House Kid.

Directly behind Crescent Holloway, who was shielding her eyes in a pretty gesture against the exploding flashbulbs, stood her personal makeup man, Simon Sachs; her press agent, Nate Sokol; and her bulking and belligerent-looking black maid, Honey Hopper.

Directly in front of Crescent—the sturdy prow of this harmlessly beleaguered sex boat—stood Rudi Zahn, her lover, her manager, and her producer, although not necessarily in that order.

Rudi Zahn, a stockily built man in his late thirties, with thinning hair and clear, direct gray eyes, raised both hands and gave the noisy photographers and reporters a friendly, give-us-a-break smile. The smile was not practiced; it was amiable and honest and suggested something true of Rudi Zahn's character, which tested surprisingly low in the slick cynicism the press expected from Hollywood types.

The reporters and photographers liked the message they were getting from Rudi Zahn and listened to what he had to say, which was: "It was a bumpy flight with a bomb scare. The movie, I mean." He mentioned a competitor's product and got a laugh. "It was so bad that people actually walked out on it." Another laugh. The jokes were old, but no one minded; Rudi didn't pretend they were otherwise.

He went on: "We're tired, but we'll stay up all night if you're on deadline. Nate's got a press kit with some quotes and pix that haven't been used yet. That's the *bad* news." Another general laugh.

The good news that Rudi Zahn promised the press corps was an early-morning conference, a screening of key scenes from the Stacked House Kid's next flick, all this graced by a buffet of delicatessen from the Stage Door with champagne for those who were thirsty and whiskey for those who weren't. . . .

Within seconds, Crescent Holloway and her group were streaming toward the elevators amid smiles and an eruption of involuntary whistles from the working press.

After midnight, when the important day began (although Gus Soltik did not feel it started until there were streaks of dawn on the horizon), he began to feel drowsy, and the infallible indicator of his mind pointed toward "home." Using a network of streets and alleys that were like the veins of his own huge body, and subway trains, and the rear tailgate of a truck lumbering along the Major Deegan Highway, Gus Soltik reached 135th Street and St. Ann's Avenue about an hour after leaving the site of the fire on Ninth Avenue in the borough of Manhattan.

It was very quiet. Rain was falling, and gusts of wind made a noise like scurrying animals in the trash in the curbs and on the sidewalk. Housing developments, the color of mud, stood in rows stretching toward a dark sky and between them stretched damp, slimy earth, unrelieved by a tree, a leaf, a stretch of grass, a child's swing, or a chair for an old man or woman to sit in thin sunlight in these barren yards that bordered prison shafts of public housing.

Gus was glad he didn't live there, glad instead to live in the rotting old tenement with Mrs. Schultz. Senor Perez gave her the money that Gus earned, and sometimes she gave him a few dollars and with that money he could buy all he really needed: hot dogs from street vendors, the cold roll heaped high with onions, a cup of snow ice with sweet bright-colored syrups, or roast walnuts and hot pretzels.

Also, he had a reserve supply of money that no one knew about. Not Senor Perez, not even Mrs. Schultz. Gus had cut a deep flap in the bottom of the heels of his Wellington boots, and after stuffing these apertures with dimes and quarters, he had pressed the V-shaped pieces of leather back into place, securing them firmly with strips of black friction tape. It gave him a good feeling to know he was walking on his secret money. It was always there if he needed to take a bus or subway or needed to satisfy his sudden, compulsive yearning for things that tasted sweet.

But Gus Soltik disliked spending those precious quarters. That was why he was glad that the kitten purring against his body in the pocket of his jacket hadn't cost him anything at all.

But while it cost nothing, it would solve a problem that had tormented him for months. How to make "greenropes" cross that street.

Gus Soltik would sleep now, to be wakened by the distant bells of St. Stanislaus. He knew he would hear Mrs. Schultz going down the creaking stairs, knowing that in her old hands she would be holding a leather prayer book and the heavy wooden rosary from the old country, on her way to his mother's dead mass.

6

GYPSY TONNELLI was a practical cop, who trusted his instincts and knew from experience that it wasn't only the "facts" or what you learned from informants that solved your cases; rather it was something you ignored or didn't see until it was too late that often provided directions to solutions. So, pacing the large, high-ceilinged living room of his apartment, he allowed his thoughts to stray, made a conscious attempt not to screen out random reflections but rather permitted external stimuli to play whimsically against all his senses. It was a few strokes after midnight, D-Day Plus One. In each of the previous four years, the Juggler had struck late in the afternoon of October 15. But they couldn't count on that. As far as Tonnelli was concerned, this was now Red Alert time. While he paced, chain-smoked, and constantly refilled his cup of coffee, Tonnelli's eyes occasionally flicked hopefully to the phone on a table beside a cheap chair, a phone connected directly to his headquarters in the 19th Precinct. As the countdown approached zero, the reports from all five boroughs had increased in volume;

so far all had been checked out, and all had proved either inconclusive or negative.

Tonnelli deliberately allowed his thoughts to wander, hoping that some significant hidden fact would sense his inattention and be trapped into a revealing carelessness of its own; the elusive lead was frequently snared in this fashion, a victim of indirect surveillance.

Detective Sergeant Boyle was at the 13th Precinct on East Twenty-first Street. He would be on duty there for eighteen straight hours, taking the occasional half-hour sleep break in the precinct-house coffee room. Late in the afternoon Rusty Boyle would break to shower, change clothes and have dinner, at which time he would be at Joyce Colby's apartment.

The alleged rape the big Irishman had checked out had developed ramifications. Boyle had told him about it. The license number of the rape suspect's car had been provided by someone named John Ransom, who had later told Rusty Boyle he was dying of cancer. Rusty had given the number to Dennis St. John from the 10th Precinct. St. John checked the tag with Motors, got an address to go with it, hit the suspect's apartment, found not only the character Hilda Smedley claimed had raped her, but four rooms full of hot TV sets, cameras, and hi-fi equipment. St. John would get all the credit for the collar, and while he had a head of solid bone, he would probably be reviewed and might be bucked up a grade or two. But none of that was Rusty Boyle's particular concern. His big Irish heart was bleeding for John Ransom, the man dying of cancer, who was forced to lie to his wife about his upholstery sales and make up

86

funny, interesting little stories about his customers, while gnawed and worried sleepless, not about himself, but how to tell his wife he was dying and how to explain to his daughter, who was in premed school, that there was no money to pay the tuition needed for the next five or six years.

Tonnelli had shocked Rusty by asking him if Ransom had a double indemnity clause in his insurance policy. There was a way to beat those riotous cancerous cells to the finish line by a couple of weeks. Rent a sailboat and go over the side. Take a drive into the Catskills, miss a curve, and take the long, final drop into the valley.

Why not? All he'd lose was hours of agony. His wife would be spared knowledge of his ordeal, and he'd be giving his daughter the biggest break of all, the chance to earn a degree in medicine. Who knows? She could wind up with a Nobel Prize.

But Rusty Boyle, the emotional and romantic optimist, had been staggered and angered by Tonnelli's proposal.

"But Jesus Christ! Supposing they discover a cure for cancer the day after he wastes himself?"

"Hate to break it to you like this, Rusty, but there really ain't no Easter Bunny."

Tonnelli's phone rang a dozen or more times within the next half hour, and as the reports flowed in, he was able to visualize and analyze the action throughout the city.

From the 90th in Brooklyn came a signal reporting men lurking in alleys. The 90th was a pigeonhole area filled with Hasidic Jews, Puerto Ricans, and stubbornly nonmobile Italian immigrants. Plainclothes and

87

uniform cops picked up the suspects, who turned out to be bullyboy Nazi types on the scene, hoping to whip the heads of some militant Jews.

At the 48th Precinct in the Seventh Division in the South Bronx, the desk sergeant got a call from a hysterical woman who demanded the police do something about two mysterious men in the apartment above her who for days had been copulating around the clock to the accompaniment of liquid and obscene noises. They were, in fact, operating what ATF (the acronym for the federal agency controlling illegal alcohol, tobacco, and firearms) describes unofficially as a "nigger" still, a phrase pejorative in relation to quantity, although not necessary to quality.

In Manhattan North (covering most of Harlem), the 26th Precinct reported a rape in an empty lot west of Tenth Avenue on 128th Street. But the girl was in her twenties, and all three of her assailants had been apprehended and they were all black, or all "chocolate," as the second laconic report had it.

East Harlem, Second Avenue near 116th Street. Twelve-year-old black girl reported missing. Found forty-five minutes later, stoned out of her skull in the men's washroom of a hamburger joint near 110th and Central Park West.

Goddamn her black ass, Tonnelli thought, but he wasn't thinking of a kid stoned in a hamburger joint, but Maybelle Cooper, who hadn't returned his call, hadn't bothered to set up a meeting at her pool hall or his HQ at the 19th. Milky Tichnor had checked in; so had Chapman and Solly Castro. All negative. But Samantha Spade hadn't checked in.

He'd collar her for that, and he'd do it with savage

pleasure. But why all the heat? he wondered. She probably knew why he never saw Adela anymore. It wasn't Maybelle Cooper that Gypsy was furious with, the black kid with the computer head, who had taught his dumb sister basic arithmetic. No, it was Samantha Spade, who knew the city and its secrets as profoundly and bitterly as he did and who probably knew damned well that Adela's Greek husband, Stav Tragis, ran a stolen car ring out of his used-car lots in Baltimore. . . .

The reports continued to come in, relayed from the switchboard operators of the 13th and 19th precincts to Lieutenant Tonnelli. In the Gypsy's mind, he could envision the operations and embrace with his imagination the gross sprawl of the dark city. He watched rivers flowing, heard the scream of police sirens, saw the revolving red glare of dome lights, pictured cops in uniform with drawn guns, taking steps two at a time to investigate the tips and squeals now being funneled into the 13th and 19th precincts at what seemed to be a cyclical rate of increase.

Ninth near Fifth. Black man forcing black girl into a maroon Mark III. Checked out negative. A pimp and his prossie.

Male Caucasian reported in women's room at comfort station in Central Park. Arrested by patrolman, cited on morals charge at the 22d Precinct on Eighty-sixth Street (Central Park's Transverse Number Three).

Missing child, Caucasian, male, age eight, residence on Fifty-fourth Street between First and Second avenues. Checked out negative. Subject found at Manhattan central bus station, hoping for ride to Detroit to visit divorced father.

Paul Wayne of the New York *Times* had called, but Tonnelli had little for him. After the Juggler's second ritualistic murder, the local press and television corps had scented a story of epic and explosive proportions in the works, given an affirmative to the one conditional "if." *If* he killed again. . . .

That was their morbid but nonetheless professional concern. And so, in the third year, when the body of Trixie Atkins had been found in a loft in Greenwich Village with rope burns on her thighs and a dreadful knife wound across her jugular vein, the thrust of the story had been escalated to intense national coverage. A year later, when Jennie Goldman was murdered on the same date after suffering the agonizing brutalities that had been inflicted on the other three victims, the story had triggered a flamboyant and righteous explosion from the media, with parallels drawn to the Zebra and Zodiac slaughters in San Francisco, accompanied by the inevitable trailing inferences of police and political incompetence. There had been nonsubtle suggestions that if patrolmen weren't "cooped up" (a police expression for sleeping on duty) in the lobbies of closed theaters or basements of school buildings, and if the deputy chiefs and assistant chiefs who served at the pleasure of the commissioner, and hence were not protected by Civil Service, had the guts to enforce stringent curfews, to haul in every known sex offender over the past decade, and if the commisioner himself were not so politically ambitious and spent less time at international councils developing his themes of "brotherhood through law and order" and "the tyranny of the philosophy of numbers in police work," well, the obvious inference was that the Juggler would have been caught long since and that Fun City would be again and forever be entitled to its innocent and sustaining nickname.

The commissioner, in fact, had been in print that morning from Stockholm. On the third page of the *Times,* below the fold, he'd been quoted as saying to a meeting of delegates: "It has been said that one death is a tragedy, but that a million deaths is a statistic. Yes, that has been said and it was said by a man whose name was Joseph Stalin. And I repudiate his convictions as I repudiate *him.* . . ."

Tonnelli was gut-certain they'd all be handed their heads by most of the media if the Juggler made it five in a row. And they'd deserve it. . . .

But the hue and cry and bullshit didn't apply to Paul Wayne. He was a cynical middle-aged pro who knew his job, and Tonnelli trusted him. It was some other papers in town that would sprinkle blood across the front pages of their sheets if it would sell five additional copies.

So he gave Wayne what he had. The tips, how they checked out, the forces and equipment that were standing by.

The phone rang again. It was Sokolsky on the switchboard at the 19th. "Lieutenant, we got a kid missing over in Brooklyn, from one of them crummy apartment buildings a block north of the Williamsburg Bridge. Age eleven, a Puerto Rican girl. Cops from the division and precinct are on it."

The Juggler had never struck outside Manhattan.

"What's the kid's name?"

"Trinidad Davoe."

"Notify the precinct commander and the division inspector that we're sending plainclothesmen over from the Thirteenth."

"Check, Lieutenant."

Before Tonnelli could refill his coffee cup and light another cigarette, Sokolsky was back on the line. "There's nothing to it, Lieutenant, that Puerto Rican kid over in Williamsburg."

"What was it?"

"A crazy, I guess," Sokolsky said. "Seems this kid got killed by a car a few years back. A milk truck, actually. The priest told the old lady that she really hadn't gone away, lots of the guys in the precinct know about this, so the old lady goes to church and lights vigil lights and keeps reporting her daughter missing. One of the guys told me she keeps the kid's bed turned down and gets up at night and finds it empty and calls the precinct to find her kid. It's kind of sad."

Crazies, a town full of crazies. Paul Wayne at the *Times* told him the crank calls were starting, and Gypsy Tonnelli thought of these as he looked at the photographs on the walls of his apartment, pictures he took as a hobby on his days off, scenes of the various boroughs that he'd grown up in and worked in and loved, scenes the out-of-towners never saw because all they wanted to do, it seemed to the Gypsy, was get drunk and wander around high-crime-rate areas where they could get mugged so they could tell the folks at home about it.

The crazies were coming out of the wood.

"Look, I ain't talking to no shit secretary or reporter. I want to talk to the editor of the *Times,* and I'll stick it in his ear, because if the cops don't catch that guy who's murdering all those little girls I ain't payin' dime one in state or city taxes anymore."

"I'll connect you to the metropolitan desk, sir."

The visitors' concept of New York never embraced that of neighborhood; their picture was inevitably a stereotype of hostile and highly neurotic people living in apartment buildings one on top of the other and sharing the elevators without ever a "hello" or a "good morning" or "it's going to be a scorcher, isn't it?"

Paul Wayne had told him of one hysterical lady who had told him in shouting Biblical accents that she and she alone was responsible for the deaths of the four girls. They had been punished by a just but Almighty God because she had sinned, had whored around the bars of Third Avenue like a bitch in season, and since she had been the angel of her family before her fall, the vengeance of God had been that much more savage and merciless. "It's all kind of a preemptive vaginal strike by the Big Cock in the Sky," Wayne had said wearily.

But in fact, Tonnelli thought, arms crossed, studying his nearly professional portraits of the boroughs of New York, Manhattan didn't match the tourist boobs' concept of it. It was as rich and diverse, as ethnically and racially sustaining as areas of the country where you had Texans and Indians and Mexicans mixed together. Or the fascinating pockets of ethnicity, the colorful and variegated customs that he had observed when he was in the Army, along the frontiers of Holland and Belgium and Italy and France. If you didn't like the weather, wait a minute and it'd change. True of his city. If you didn't like the food, the look of the streets, the people, the way they dressed, take a walk and find something else.

Paul Wayne had told him of other calls.

"I marvel at your stupidity, all of you phony liberals, though I am not going to assume your 'bigotry' and assert that you are not sincere. But it is so simple it makes me laugh. If 'they' would just let James Earl Ray out of solitary, you wouldn't have a country where four little girls can get their throats slashed by the 'animals' that are the darlings of all your Northern cities."

Lieutenant Tonnelli inhaled deeply on his cigarette and looked at photographs he had taken of Queens around Jackson Heights and the Carroll Gardens in Brooklyn and the playgrounds and wading pools at Hillside Home in the Bronx. Much of the views were imperfect. There was always the evidence of common humanity in graffiti and litter, but there was strength everywhere, too, in an evident will not only to endure but to survive, exemplified nowhere more powerfully than in vistas and scenes that Lieutenant Tonnelli had found in Grymes Hill, Staten Island, a neighborhood still splendored by gulls and water and views of seaports and shipping lanes.

But the tourists saw none of that. Probably because they didn't want to. New York was a safari for them, with cabdrivers their white hunters, scaring the shit out of them with stories about certain areas of the West Side and Central Park. And it wasn't just the tourists; it could be pros. Sokolsky had called in earlier tonight to tell him about a retired Camden, New Jersey, detective named Babe Fritzel. Fritzel had come into the 19th Precinct, a well-set-up man despite his seventy-odd years, Sokolsky had reported, with shrewd, tough eyes and a full shock of white hair. Babe Fritzel still had a gun, a gold badge, and a two-way radio, and he'd come over to Manhattan from Teaneck, New Jersey, to offer his service to the NYPD to "get the bastard" who was cutting up little girls in the city.

"You know somebody named Unruh, Lieutenant?"

"Unruh?"

"Yeah, Unruh, that's what this guy Fritzel said."

"Well, there was a Howard or John Unruh who walked out of his house in Camden on a nice, sunny day, hell, this was before our time, Sokolsky, way back in the fifties, maybe even before that, and he shot and killed thirteen people, a lot of them kids, I remember."

Sokolsky seemed pleased to corroborate his lieutenant's last comment. "This guy, Babe Fritzel, told me one little kid was sitting on a rocking horse in a barbershop waiting to get his hair cut when Unruh blasted him. Fritzel was one of the cops who collared Unruh."

"You told him to get lost?"

"Told Mr. Babe Fritzel to go back to Teaneck and watch the show on TV in living color."

"What the hell is wrong with everybody?"

Sokolsky had hesitated a moment and then, clearing his throat, had said, "Well, Lieutenant, my idea is that—"

"Oh, for Christ's sake," Tonnelli said, and put the phone back in its cradle.

Tonnelli's doorbell rang. He checked the .38 in the holster on his belt, turned two locks, and opened his front door the six inches allowed by the burglar chain and found himself staring into the luminous, white-circled eyes of Samantha Spade, which were shadowed only slightly by the floppy brim of her red velvet hat.

"Real big of you to drop by," he said.

"Might have something, Lieutenant," Samantha said. "Buy a lady a drink?"

"You're on," Tonnelli said, and unhooked the burglar chain.

"It was on Eighth Avenue, up around a Hundred and Eleventh or a Hundred and Twelfth, six—maybe eight—months ago," Samantha said.

Samantha still wore her flared black leather coat and the black denim pants suit with sequins glittering in patriotic designs, but she had added a half dozen thick gold bracelets to her wrists.

"Bourbon all right?"

"With a splash of water."

Tonnelli went into his small kitchen and made two drinks and brought one back to Samantha, who reclined languidly in a deep leather chair, her legs crossed, the overhead lights glistening on her white boots.

"Go on," Tonnelli said.

"Where was I?"

"Eighth Avenue between a Hundred and Eleventh and a Hundred and Twelfth."

"One of my sharks was making loans in that area, laying the bread on guys from a car. Couple of my studs, Coke and Biggie, were keeping the line nice and orderly, taking down names, addresses, the amount of loot and collecting signatures. Most of the guys were old customers, brothers, and a few Puerto Ricans, so this big honkie, well—he stood out. I mean he was like a rebel yell at some spade corn boil. He was big, Gypsy. Six-four, my guys told me. And from what they said, a chest and shoulders like yours. He was wearing a leather jacket and some kind of a funky cap. My studs told me later he looked out to lunch permanent upstairs."

Tonnelli was taking notes on a legal pad. "How about his age?"

"Thirty, thirty-five. Anyway, the big honkie seemed to think it was like Santa Claus handing out the money. When he gets up to the paymaster, he reaches for some loot. They tried to get his name, find out where he worked, but they couldn't get through to him. Finally, they gave him a piece of paper and a pencil and told him to write all that shit down, and that's when he went ape."

"But did he write anything?" the Gypsy asked her.

"He tried to, but apparently he didn't know *how*, and that's what sent him around the bend. He just exploded, knocked two of my studs down, and it takes some kind of man to do that little thing. Then he smashed the windshield of the car with his fist and ran south down Eighth Avenue. The brothers took after him, you better believe it, but he split into Central Park. That's where they lost him."

"Where exactly, Maybelle?"

"There's an awful lot of hiding places between Central Park West and the Harlem Lake. You'd need dogs to find anybody."

"Your guys have anything else on his physical description?"

She frowned faintly and gently rubbed her jaw with long, tapering fingers. "Not really, Vince." Still frowning, she ticked off items. "He was big. He was white. Leather jacket, silly-looking hat, I think they said yellow."

"That's important. Are you sure they said that? That he was wearing a yellow cap?"

"How the shit you expect me to be sure of anything happened six months ago?"

Tonnelli sghed. "You always had a rotten temper and brass knuckles on your tongue."

"Hush," she said, and her expression became thoughtful. "I remember a couple of other things. The one word that came through clear sounded like a man's name. It was Lanny."

"Just that. No last name?"

She shook her head. "Just Lanny. And one of my guys told me this weirdo had real small eyes and a kind of bulging forehead."

"Your people ever see him around again?"

Samantha shook her head. "And you can believe they were looking."

"Fix yourself another drink if you want, the bottle's in the kitchen. Can't say for sure, but what you got might be some help."

As Tonnelli went to the telephone, Samantha stood with languid, slimly muscled grace and wandered toward the kitchen. Thanks a lot, Gypsy, she was thinking, realizing with an anticipation she dreaded that soon the first fires of migraine would ignite in her head. Emma and Missoura, you lazy niggers, you should have walked home through the rain. . . .

Lieutenant Tonnelli gave his orders to the operator at Central. "I want you to patch this description through to every precinct and division, to all boroughs. I want it to go first to Detective Sergeant Boyle at the Thirteenth and to Detective Clem Scott at the Nineteenth. Arrest

98

on sight with drawn guns a male Caucasian, thirty to thirty-five years of age. . . ."

In the neat and functional kitchen, Samantha added a mild splash of bourbon to her drink and strolled back into the living room, looking about curiously at Tonnelli's photographs, the worn leather furniture, and the framed pictures of Tonnelli's parents which stood on a marble mantel above the gas-log fireplace.

Tonnelli replaced the phone in its cradle and glanced appraisingly at Samantha, while the tip of his forefinger ran slowly up and down the scar that streaked the left side of his dark face. She interpreted the question in his eyes and sighed with weary finality.

"What else you want, Gypsy?"

"There's a police sketch artist standing by at my headquarters," Tonnelli said. "Your studs may have spotted the bastard we call the Juggler. My question is: Will they work with a police artist and help us come up with a picture?"

In for a penny, she thought, and rubbed her forehead as the first needles of pain began their precise probings of her brain.

"Coke and Biggie'll help out, Lieutenant," she said. "I'll get 'em over to the Nineteenth."

Because of her pain and the knowledge of what caused it, she felt a need to hurt him; her smile became cool and disparaging as she glanced about the room.

"So this is how the great Vincent Tonnelli winds up, All-State guard, honest cop, a bachelor in a two-room pad with some chairs and sofas that would go under the hammer for about fifty bucks."

Tonnelli smiled and flicked an imaginary speck of

99

dust from the sleeve of his cashmere jacket. "I wear it all on my back, Sam."

She looked at him curiously. "Saving your ginzo voodoo streak, you usually walk the cool side of the street. What's your hang-up now? Why you want to nail this bastard to the wall in strips?"

"I'm a cop. It's my job."

"Bull, baby, I make a living reading people, and knowing you, Gypsy, I could do it by Braille."

"It shows then?"

"Believe it. It comes through."

Over the years, Tonnelli had carefully studied his emotions and reactions, well aware that the intensity of his anger could escalate to a dangerous sickness, a plateau at which it might become a liability rather than an asset. He had seen that happen to cops who had lost their partners and had blamed themselves for it. They wanted victims to ease their rage and guilt. But after a certain point, considerations of innocence and involvement became irrelevant, and any victim would feed their need for revenge.

At first Tonnelli had believed his passion had been rooted in the simple violations of his turf. The murders had been committed in his village, in Manhattan. It was the taboo of territory, of tribe, of temples and shrines. But as the years passed, Tonnelli realized it was more than that.

"Say, how's that sister of yours?" Samantha asked him. "Adela? I heard she got married and has a lot of kids."

That was so close to his pain that her words struck him with an almost physical impact. A lot of kids, sure, he thought bitterly. Three nieces, two nephews. His

100

only kin and blood. When he'd walk by toy stores, he'd stop and look at things he'd like to buy for his nieces and nephews but couldn't. Big Raggedy Ann dolls, trains, windup animals that jumped through hoops, model airplanes you could fly by remote control. Hell, he'd once thought about getting a department loan and taking them all out to Disneyland. Or having them over here when he had three-day weekends. They could go to restaurants and ride around in his unmarked car and listen to the police calls. He could show them the photograph albums. The old man in his apron and the cheeses hanging from the ceiling in his market on Fulton Street. And the colored photograph of his mother without a streak of white in her hair at sixty and a temper that didn't go with those big, soulful eyes. And never a crooked dime out of that store or in their home. He knew damn well Adela wouldn't have any of those pictures, wouldn't even want them.

He would never know his nieces and nephews, never hold them in his arms, and that was why he would destroy the Juggler, because that madman's victims were surrogates for the kin he could never know and love.

"So how is she, Gypsy?"

"She's fine, just great," Tonnelli said quickly, too quickly, Samantha realized, and decided not to press it. She knew, in point of fact, that Adela Tonnelli was married to a Greek used-car dealer who fenced hot heaps up and down the Atlantic seaboard, and the Gypsy must know that, too, which meant he didn't see his sister or her kids anymore.

Tonnelli wasn't the worst of them. In fact, he was the best of them, and her need to hurt him was gone.

101

If there was anything good about cops, it was studs like Gypsy Tonnelli. He was straight and honest and wouldn't mark a man for life with the butt of his gun for kicks. There was a ton of weary pain in Tonnelli, and that was a town Samantha had played, and she knew all its dirty streets and alleys. At times she was so sick and full of despair from listening to one whining loser after another that it flawed her physically; there were nights when her headaches and muscle cramps almost drove her insane, and it was pills and the bottle then, and not being able to hate Whitey enough, and the annealing but sick and unrealizable dream of being on a warm beach with clean air around her and only the sound of slowly curling waves under a big, blue sky, and maybe—and this was the sickness—having someone like little Manolo to take care of and protect, and hell, maybe even love. . . .

Tonnelli knew from the masked compassion in Samantha's expression that she probably knew all about Stav Tragis, his sister's husband, who fenced hot cars and sold them to red-necks and Okies in North and South Carolina. And he was grateful that she was obviously not going to hit him with it, not sting him with the fact that he couldn't see his sister or her children anymore because she was married to a common thief.

"You know, Sam, why don't you try my side of the street for a while?" Tonnelli asked her. "Who knows, you might get to like it."

"You forget, Gypsy, us black cats don't have no spots to change. And for Christ's sake, Pope, the next time you ask me over, would you spring for a bottle of scotch?"

One of the offices in Tonnelli's headquarters in the

102

13th Precinct House had been converted into a "darkroom" by a police sketch artist, Detective First Grade Todd Webb. He had set up a portable screen and a sixteen-millimeter projector, and all functional witnesses were present, save Joey Harpe, who would be along within a few minutes, since the little Irisher and his parents were already en route to the 19th in a squad car.

Lieutenant Tonnelli stood alongside Patrolman Max Prima, whose back was like a ramrod and whose eyes were wide with an almost comical respect, which were his reactions to the top brass on the scene, Deputy Chief of Detectives Walter Greene and, an even more significant figure, the borough commander of South Manhattan himself, a two-star cop, Assistant Chief Inspector Taylor "Chip" Larkin, who, with his slight frame and silver-white hair and rimless spectacles, looked more like a parish priest from his native county of Cork than the chief of all police in the southern half of this sprawling, million-footed city.

Coke Roosevelt and Biggie Lewis stood apart from the police, talking to each other in soft, chuckling voices; if they found it a distinction to be in the presence of such exalted police officers, they were concealing it nicely.

At last—it was then about three fifteen on the morning of October 15—the office door opened, and the little Irish boy, Joey Harpe, came into the room with his vaguely apprehensive parents.

It was Joey Harpe who had seen the man who had murdered Jenny Goldman in the basement of a building on Twenty-ninth Street between Lexington and Third Avenue. . . .

With all lights turned off, Detective Todd Webb went

to work, flashing various shapes of skulls on the screen, long, square, round, and oval, until a consensus was reached by Patrolman Prima, the small Irish boy, and the two big blacks that the man they had all mutually observed had a head that was nearly as round as a bowling ball.

Detective Webb left that outline on the screen and began with deliberate speed to add and subtract from it various kinds and shapes of mouths, noses, and eyes and ears, until at last, after considerable argument and disagreement, the functional group of witnesses settled on a front and profile sketch of a man's face with these characteristics: small eyes, a heavy forehead, scraggly blond hair, a corded, powerful neck, and comically protruding ears.

Copies of this sketch would be processed and distributed by squad cars to every precinct of every borough of New York City.

They would not be distributed to local newspapers or television stations.

This was Chief Inspector Chip Larkin's decision.

As an impeccably schooled and highly intelligent police officer Chief Larkin knew that the Juggler could be classified medically as a Constitutional Psychopathic Inferior, whose shames and humiliations, whose rages and angers, induced by his own construct of physical chemicals, would helplessly and forever drive him into antisocial violence. They would catch him, of course, because he would continue on his course of savage and sadistic murders until they did. But Chief Larkin wanted him stopped tonight, not ten years from now. Ten young girls from now. . . .

And that was behind his decision not to release the

sketches of the Juggler to newsmen. They would need surprise and secrecy to bait traps for the Juggler.

"Thank you, son, and thank you, gentlemen," Chief Larkin said, and then he turned his parish priest's smile on Patrolman Max Prima. "That was a good, sharp bit of work, Officer."

In a move that surprised all of them, young Joey Harpe whipped out a notebook and a pencil and asked Biggie Lewis and Coke Roosevelt for their autographs.

7

THE kitten, purring, made its way slowly across the brown blanket of Gus Soltik's bed, stopping occasionally to peer about alertly and cautiously at its new environment. Near Gus Soltik's wrinkled and soiled pillow the kitten found a bit of food, a crumb of a doughnut with sugar on it. It sniffed at it, and while it licked at the grains of sugar, the door opened and Gus Soltik came in from the second-floor corridor with a saucer of milk in his big hands. He closed the door, locked it, and placed the dish of milk on the floor.

The room was close and warm, and there was an animal smell to it. Gus Soltik removed his yellow cap and pulled off his brown sweater, and the light from the single overhead bulb gleamed yellow on Gus Soltik's thick, wide shoulders, which were spotted with tiny clusters of pimples. He picked up the kitten, which was warm and soft in his great hands, and squeezed it gently, increasing the pressure till the little cat whimpered. "Not hurt," he said, speaking slowly and quietly, and then he placed the kitten on the floor beside the saucer of milk.

The kitten caused words to form in Gus Soltik's mind.

"Cages" and "Lanny." The kitten made him think of the "cages." They roared and frightened people, but Gus Soltik knew in some fashion they were helpless. They were him. Like him. He could frighten, but he was helpless. It created an agony of bewilderment and confusion in his head when he saw clerks making the cash register ring, adding up numbers, changing the paper money into the hard, shiny money. He could lift crates from the floor that none of the others could, but they had to point to where they wanted him to put them down. He never knew.

"Lanny." And food. Lanny had tried to explain to him about the animals that played the musical instruments around the clock. But he couldn't understand the music and distrusted it. But Lanny talked quietly. Lanny worked in the big building near the zoo and the pond. He liked Lanny, and once he had brought a sack of old food from the store. Green stuff and oranges and potatoes they put in the alley when the store closed. The food was for the cages. Gus Soltik wanted to do something for them because Lanny was good to him. But Lanny explained, slowly and quietly, that only certain people could give food to the cages. He felt none of the helpless anger that was like a fire in him when such things happened. When he didn't understand, Lanny talked slow and smiled, and it was different. . . . And once, and this was their secret, Lanny had shown him how to start and drive the truck.

With the back of his hand, Gus Soltik massaged the welt in his low, round forehead which had been caused by the tight, restricting rim of his yellow leather cap. He spoke again to the kitten, saying, "Not hurt," and smiled in an earnest and surprised fashion when the little animal began to lap at the milk with its darting pink tongue. It was a pretty cage, he thought, black with a white spot between its eyes. "Not hurt," he said again.

Gus Soltik's voice was high and shrill, a ludicrous sound emerging from that massive corded throat, but the sounds he made were only high and straining when he was excited, and he was so excited now that his hands were trembling and there were blisters of sweat on his forehead and the backs of his hands.

It was time. He thought of a green skirt and white legs, and a mask of lust glazed his eyes and, like a muddy dye, deepened the raw red color in his cheeks.

Moving with strides uncommon to a man of his height and size, he went to his closet, where a battered airlines travel bag hung from a hook alongside his mother's dress.

Unzippering the bag, Gus Soltik placed it on his bed, noting as he did that the kitten was continuing to drink the milk. He had found the bag one night in a trash can on Park Avenue near Fifty-seventh Street. The sides of the bag were frayed, and there were several rips in the stiff plastic fabric, but it had a strong zipper and a sturdy handle.

Gus Soltik glanced slowly around his meagerly furnished room to be absolutely certain that he remembered all his hiding places. Some things were there, he knew, allowing his glazed eyes to remain fixed on a chest of drawers. Another thing was in the shoebox on the table under a window which was covered by a faded green shade.

Suddenly he felt a stir of panic; it was as if a damp cloth had been rubbed with a powerful hand across his mind, completely erasing his memory of his last name.

"Gus . . . Gus . . . " he said, the words tense with his fears.

109

And with this sickening lapse, this dreadful loss of identity, came still another desperate realization; his mind was blank, and there was a roaring in his ears because he knew he not only had forgotten his last name but had forgotten the hiding places of the two most essential things. . . .

He couldn't run downstairs to the mailbox and look for his name. Not without putting on his sweater and cap. Mrs. Schultz would shout at him and want to know why, but if he stood here, trembling like an animal trapped in a circle of fire, his despair might become so unendurable that he would be forced to pound his head against the wall until he lost consciousness.

Abruptly he was seized by a terrible thirst. He ran into his bathroom and opened the mirrored door of a tiny medicine cabinet, and while he reached for a plastic glass, his eye fell on an object partially hidden by a pair of empty cookie boxes. When he saw those glistening loops of steel, he almost sobbed with relief.

And at the same instant he was able to speak his own name clearly and confidently: "Gus Soltik."

His thirst had gone. With sure, confident fingers, he lifted the handcuffs from behind the cookie boxes and returned to his bedroom and gently placed the linked steel wristlets into the tattered airlines bag. He had bought the handcuffs in a novelty shop on Forty-second Street, and while they were sold as toys, they would effectively manacle the thin wrists of a child.

Moving now with extreme care, determined to make no mistakes, there was a sense of both ritual and economy in the manner in which Gus Soltik opened the bureau drawer and lifted out three items which had been hidden under one of his shirts: a coil of slim nylon rope, a roll of wide adhesive tape, and a pipe lighter whose tiny metal jet could generate a three-inch surge of white-hot flame. After carefully placing these objects in the airlines bag, he removed the lid from the shoebox and sifted through a clutter of torn-up newspapers until his fingers closed on the handle of his heavy hunting knife. Slipping the knife free from its sheath, he checked the edge of the razor-sharp blade with his thumb. As he returned the blade to its sheath and dropped the hunting knife into the airlines bag, there was a knock on the door, and Mrs. Schultz called to him from the corridor.

"Come on down to the kitchen, Gus."

Not remembering whether or not he had locked the door, Gus moved with a speed spurred by terror, scooping up the cat and plunging it into the airlines bag.

"I got some coffee and doughnuts," Mrs. Schultz said. "I got the jelly kind."

Gus put the airlines bag in his closet and closed the door, and then, trembling with panic, he picked up the saucer of milk and ran into the bathroom, dumping the milk into the handbasin and rinsing it away with sluicings of tap water.

In the corridor of the old tenement, which creaked endlessly with the final settlings of time, Mrs. Schultz stood in front of Gus Soltik's door, her normally placid and passive features darkened with an anxious frown.

She was a stout old woman with thick gray hair, which she wore knotted with a rubber band at the base of her neck. Balanced on the bridge of her bulbous nose were narrow steel-rimmed spectacles which did little to aid her rheumy old eyes. This didn't concern her; she had no occasion to read anything these days and they were fine for yardwork and TV shows, and she liked the way they looked, bright and glinty on sunny days. She tried

Gus' door and found it locked and felt a stir of anxiety.

"What you doing, Gus?"

"Putting clothes."

Mrs. Schultz noticed that his voice was high and shrill, which was bad. It meant he was nervous. The best thing to do was just leave him alone, pay no attention. . . . That's what Gus' mother had told her, and who would know better than a boy's own mother?

"It's ready when you want it," she said, and went back down the stairs and into the kitchen on the first floor of their silent old tenement.

Mrs. Schultz sat in the kitchen, waiting for the sound of Gus Soltik's heavy footsteps on the stairs. The room was warm, and the rows of African violets she kept on the windowsills that overlooked the cluttered backyard charged the air with damp fragrance.

Mrs. Schultz felt sorry for Gus tonight because she knew he was in one of his troubled moods, but the emotion was not strange to her because she had spent most of the seventy-three years of her life feeling sorry for other people.

Her parents had brought her to New York from Germany when she was only a child, a dozen years before the First World War, and ever since, she had lived in New York in a succession of slums and tenements and ghettos. She never complained because her father and mother had told her she must be grateful because she lived in a free country.

Mrs. Schultz had made it her life's work to help others. She brought soups to ailing women and collected clothing for ragamuffin children. She tried to console the wives of the crazy Irishers, who drank from Saturday night until Monday morning and sometimes tore up their pay as if they hated the sight of it. The

112

Irishers' wives, the young ones anyway, were always the prettiest in the block, with their black or red hair and creamy skins and wild, frightened eyes. She brought sassafras tea and lemon cakes to the sorrowing Jewish women when they were having their cherished babies, and she hounded Sergeant Duffy to let the drunks out in time to get to their jobs.

Gus Soltik had no father that anyone knew anything about. His mother had rented a room from Mrs. Schultz almost twenty years ago, when Gus was a huge, awkward ten-year-old. They had lived in adjoining rooms on the second floor and were no trouble at all, except when Gus got into his queer moods, where he might lash out unexpectedly at anybody who happened to trigger his crazy temper.

That arrangement had ended one misting night about five years ago, when Mrs. Soltik had been struck and killed by an automobile at the intersection of Eighth Avenue and Fifty-fourth Street. The driver, Marla Collins, a nineteen-year-old secretary, had been questioned and released by police. Mrs. Soltik, who was given to drink and strong language, had staggered from between two parked trucks directly into the path of Miss Collins' car, and the girl testified there was no way in the world she could have avoided hitting the big woman.

After the accident Gus Soltik had hidden himself in the basement of the tenement for a week. He hadn't gone to the church or the graveyard. He wasn't angry. That came later. He was frightened. He was afraid someone would come and take him away, now that he was alone.

Mrs. Schultz coaxed him back upstairs with a tray of rice pudding and hot milk flecked with cinnamon. She had a bouquet of flowers for him. He didn't know their names, but they were the colors of this time of year, yellows and reds like the leaves of the trees. They had been sent to the church by Marla Collins. With the flowers was a simple white card with Marla Collins' name and address on it and a message written by hand which Mrs. Schultz read to Gus. "My sorrow and my prayers are with you today."

Later Gus put the flowers and the little card in the closet on a shelf above his mother's black dress.

It was a long time before the fear of being taken away left him. And then the almost unbearable anger began to grow. He looked at the card beside the withered flowers and saw the numbers. He made out the 6 and the 9 and he knew that was Sixty-ninth Street.

Gus Soltik found out where she lived, a basement apartment with two other girls. He went there nights and watched the lights in the apartment. But one night they were all dark and the shades were down. He climbed a wall behind the building and forced open a door. The apartment was empty. There was no furniture. She was gone. And he never found out where. He looked for her on the streets and on the sidewalks, but he never saw her again, and as the days grew colder and the first anniversary of his mother's death drew near, Gus Soltik began looking for someone else.

In the five years since the accident Gus Soltik had lived alone with Mrs. Schultz. Mrs. Soltik, before her death, had once told Mrs. Schultz that because Gus wasn't right in the head, there was no way he could "go" with girls. His great, hulking size and blemished complexion frightened them, and their fear roused a terrible frustration in him. He had hurt a girl on a

114

school playground once, twisting her arm so hard and vengefully that he had dislocated her shoulder.

In an attempt to prevent any more of this kind of trouble, Mrs. Soltik had warned her son to keep away from girls. She had told him—driving the "facts" home in her grating, menacing voice—that girls carried razors and bottles of acid in their purses, and if he ever tried to bother them, even go near them, they would slash at him with the razors and throw the burning acid into his eyes. Then the police would blame him and arrest him and hurt him.

Mrs. Schultz did what she could for him. She wished he would go to church with her, but all she could do was make sure his clothes were clean and that he got enough food and the sweet things he liked, the cakes and cookies. But she couldn't coax him into taking baths.

She heard his slow, heavy footsteps on the stairs and stood to pour him a cup of coffee.

In the narrow hall outside the kitchen, Gus put his bulging flight bag behind an old-fashioned hall tree and then went into the fragrant kitchen and sat down at the table with the old woman.

He was wearing his yellow leather cap, denim pants, Wellington boots, and the heavy brown turtleneck sweater.

"It was pretty," she said. "All the incense and the candles and the singing. And three priests."

It frightened him to think about it. His mother and the fires.

"Going out?" she asked him.

Gus Soltik stared at his steaming cup of coffee. "Walk."

Mrs. Schultz knew it was risky to ask him questions

when he was in one of his "moods" because it could cause him to erupt in emotional explosions; but she was worried about him, and in some profound, unquiet way, she knew in her old bones that it would be best if she knew where he was going to be that night. And so she risked a final question.

"You gonna see Lanny?"

He shook his head, and when he looked up from his coffee cup, she saw the angry glaze masking his eyes. "Walk," he said again, but now his voice was rising in volume and intensity and his big hands held the edge of the table with a power that whitened his knuckles.

Just leave him alone, leave him alone. That was best, so the old woman muttered something about taking out the trash and went quickly and silently from the room in her worn felt slippers.

There were no words to describe—no words in Gus Soltik's limited lexicon, that is—the great white void inside his head and the clamorous shapes of terror and excitement that filled the caverns of his mind with almost physically unbearable hungers and compulsions. He thought of slim white arms and legs and the green fabric of a school uniform. "Greenropes." With those images coiling hotly through his body, he stood so abruptly that his chair tipped over with a crash, but he was unaware of this, unaware of anythig but his savage, growing needs.

Picking up the flight bag from behind the hall tree, Gus Soltik let himself out of the creaking old building and ran down stone steps to the sidewalk.

It was late afternoon, October 15, and the last thin rays of sunlight fell like a golden blessing over the dirt and refuse that littered the curbs and streets of this bitter and defeated city slum.

116

8

MANOLO RAMOS, in a suite in the Plaza, lay in the warm and urgent embrace of a florist from Detroit, Michigan. The man, whose three sons attended the University of Pennsylvania, whispered in Manolo's ear, "Would you do that for me?"

Manolo arched his delicate eyebrows and allowed his exquisite features to register a mixture of surprise and admiration.

"You a crazy stud, you know that?" Manolo said softly.

"Will you do it?"

Manolo looked at his gold wristwatch and shook his head slowly. "It's been too long, daddy."

"I'll pay you extra." The man had begun to pant like an exhausted swimmer. "I'll double what I gave you. Please do it. *Please.*"

That would make Samantha happy, Manolo thought sullenly. Overtime for the big black bitch, collected from my sweet ass.

Last night and today, he had earned close to three hundred dollars. Almost halfway home. But maybe she'd give him a break; she seemed kinky enough yesterday to want to make it with him.

As Manolo's practiced hands and lips catapulted the florist to a pinnacle of frenzied ecstasy, he was wondering if there was anything for him with Samantha, if he could make it with her, make it straight. Maybe, he thought, remembering with a blend of guilt and excitement how effortlessly she had turned him on yesterday. . . .

"Oh, God!" the man cried in a soft, shuddering voice.

But if he didn't score heavy, Manolo thought, he'd have to try the park again tonight. Maybe even the Ramble, where he might luck onto a coke pusher. Some of them were rich enough and hot enough to trick all night. That way he could be even with big Sam by tomorrow.

"Here we go!" the man screamed into Manolo's ear, his voice threaded with exultant anticipation.

You go, big, fat, crazy shit, Manolo thought, and looked critically at the back of his left hand, the rosy fingertips gleaming dully in the illumination of a bedside lamp.

In the same hotel, at approximately the same time, but on a higher and more prestigious floor, a young waiter named Lee Chang pushed a dinner cart in the direction of the suite occupied by Rudi Zahn and Crescent Holloway.

Chang had been given the heady details of their arrival the preceding day. Waiters, bellhops, desk clerks, all had been gossiping like scandal-starved voyeurs about Crescent's shrewdly democratic manners and her clothes, a creamy white flannel pants suit trimmed in honey-colored mink, the tabby-striped hair, her great lavender eyes, and the hips, thighs, and

118

breasts which seemed to be linked but oddly separate continents of sexuality. And they had chattered about her luggage, sixteen pieces of matched Hermes, and her personal maid and hairdresser, her cheerful, balding manager and lover, Rudi Zahn, and what the florist had sent up and what they had ordered from room service the night before—oysters, caviar, and three bottles of chilled Bâtard Montrachet.

Chang had hoped for a glimpse of Crescent Holloway, but it was Rudi Zahn who opened the door and waved him inside.

Tall, narrow windows gave out on immense, spectacular sweeps of Central Park. The living room was cluttered with flowers and luggage and bowls of fruit wrapped in bright ribbon and foamy clouds of cellophane, the donors' envelopes unopened, thrown aside like small unrespected flags.

Chang noted with disappointment that the large double doors leading to the bedroom were closed.

Rudi Zahn signed for the early supper—baby lamb chops, white asparagus, and Mouton Rothschild '59—and within seconds Chang was once again in the long corridor, alone again, except for his dashed little hopes and dreams.

Rudi Zahn had drunk sparingly the night before and was in excellent spirits, physically and mentally. Crescent, on the contrary, had finished two bottles of the Montrachet, and Rudi anticipated trouble with her, particularly if she had got into any of the scripts he had left pointedly on her bedside table.

(Nate Sokol had handled the morning's press conference. Film clips and delicatessen and champagne and whiskey had been a benign substitute for the

Stacked House Kid, who, Nate Sokol had explained, was down with a mild bout of flu.)

Rudi had waked at three thirty in the afternoon and, after a half hour of calisthenics, had shaved, showered, and put on a gray flannel suit over a tattersall vest, a combination he thought would complement the smart "British" look of his brown suede shoes. Rudi had ordered this light supper, not because Crescent would be hungry yet, but because nibbling at the food would allow her to savor the wine without any pangs from her conscience.

Not that her conscience ever won out. She ate and drank like a willful, undisciplined child: hot dogs and Cokes for breakfast, bags of roasted almonds, liverwurst sandwiches washed down with scotch as after-dinner snacks. Her handbag was always bulging with candy, and her portable dressing room (practically a bungalow) was stocked like an East Side delicatessen. Yet her skin remained flawless and creamy, her body was firm and slim, and her lavender eyes glowed with calm, serene health, like those of a contented Persian cat.

He pushed open the double doors and pulled the dining cart into her bedroom. "Hello there," he said to Crescent, who was sitting up in their huge round bed, looking with what he judged to be active dislike at the script she was holding.

"Where do you get this shit from?" she asked him.

"What shit?"

"I mean this script shit," she said. "I mean, who writes this cunty drivel?"

"There is one thing to remember about each of those scripts, sweetie," he said and poured a glass of wine for her.

"Thanks. What's that?"

"Each of those scripts is accompanied by a firm offer, and each offer tops anything we've got so far."

"But why does it always have to be such crud? Honest, Rudi, there's a scene in this bomb—what's it called?" She turned the script around to look at the title on the cover. Then she stuck out her tongue at the script. "'Boobs in the Woods.' Well, there's a scene where I'm attacked by vibrators. And are you ready for this? I adore it. Can't get enough of it."

"Look, sweetie. We're not selling you as Bergman or Katie Hepburn," he said. "You're everybody's roll in the hay, the little girl who shivers and squeaks when she's kissed, who can widen her mouth into a perfect circle and make guys think dirty."

"But *you* don't have to act in these stinkers, Rudi."

He gave her another glass of wine. She gulped two big swallows and then, more petulant than angry now, said, "Do you realize what it's like to know that the grips and gaffers are embarrassed for you?"

Crescent looked miserably at her empty glass. "What are you so afraid of, Rudi?"

"I'm afraid of not making these three deals," he said untruthfully, surprised at the question.

"But I don't have any friends anymore," she said, sighing again like a hurt child. "I'm thirty-three, and I've got to keep acting like I'm twenty. I'm sick and tired of training around the year like a goddamn racehorse. I want to eat and drink what I please—"

He cut in. "Well, if you're on a diet now, I'd hate to be around when you go off it."

"You just don't want to get involved with anything or anybody. Just collect the loot, so we'll be safe and secure

121

when we're *what?* Living in some rest home?" She sighed again. "I can't wait. You and me going hand and hand up the path, where the staff of Ye Olde Bedpan Manor is waiting for us with big, happy grins."

Rudi smiled at this, but he didn't want her to start feeling sorry for herself; self-pity was vanity's sniveling little sister, he knew, and Crescent was more malleable in moods of arrogant self-esteem and sexual exuberance than she was when her spirits plunged into these states of self-deprecation.

"Have some more wine," he suggested, and when she nodded, he filled her glass.

But Crescent was not ready to be cheered up. "I don't even see my family anymore. You don't have any family, so you don't know what that means, Rudi."

"My family went up in smoke in Poland," Rudi said coldly.

"Oh, shit, I'm sorry, Rudi." She looked contritely at him. "That was a lousy thing for me to say."

She was going the wrong way again, he realized, loose and sloppy.

To correct this, Rudi said, "I wish you would occasionally think, *think,* if you know what the word means, before you shoot off that big mouth of yours."

"Well, Christ, I *said* I was sorry." Then her temper got the better of her, and she threw her long golden hair back from her forehead and glared at him with what she fancied to be her "tigress" look. "Just who the fuck do you think you are, Rudi Zahn?"

"Very nice display. Very nice and tasteful," he said quietly.

"Don't give me that well-bred gentleman shit," she

122

screamed at him, challenging now, brandishing her sex like a weapon. "Where the fuck would you be without me? Without your sluttish dummy? You'd be hocking around the studios with flop sweat shining on your bald head, laying secretaries to get ten minutes with their bosses."

She would be all right now, Rudi knew. When he returned, she would be her normal cheerful self. No gloom, no depressions. They would have a pleasant dinner, here or at 21, and she would be happily drunk by bedtime and would be grateful if he made love to her.

"Charming," he said, and gave her a little bow. "You're so delightful I'll let you enjoy yourself without any distractions. I'm going for a walk."

"Well, take these shitty scripts with you then," she said, and hurled two of them after him. One of them struck his shoulder and fell to the floor. He picked it up, put it on a coffee table, and strolled into the living room of their suite.

"Please come back, Rudi. *Please.*" She raised her voice to make sure he would hear her, but her anger had evaporated, and her tone was as pleading and helpless as a frightened child.

When she heard the door of the drawing room open and shut with a dry click of finality, she threw herself sideways on the bed, cradling her face in her crossed arms. She knew that Rudi used her, manipulated her moods and responses, playing her like a goddamn yo-yo, but there was little bitterness in her reflections because she knew his private hells.

But it was hard. Hard to be thirty-three and charged

with sexual excitement and still have to compete for Rudi's love with an eight-year-old child who had died almost thirty years ago. Ilana. She was burned into his soul like a brand. He was chained to her memory.

Well, she'd keep trying, get herself beautifully turned out, and when he came back from the park, they'd go to 21 for dinner.

She sat up smiling and poured herself a glass of wine. They'd have champagne with a splash of vodka and maybe Little Neck clams and prime rib.

And then they'd come back here and be so good to each other. . . .

In the East Eighties, between Park Avenue and Lexington, a street vendor sold pretzels and cones of shaved ice liberally drenched with sweet fruited syrups.

The "clock" in Gus Soltik's head told him there was time. So he bought one of the paper cones of sweet ice, extending his hand and letting the vendor pick the proper coins from his rough palm.

A police car cruised smoothly past the vendor, slowing with the rush-hour traffic.

The patrolman in the passenger seat was a uniformed officer in his forties, Joe Smegelski, a veteran with smoothly tanned features and calm blue eyes.

"Jesus, Mary, and Joseph," he said quietly, and tapped his partner on the arm. "Pull over to the curb, Abe. Take it nice and slow."

"What's up?"

"Just do what I tell you. Nice and easy." Smegelski opened the glove compartment, pulled out the police artist's Xeroxed sketch of the Juggler.

"Could be this character's back there on the southwest corner of Lex and Eighty-third. Check your mirror."

Abe angled the squad car to the curb and at the same time glanced up at the rear-vision mirror.

"Let's pick him up," Smegelski said. "Take the north side of the street; I'll take the south. Don't look at him. Play it like it's coffee-break time."

The policemen left their squad car and sauntered along opposite sidewalks on a course that would bring them to the hulking figure who resembled the sketch artist's portrait of the Juggler.

But at this moment, with the interval of savage rapture so close to culmination, Gus Soltik's instincts were as alert and sensitive as a jackal in the terrain of its predators.

Mingling casually with the normal flow of pedestrians, the policemen were converging casually on him, and when Gus Soltik saw them and sensed their deliberate lack of interest in him, alarm bells clamored through his nervous sytem. It was like that terrible night in the basement when the big man and the man with a scar had wanted to hurt him. . . .

Gus Soltik turned and bolted south into Lexington Avenue and in his terrified flight collided with a pair of window-shoppers and knocked them sprawling onto the sidewalk.

"Police! Halt!" Smegelski yelled, and drawing his gun, he sprinted to the intersection with Abe close behind him. They ran along the sidewalk twenty or twenty-five yards behind the Juggler, unable to risk a shot because of the crowds.

Gus Soltik plunged from their view into an alley, and

by the time the officers reached this narrow passage he was already straddling a ten-foot brick fence.

"Freeze!" Smegelski shouted at him, but the huge man leaped from sight a split second before shots from Smegelski and Abe's police specials blasted splinters and explosions of red dust from the brick wall.

9

IN his headquarters at the 19th Precinct, Gypsy
Tonnelli gave rapid orders to Sokolsky at the switchboard. "Send a signal to the Fourth Division, the
Twentieth, the Twenty-third and the Twenty-fifth
precincts."

Units from the 19th were already in the street, and
the forces he was presently committing would box
Eighty-third and Lexington on the cardinal points of
the compass. While Detectives Clem Scott and Carmine
Garbalotto waited for orders (Augie Brohan and Jim
Taylor had already gone), Tonnelli mentally checked
and rechecked the distributions of his units. Here, the
19th, was the southern flank, the Fourth Division and
the 20th Precinct held the western line, while the 23d
and 25th comprised the northern and eastern boundaries.

"Carmine, you and Clem take as many uniformed
cops as you need and start rousting the supers. Alert
them and their engineering staffs to check the
basements of their buildings for signs of forced entry."

When the detectives had gone, Tonnelli paced the
floor, reexamining every decision he had made, trying

to be sure he had forgotten nothing. Then he stopped, suddenly becoming aware of a stockily built, neatly groomed white-haired old man standing in the door of his office.

"Yes?" Tonnelli said to him, puzzled by some quality of tension and expectancy in the man's expression.

"I'm Babe Fritzel," the white-haired old man said. Sokolsky looked wearily at the ceiling. "I was here before, talked to your guy on the switchboard. He didn't seem to understand that I came all the way over from Teaneck, New Jersey, to lend you guys a hand. I was a cop for twenty-eight years in Camden. You may not remember, but I was the guy that finally put the cuffs on Howard Unruh after he'd killed thirteen people. Lot of them kids. One lady he killed in a car waiting for the light to change. He had a firing range in his basement, the wall three feet thick with sandbags."

Tonnelli stared at him and shook his head slowly. "We took him to Cooper Hospital in Camden," Fritzel continued, apparently oblivious of Tonnelli's negative reaction. "They treated him for a minor bullet wound, and then we took him to the New Jersey Hospital for the Insane in Trenton. I still got a gun and a permit to carry it, and a two-way radio. And the way I look at it—"

Tonnelli cut him off with irritable, chopping gesture of his right hand. "What you got over there in Teaneck, Mr. Fritzel? Chickens or a truck farm?"

"Neither, but I keep busy. Some gunning in the fall, and weekends I help the bartender at the Elks' Club."

And, Tonnelli thought, you miss those flashing red dome lights, the smell of cordite after a shoot-out, the good old days.

"Look, you were a cop and obviously a fine one,"

128

Tonnelli said to Fritzel. "So you know what I got to say. Which is wish us luck and go on home."

"I figured you'd say that." Fritzel glanced wistfully around the office, watching with a sadly detached interest as a policewoman, Doris Polk, hurried from her inner office with a memo for Sokolsky.

"Good luck, Lieutenant," Fritzel said, and with a little salute which included Tonnelli, the office, and his own past, he turned and walked slowly toward the elevators.

Sergeant Rusty Boyle found a parking space in front of Joyce Colby's apartment building, which was in the East Sixties between Park and Madison.

He cut the motor but made no move to leave the car. He sat thinking about what he had decided to do. He didn't know whether it was right or wrong, but he was determined to do it. Sergeant Boyle sighed and rubbed a hand through his thick red hair. On balance, he was a reasonably uncomplicated human being, but there were times when he didn't understand a certain compulsive need to render sympathy and compassion to the helpless, shit-upon losers he met as a cop in the crowded and often merciless streets of New York.

Boyle picked up his dashboard phone and asked Central to patch him through to a number he had looked up earlier at the 13th Precinct.

To a certain extent, Tonnelli was undoubtedly right. Ransom should at least be advised of his options. Whether or not he chose to exercise them was another matter. But somebody had to tell him— No, that was too strong. Somebody should just give him a hint there was another way to go, that he just didn't have to wait until the fire inside him burned up his life.

129

The connection was made. The phone rang three times. Then he recognized Ransom's voice.

"Hello?"

"John Ransom?"

"Yes, that's right."

"John, this is Sergeant Boyle. Rusty Boyle. Remember we had a talk yesterday?"

"Of course." Ransom's voice was suddenly warm; Rusty Boyle could imagine that he was smiling.

"Well, here's why I'm calling. I got to thinking. This is something you might check out. I mean, what hit you is just as much an accident as if it was a truck. Maybe you could ask your doctor about it."

"I appreciate your interest, but I don't see what good it would do."

"Maybe not. It was just a thought. It might have some effect on your pension—"

Ransom laughed weakly. "If I had one, Sergeant."

Please take the hook, Rusty Boyle thought. Please. Don't make me a goddamn accessory before and after the fact.

"But I can't say how much it helps to have you call me like this, Sergeant. I've never talked about it with anyone except the doctors. That's the hardest part of it." Ransom's voice was trembling emotionally. "Carrying it around with you and not being able to talk about it."

All right, Boyle thought, you're in this far, so use a sledgehammer.

"I thought 'accident' because that might apply if you've got a double indemnity clause in your insurance policy. . . ."

Ransom was silent for a dozen or more seconds, but

130

Boyle could hear the altered rate of his breathing; it was ragged and uneven, and unless Boyle was imagining things, it was threaded with a touch of apprehension. At last, Ransom said, "I believe I understand what you mean, Sergeant."

"It's just something you might check out. . . ."

"I intend to, Sergeant. Thank you"— Ransom's voice was close to breaking—"and God bless you."

As Rusty Boyle let himself into Joyce's apartment, he was remembering the first time he had met her, five months ago when she had called the precinct to report a burglary. A ring with a sentimental value but very little else was missing. He had filed a report and forgotten about it. But he couldn't forget Joyce Colby. She was slim and tall, in her late twenties, with a fair complexion that was in flawless complement to her fire-engine red hair. And she was honest and intelligent, and Rusty Boyle loved her so much that she could melt his heart with a laugh or a gesture.

She had been married at eighteen to a construction worker, who had been killed in a fall from the forty-second floor of a building being put up near Times Square. From that experience and from Rusty Boyle's own occupational hazards, Joyce believed that brave men were always in danger, simply by virtue of their maleness and courage, and she considered it not only her privilege but her duty to reward such men with understanding intelligence and share with them the sexual excitements of her body.

When he closed the door, she called a hello to him from the kitchen.

She was wearing green velvet Levi's and a white silk

shirt buttoned only at the waist, and when he kissed her and took her in his arms, the lovely swell of her breasts charged his whole body with excitement. When she turned away from him, however, he noted a touch of resignation in her manner.

"Anything wrong?"

She smiled and shook her head slowly.

He picked up a bottle of scotch and two glasses from the bar adjoining the sink, but she shook her head again and put a hand on his arm.

"There's a steak, an avocado salad, and a bottle of good cold wine," she said. "But later."

"Goddamn it to hell," he said.

"That's right. Tonnelli called."

"Goddamn it," he said again, but he was already on his way to the front door.

10

IT was late afternoon on October 15 that Barbara Boyd's nerve failed her; she told the cabdriver to let her off at Sixty-fifth Street, several blocks from her apartment, and after giving the man a bill without even looking at its denomination, she walked swiftly along the sidewalk toward the Grosvenor Hotel, where she knew there was a small, intimate piano bar just off the lobby.

Luther would have listened to the tapes a dozen times by now, she thought, analyzing and weighing her every word, listening alertly for a revealing pause or stammer, a nervous laugh, or contradictions in what she knew he would think of as her "evidence."

She sat at the end of the bar with her long legs crossed, twisting the stem of her martini glass with restless fingers, a flex of nervous energy. When she was at ease (which she wasn't at present), there was a lithe and almost feline grace in her movements, a challenge in the directness of her eyes and in the clean planes of her face. She was wearing a bottle-green tweed suit and a blue scarf knotted loosely about her throat, and if it hadn't been for the nervous tremor in her fingers, a casual observer would have taken her for an artist or designer or possibly an actress sipping a drink while waiting to keep a rendezvous with some fortunate man.

At this hour there were only a half dozen customers along the bar, and one of these, a large, florid man with cold eyes, was staring with frank and deliberate interest at Barbara's elegantly slim legs. In the rear of the room the piano player was singing a medley of Noel Coward songs.

". . . I'll see you again. . . ."

His voice was sad and muted, the words as blue as the air in the smoke-filled little bar.

Her thoughts were sad and splintered with pain, like the music.

What was London, where she had first met and loved Luther Boyd, if it was not as she had once read, the mighty fleet of Wren, with top gallants and mainsails of stone? . . .

And for some idiotic reason, maybe only because they had been so happy sitting in the lounge bar of the Dorchester, she had said to him, "Time held me green and dying, though I sang in my chains like the sea."

And he had asked her, "Is that T. S. Eliot?"

"No, Dylan Thomas," she had said, and he had made a note of the quotation and the name in his small leather appointments book, and she had liked him for that, had found it touching.

The martini did nothing to ease a bruise that seemed to be in the center of her heart.

Kate had been *their* child, but Buddy had always been *her* child even though Luther had adopted him and given him the Boyd name. But was that a fair assessment or just her depressed imagination at work?

134

The psychiatrist had asked her if she had any feelings of guilt about not having given Luther Boyd a son. She hadn't been prepared for that question and hence had blurted out a quick and honest answer: "No, I'm glad I didn't, Doctor."

Why had she said that? It was simple enough, and one didn't need diplomas on the wall from Harvard and Vienna to interpret it. She could not bear even the thought of losing another son.

She asked the bartender for a second martini, knowing she needed this additional crutch for her meeting with Luther, but as she did so, she experienced a revulsion for her own weakness and an active dislike for the person she seemed to be turning into, a neurotic female taking liquid courage under the insolent stares of the florid man at the other end of the bar, who, she knew quite well, would offer to pay for her third drink. . . .

11

"GOD created man, and finding him not sufficiently alone, gave him a female companion so that he might feel his loneliness more acutely."

Luther Boyd closed the book he was reading with an irritable snap of his powerful hands and dropped it with a dismissing gesture on the table beside his deep leather chair.

"—feel his loneliness more acutely. . . ."

A draining, weakening thought. . . . He had made an honest effort to involve himself in poetry and ballet and opera because these were art forms Barbara was passionately fond of. But how far could a man force himself? At what point did his simulated interest, his patient study of areas that bored him, wear into thin hypocrisy?

Since he tried to be honest with himself, he reluctantly conceded that it had once been a stimulating challenge to examine musical scores as if they were campaign maps, searching out the trivial or complex reasons behind the writings of plays and novels and operas.

He remembered an afternoon in a hotel in London

(where had it been, the Connaught?), he could recall even now the look and texture of the warm sunlight on the backs of Barbara's slim hands, and as he thought of her then, her eyes shining with grave amusement, quoting words from Dylan Thomas, Luther Boyd felt a stab of poignant pain at all the promises and pleasures they had lost in only these last brief years.

He stood and paced the study of his apartment above Central Park, choosing another book from his shelves, a military manual detailing General Grant's strategy and tactics while driving his Army of the Tennessee against Forts Henry and Donelson on his battering course through Shiloh to Vicksburg.

There was a lesson in guerrilla warfare to be learned from the confusion of the rebel commanders facing Grant, the mismatched triumvirate of Generals Floyd, Pillow, and Buckner. They had allowed a massive victory to evaporate, to slip from their collective hands that night; faulty intelligence had been part of it, but more important, they had been deceived by chimerical phantoms which had convinced them that the Union forces were still in position, thus causing them to sound retreat against an enemy that had already withdrawn from the field.

But what they took for the enemy had been only the banked Union campfires, whipped into flames by gusting winds to create the illusion of a continuing hostile encirclement.

Boyd checked his watch as he heard, above Kate's hi-fi, the musical chimes of the front door. This would be Barbara, he thought, as he rose and went into the living room, Injustice is relatively easy to bear, he had once read; what stings is justice. Was that why his mood

138

was so wounded and angry? Because there was justice in Barbara's position? So let's get this the hell over with, he thought. As Patton said, a pint of sweat can save a gallon of blood. . . . Don't think; act.

"I think we've wasted too much time and energy in accusations," Luther Boyd said to Barbara. "Do you want a divorce?"

He stood with his back to her at the windows of the long drawing room, staring at but not seeing the golden glow of the last sunlight in the crowns of towering elms and maples in the park.

Barbara was at the bar making herself a drink. Because his question terrified her, made her feel lonely and shaken, she managed a defiant smile and said to him, "Can I fix you a touch, Luther?"

"I'm trying to be serious, Barbara."

"You don't have to *try* to be serious, Luther. You *are* serious."

"What about it? Yes or no?"

She was frightened at the thought of leaving him, but she was determined to do it, simply because she couldn't bear his leaving her again and again and again. . . . She had been alone when Kate was born. She had been alone when the wire had come that Buddy was dead. She had been alone on too many nights when her body ached for his love. And she had been alone with him too often when he sat in the same room with her with his thoughts lost in the history of centuries-old campaigns and wars.

He would always leave. The flags on the horizon, the distant thunder of artillery, the challenge of decisions and battles were magnets he couldn't resist.

And she didn't want him to leave her. But there was no word from her, no cry, no appeal that had the magic of the lures that streamed like plumes from his concepts of honor and duty, and yes, she thought bitterly, yes, always, the fire-engine excitement of armies on the march. . . .

She put her drink down on the bar, walked across the room, and stopped behind her husband.

"Luther, at the risk of boring you out of your mind, can I try to explain one more time why I've come to this decision?"

Boyd turned and looked steady at her. "Of course," he said patiently. "This is truly important to me, Barbara."

While she was trying to collect thoughts that scattered around in her head like mice, there was an excited yelping from the corridor, and Harry Lauder burst into the room, tugging at the leash in Kate's hands. Kate ran to her mother and gave her a hug and a kiss while Harry Lauder circled them both with yapping enthusiasm.

Kate knew that her mother and father were being what people called "civilized" about their problem, but she thought it was grossly unfair that she wasn't allowed to talk to them about it, that she was expected to be just as "civilized" as they were.

"Mommy, I'll only be gone ten or fifteen minutes. Will you wait here for me?"

"Of course I will, darling."

"Remember the ground rules, Kate."

She repeated them in a singsong but cheerful voice. "Stay on the east side of Fifth Avenue, in your own block where Mr. Brennan can keep an eye on you."

"Right," Boyd said.

In the lobby, Mr. Brennan pulled on a heavy blue overcoat decorated with gold epaulets and went outside with Kate and, standing under the canopy, looked with affection after the girl who was skipping down the block with her little Scottie.

The wind was fresh and cold on her cheeks and sent strands of her silken blond hair streaming behind her like pennants.

Across the street the same winds played in the big trees of Central Park. Leaves were blown high in the air to spin with errant thermals and finally to drift down into the thick shrubbery bordering the sidewalk along this block of Fifth Avenue. There was a fall fragrance in the air, threaded with the delicate, smoky tang of roasting chestnuts. The elderly vendor had positioned his cart a block south of Kate's building and was stamping his feet against the cold, his breath hoary in the deepening twilight winds.

Kate, at the opposite end of the block, north of her building, was snug against the weather in small sturdy boots, a blue jump suit, and a red quilted ski jacket with decorative zigzag stitchings on the collar and sleeve. She also wore her green suede shoulder bag because there was a dollar bill in her wallet, and she wanted to buy a bag of hot chestnuts before she went back up to her apartment.

Traffic was light on the avenue. Harry Lauder began barking at something or someone in the bushes across the street in Central Park.

"No, no, no," Kate said, and pulled him back from the curb. She walked south toward her building then, giving Mr. Brennan a wave and a smile.

She called a greeting to the chestnut vendor, who returned it with a bobbing nod. He was a mute, but his hearing was unimpaired, and he seemed to enjoy the traffic and activity of the street and his limited exchanges with the little blond girl and her Scottie.

Rudi Zahn was a precise and orderly man who took his exercise seriously. He did not stroll through Central Park idly cataloguing birds and trees and flowers, but instead strode the pathways with long, decisive strides, almost as if marching to the cadence of distant martial music. It had rained in the late afternoon that day, a miniature autumn squall, which had had the positive effect of rinsing the air and leaving it as clear and bracing as winds over freshwater lakes.

Rudi was thinking about Crescent Holloway, which in turn led him to remember the pale and ravaged face of Ilana, one of the four survivors from a dozen-odd families who had been deported from Rudi's village in Bavaria to concentration camps in Poland. At age five Rudi had adored Ilana, who had been a slim, vivacious eight-year-old, charged with tomboyish energies and excitements and graced with a buoyancy of spirit that seemed indestructible to everyone who knew and loved her. She was everyone's pet, and when the soldiers came, it seemed somehow a special and dreadful outrage that Ilana should be taken away with the other seventy-four Jews of the village.

Rudi's parents and his older brother and sister had

been in that group of seventy-four Jews. But even that had not seemed as incredible and horrifying as the violation of Ilana.

Rudi had been spared through the intervention of the parish priest, who—having been a longtime friend and chess opponent of the rabbi—gave the little boy sanctuary in the basement of the church until the crowded trucks with their wailing cargo had rolled out of the village.

The gray and frightful years had gone by like slow, ominous shadows, and then the Americans came and after them, the survivors, Ilana and three other children, the only ones left from the dozen families who five years before had charged the streets and shops of the village with their exuberant energy.

And one day an American Army captain, second cousin to the mother of one of the exterminated families, had come to the village in a jeep with a driver and a large American sergeant who wore three rows of campaign ribbons on his Ike jacket and a .45 automatic on his cartridge belt.

The four survivors and Rudi had joined the captain and the sergeant in a cold room to drink American coffee and to eat American chocolate while Ilana told the captain, who was small and wore bifocals and whose name was Adler, what had happened to the people of the village, including the captain's relatives.

Ilana was now thirteen, shrunken and destroyed, but still beautiful to Rudi, with despairing, haunted eyes which seemed to him the most dreadful symbols of what had been inflicted on her and all the others.

Ilana spoke in German with occasional lapses into

Yiddish, and Captain Adler translated her words into English in a voice that was racked by emotion and broken on occasion with stifled sobs.

"There were two lines," Ilana said, and Captain Adler translated the words to the American sergeant. "One was for the healthy who could work; the other was for the old and sick and crippled, no matter how young they were. That line went into the gas chamber. The two lines were only six feet apart, separated by soldiers. My mother was walking to the gas chamber. I was in the other line. When the soldiers were not looking, I got into the line with my mother. I wanted to die with her. I told her that, and she said she would help me. She put her coat around me so the soldiers wouldn't see. She was crying, and I could feel her heart beating very fast. But before we reached the door to the gas chamber, my mother pulled her coat away from me and threw me into the arms of a soldier. She screamed that I must try to live. I fought the soldier and tried to get back to my mother; but she was gone by then, and the door had closed. I couldn't see her. They shoved me into the other line, and I tried for the next years to do what my mother had asked me to do, to try to live."

But that grotesquely unfair and demoralizing struggle had been an empty victory; Ilana was dead within ten months of her release from the camp, her lungs betraying her unquenchable spirit.

This was the dreadful fear that had been burned into Rudi Zahn's consciousness, and this was what Crescent Holloway could never understand; she had never in her life been vulnerable and helpless, and she couldn't conceive how that experience could cripple a person's character and confidence.

144

Money, with its consequent privilege and power, was the only specific against such terrors. . . .

In the lobby of Kate Boyd's building the elevator doors opened and Mrs. Root Cadwalader stepped from the car with a bulky piece of luggage. She put the bag down and waved to Mr. Brennan, who was standing under the canopy in front of the building.

Mr. Brennan glanced through the revolving doors and saw Mrs. Cadwalader beckoning to him at the same instant that Kate noted what had caught Harry Lauder's attention on the opposite side of Fifth Avenue.

It was a kitten, crawling uncertainly along the sidewalk, a white fur star gleaming on its black forehead.

Mr. Brennan hurried into the lobby and picked up Mrs. Root Cadwalader's suitcase. "You'll be needing a cab, Mrs. Cadwalader?"

"Yes, please, John. I have a seven thirty flight to Chicago."

"Visiting your grandson then? How old is he now?"

"Sixteen, John."

"Good heavens, where does time go? I remember him roller skating on the sidewalk here, just a lad."

"Well, he's sixteen, and he's got a driver's license to prove it. He's meeting me at O'Hare in Chicago."

During these exchanges between John Brennan and Mrs. Cadwalader, Kate had stopped to stare with longing eyes across the avenue at the little kitten, which she felt certain must be lonely, hungry, frightened by the sounds of horns and traffic.

She had been forbidden by her father to cross Fifth

145

Avenue, but she was rationalizing that injunction now, telling herself that he couldn't blame her for going to the rescue of a helpless little animal. Kate had been trained by her father to take care of dogs and horses, to make sure that they were fed and dry and warm, that their stalls or runs were clean, before going inside for her own bath and dinner. These were not chores you depended on grooms to perform, because a horse or dog trusted and obeyed the person who took care of it. That was not a responsibility to delegate to anyone else, her father had always insisted. Get in the habit of doing those chores yourself. And with these thoughts came another, prompted by a verse they were reading at Miss Prewitt's: "Down to Gehenna and up to the throne, he travels the fastest who travels alone."

The words thrilled her and made her feel strong and invulnerable.

Tightening her grip on Harry Lauder's leash, she waited for a break in the traffic and then ran across Fifth Avenue to the sidewalk that flanked Central Park.

Harry Lauder barked so noisily at the crying kitten that Kate bent and gave him a sharp tap on his muzzle. But then the Scottie began to bark at something or someone in the thick shrubbery behind the four-foot black stone wall bordering this stretch of the park. And when Kate reached down to pick up the kitten, her dog leaped away from her and his leash slipped through her gloved hand. In an instant he was gone, scrambling first onto a park bench and then to the top of the wall, where he jumped from sight into thick tangles of spicebush and shining sumac.

Kate called for him him to come back, her voice high and urgent, but the sound of his thrashing progress through the grove of underbrush warned her that he was already deeper into the park.

What a *mess!* she thought. If he got lost, she'd be blamed for it. And she'd deserve it. But if she took time to go and get her father, they might never find him.

She knew there was an entrance into the park just to her north. Kate hesitated only an instant, and then she put the kitten on the park bench and ran as fast as she could toward the next intersection.

Calling her dog's name in a high, anxious voice, Kate ran along a cobbled pathway through the park and when she turned and ran back toward the area where he had got away from her, she was under huge English oaks whose shadows fell about her like great dark wings.

She stopped at aproximately the place where Harry Lauder had scrambled into the park and stood listening for sounds of him above the noise of the traffic on Fifth Avenue.

Then, while she stared about helplessly, she heard the Scottie barking, but he was a long way off, it seemed, his yelping coming faintly from a dark stand of trees near the East Drive.

Calling his name again, she ran toward the sound of his barking, her slim body blending and finally merging with the shadows until only her fair, streaming hair could be seen reflecting the last of the day's sunlight.

And watching that plume of blond hair and waiting for Kate among that thicket of trees stood Gus Soltik, the barking little dog helpless in his huge hands.

But an additional element had threaded itself into his emotional complex of lusts and compulsions and angers. And that was fear. In his dim mind, he knew

147

someone had told on him. . . . Men who would hurt him had chased him and shouted at him, with guns. . . . He had run away from them in an alley. But they were looking for him. Who had told them? . . .

But it was all right now. "Greenropes" would follow the sounds of the dog, and he would draw her deeper and deeper into the park to a place he knew that was dark and silent, where no one would ever hear her.

12

CENTRAL PARK is potentially one of the more glorious and gratifying natural ornaments in the city of New York.

A long green rectangle consisting of eight hundred and forty-odd acres, it is enclosed on three sides by what may be the most prestigious and expensive real estate in the world. One might argue that the Rue Faubourg St.-Honoré in Paris is more elegant and graceful or that the immense sweep of the Nash and Royal crescents in Bath, England, is more architecturally impressive and more spiritually satisfying, but the streets and avenues that embrace three sides of Central Park are clearly without peer in the world of commercial fashion and commercial art, in the fields of law and medical research, of finance and entertainment and publishing. In addition to its vast mass of mighty high rises, its shops and restaurants have long been legendary magnets to elite foreigners and Americans with the money to pay for their products.

The northern end of Central Park at 110th Street runs on a broad half-mile-wide front into the area of Manhattan known as Harlem, an immense ghetto housing the city's more than million-odd blacks.

Central Park provides a home and a handsome background for honeysuckle and American elms, ginkgo trees and Atlas Mountain cedars, Osage orange and massive green ash, black locusts, and fragrant tulip trees.

In most seasons the park is a haven for robins and redwing blackbirds, pied-billed grebes, green herons, spotted sandpipers, yellow and parula warblers, red-shouldered and broad-winged hawks, emerald-winged teals, and the normal proliferation of permanent residents, starlings, cardinals, mallards and, of course, the city's sparrows, owls, and pigeons.

Originally, the land given to the designers of Central Park in the middle of the nineteenth century was a discouraging expanse of urban litter, studded with squatters' shacks, hog farms, and bone-boiling works. Also among these malodorous swamplands were sewers and cesspools covered with bramble nearly as impenetrable as huge clusters of rusted iron.

The granitic bones of the city itself thrust upward through this morass in formations of grotesquely beautiful black rock. These natural constructions create grottoes and escarpments, valleys and gullies choked with vegetation, and caves and ravines so convoluted and labyrinthine in their patterns that guided tours were essential before several decades of order had been imposed upon this rugged, inhospitable landscape.

The Ramble, a forty-acre area between Seventy-fifth and Seventy-seventh streets, directly north of the lake and boathouse, is a sanctuary for birds and animals, a wild and shadowed expanse of trees, juttings of steep black rock, and terraced serpentine walks which create a mazelike effect but which eventually lead pedestrians to

150

bridges and access routes on a circuitous course toward Central Park West.

But Central Park, despite its beauty, despite its variety of natural attractions, is usually deserted after dark. Occasionally, couples will stroll along the pathways near the southern end of the park, where there are hansom cabs, the reassuring glitter and crowds of Fifty-ninth Street, and the huge, graceful bulk of the Plaza Hotel.

But few prudent citizens would consider venturing north beyond the upper Sixties because at night the park is infested by human predators that prey on anyone foolish or reckless enough to stray into their terrain.

Uninformed or incautious tourists, wandering drunks and questing homosexuals, narcotics pushers, sexual freaks, masochists of all varieties, the strange and lonely neurotics who exist in all sprawling cities—these are the potential victims of the rapists and muggers who are hidden in the nighttime shadows of this immense, graceful sprawl of lakes and meadows and trees.

In this darkness Central Park (save perhaps for battlefields of warring nations) is potentially one of the more dangerous stretches of real estate in the world.

13

LUTHER BOYD checked his wristwatch. It was close to six thirty.

Barbara was pacing restlessly, her hands locked around her elbows in a curiously defensive and vulnerable gesture.

They has been circling their problems with words since Kate had gone off with Harry Lauder and still hadn't come to the heart of it. God knows, it wasn't all Luther's fault, she thought, because he had been bred to treat people as statistics.

Barbara wondered if she were listed in his precise mental files as a slender object which catered to his tastes in food and drink and—asterisk and foot-note—object also programmed for sexual activity.

"Didn't Kate say she'd be back in about fifteen minutes?" she asked him.

"Yes," Boyd said. He had been concerned about her absence for the last ten minutes or so to the extent that he had hardly been listening to Barbara's catalogue of disillusionments. But he realized now that she had also been participating in the charade; he knew her well and suspected that her present aimless, almost erratic manner reflected an anxiety she was perhaps afraid to articulate.

It was then the phone rang. Luther Boyd picked up the receiver and said, "Yes?"

"It's John Brennan, Mr. Boyd. Is Kate up there with you?"

"No, she's not, John."

"I had to carry out some luggage for Mrs. Cadwalader, then get her a cab." The old man sounded worried. "But I didn't have my eyes off Kate for more than a minute or so."

"She's not out front on the sidewalk?"

"No. I figured she went upstairs while I was whistling for a cab."

"Any sign of Harry Lauder?"

"Not as far as I can see, Mr. Boyd."

Barbara walked across the room to her husband, her eyes searching his face.

"What's the matter?" she asked him. "Is it Kate?"

"Thanks, John."

"I don't understand this, Mr. Boyd. But I feel terrible about it."

"You've got responsibilities to all your tenants, not just the Boyd family." He hung up on John Brennan's further apologies and looked at Barbara.

"Kate's wandered off," he said.

"But where?"

Boyd rubbed his jaw, a gesture which alarmed Barbara, for she knew it was one of his few physical reactions to stress. "You tell me," he said.

"Wait. Maybe she went up to see Tish Tennyson."

"You have her number?"

"Yes, I'll get it." Barbara hurried along the hall to

154

Kate's room, collected Kate's address book, and returned to the drawing room, flipping the pages. "Here it is," she said, and gave the book to her husband.

Luther Boyd dialed the number and spoke with Mrs. Tennyson and with Tish. But Kate hadn't been to the Tennysons.

Boyd dropped the receiver into its cradle, and when Barbard noted the stillness of his expression, the cold appraisal in his eyes, she experienced an uncomfortable twist of fear. "This isn't like Kate, Luther. You know it isn't."

"You stay here in case there's a phone call."

This was not a request or a course of procedure to be discussed; this was a bird colonel talking to the troops, and Barbara nodded quickly.

In the lobby Boyd cut off still more apologies from Mr. Brennan. "Forget it, John. It's not important now. But this is: Where was Kate when you saw her last, and what time was it?"

"She was a half block north of here, on this side of Fifth." The old man frowned, then nodded with obvious relief. "That would have been just a minute or two before six o'clock. Because Mrs. Cadwalader told me she was giving herself an hour and a half for her seven thirty flight at Kennedy."

Boyd checked his watch, noted that it was a few seconds past six thirty-five. Which meant Kate had been off on her own about thirty-seven or thirty-eight minutes.

He hit the revolving door with the heel of his hand, and it was still spinning when he walked to the curb and looked up and down the avenue. Traffic was normal, a half dozen pedestrians on the sidewalks, a man in

155

uniform removing a box of flowers from the rear of a florist's van. Boyd noted the chestnut vendor standing beside his cart at the intersection south of their building. He walked to him and said, "Did you see a young girl"—he indicated Kate's height with his hand—"wearing a red ski jacket and walking a black Scottie?"

Halfway through the sentence, the old man shook his head helplessly and pointed to his mouth.

"You can't speak?" Boyd asked.

The old man nodded quickly. He repeated Boyd's gesture by which he had indicated Kate's height and pointed across the avenue to Central Park.

"She went into the park?"

Instead of responding with a nod or headshake, the old man knelt and made a scrambling motion with his fingers on the sidewalk.

"The dog?"

The old man nodded rapidly.

"The dog went into the park?"

The chestnut vendor put his right forefinger into the palm of his left hand and made a fist over it. Then he abruptly jerked the forefinger free from his own grasp.

"The dog pulled the leash from the girl's hand?"

The old man nodded again.

"The dog got away from her, ran into the park."

Again a quick nod.

"And she followed him?"

The old man's expression reflected impotence and frustration. He pointed across the avenue to the approximate place that Harry Lauder had scrambled across the wall and disappeared into thickets of shining sumac. As Boyd looked at him questioningly, the old man gave him an emphatic shake of his head and

156

pointed north to a footpath which entered the park two blocks from where they were standing.

Luther Boyd saw exactly what had happened, as clearly as if he were watching the sequence of action on a motion-picture screen.

He thanked the old man and stared at the sprawl of the park, while he examined the first three scenarios that occurred to him. One, Kate was in the park searching for the Scottie. Two, she was lost and was trying to find her way back to Fifth Avenue. Three, she was in trouble, hurt or restrained, physically unable to leave the park.

He rapidly sorted out his options: to go after her immediately or risk a few precious moments to prepare himself for potentially dangerous contingencies.

Luther Boyd had been trained to face facts, and because of that discipline, he had already accepted his third scenario as the most logical explanation for Kate's absence.

Barbara turned to him nervously when he let himself into their apartment. "Where is she?"

"Somewhere in the park."

"Oh, God. Why would she do that?"

Boyd went along the hallway to his bedroom and kicked off his loafers, while Barbara hurried after him, her high heels sounding with a clatter of panic on the parquet flooring.

"Luther, what's happening?"

He sat on the edge of the bed, putting on a pair of tennis shoes. "For some reason, she crossed Fifth Avenue. Harry Lauder got away from her and ran into the park."

Luther Boyd stripped off his jacket and pulled on a

157

black windbreaker. "The wall is too high for Kate to manage, so she went up a block or so to an entrance."

"But *when?* How long has she been in there?"

Boyd opened the top drawer of a highboy and removed a Browning 9mm automatic pistol, and after checking the thirteen-shot magazine and the safety, he slipped the piece under the waistband of his slacks. From the same drawer he picked up a flashlight and tucked it into his rear pocket.

Barbara's eyes were dark and haunted against the natural pallor of her face. "Goddamn it, are you trying to torture me? How long has she been in the park?"

"Forty minutes," Boyd said, and went into the bathroom and from the medicine cabinet collected a compact but sophisticated first-aid kit.

Barbara's voice was trembling, and her eyes were bright with tears. "Did you call the police?"

"No," he said.

"Why in God's name didn't you?"

"Hysterics won't help Kate," Boyd said, and put his big hands on her shoulders and shook her until the glaze of terror faded from her eyes.

"Now listen to me and understand me," he said. "We aren't calling the police. If she's in trouble, the faster I get to her, the better her chances are. We don't want a task force blundering around out there. This is a one-man job. And it requires speed. Whatever's happened, I'll find Kate. That's a promise. This is the kind of shit detail I'm good at."

And he was gone.

In less than three minutes, Luther Boyd had picked up Kate's trail in Central Park.

His knowledge and awareness of his daughter's

character and habits were precise. And his tracking abilities and instincts had been honed to near perfection by decades of application and experience.

He knew Kate would head south on a straight line to where her Scottie had leaped a wall and scrambled into the park.

As he ran silently and effortlessly through the shadows of huge English oaks, his flashlight picked up the imprint of Kate's small boot beside a drinking fountain where the earth was especially moist and soggy. When he reached the area where Harry Lauder had entered the park, he heard nothing but the wind high in the crowns of a quartet of gum trees and, above that, the muted traffic on the avenue. Knowing Kate's resilience and guts, Boyd realized she wouldn't give up at this point; she had a dangerous conviction that the world was full of nice people, and she was just reckless enough to continue searching for Harry Lauder through this dark and dangerous jungle.

Luther Boyd, eyes tracking the ground, ran in slow but ever-widening circles until he picked up another imprint of Kate's boot, this one pointing at right angles from her original course. She was traveling west now and running, which he determined by the length of her strides.

He thanked Providence for the drenching afternoon rain which had cleared the park of most pedestrian traffic. Normally, in fair weather, there would be a variety of footprints evident in this safe and attractive area of the park. But much of those signs had been erased by the rain, and the ground was fresh and pristine and so spongy and porous that he could follow the track of his daughter's small boots as easily as if she were running across wet sand.

159

Directly ahead of Boyd, perhaps a hundred yards away, was a tall stand of dark trees. And it was toward these that Kate had been hurrying, obviously following Harry Lauder's noisy trail. But when he entered the grove of trees (mulberries, he knew from the sandpaperlike touch of the leaves), there were signs of Kate but none of the Scottie, and this puzzled him. If the dog had been underneath these trees, there would be evidence of it, leaves and soil scratched and scattered in a half dozen places. But while he spotted the imprints of Kate's small boots, he saw nothing to indicate *why* she had rushed so confidently toward this particular grove of trees.

He tried to sort it out. Two things would have drawn her here: sight or sound of Harry Lauder. Since she couldn't see him at that distance at this hour of night, she must have heard him. From which it could be inferred that the Scottie *had* been among those trees. Then why no sign of him?

Suddenly, Luther Boyd was sickened by a conviction of what might have happened. He began looking for something else, and he found what he was looking for at the far edge of this stand of trees, the imprints of a huge pair of boots. He knelt and examined them closely under the beam of his flashlight. Wellingtons, he surmised, with stacked heels. And clearly defined in the mud were jagged notches on the bottom of those heels, V-shaped indentations that had been cut unevenly into the leather with some kind of sharp instrument.

He saw it all then. Someone had stood here waiting for Kate, watching her run across the open meadow toward the trees. A big man, a heavy man, to judge from the size of the Wellingtons and their deep imprint in the soggy earth, and he had stood here holding the

160

Scottie in his hands, using the barking dog as a magnet to draw Kate to him.

Luther Boyd glanced rapidly in all directions, scenting the chill night wind like an animal. There was traffic on the East Drive, and there were probably couples strolling about somewhere in this reasonably safe area of the park.

So it was logical to assume the man wouldn't make a move here. Using the dog as a lure, he would try to draw Kate deeper into the park, across the East Drive, and probably north then to areas that were remote and isolated and silent.

Rising quickly, Boyd began tracking those Wellingtons with the V-shaped indentations in their heels, and his deduction was proved correct almost immediately, for those huge footprints led him toward the East Drive. When Boyd picked up the imprints of Kate's boots on the same line he knew with certainty that his daughter was running headlong into the trap being set for her.

And because Luther Boyd had been reared by religious parents, words came to him from the verses of Matthew: "It had been good for that man if he had not been born."

But because he had spent the majority of his life in barracks and on battlefields, the remorseless purity of that threat was accompanied by a thought of his own, grim and savage: I'll find you, you big bastard, and when I do, you'll wish to God you'd got your kicks from a madam with whips and leather.

Barbara Boyd paced the drawing room of their apartment, her nerves drawn painfully tight with tension, and while she tried to resist the impulse, she was drawn helplessly toward the windows to stare at the bleak and now-terrifying darkness of Central Park.

But with her fear and anguish had come a searing confusion. What was it he had said? That he was good at details like this. . . . She hadn't thought of him in that way before, as a man so strong and competent that other men sought him out when there were dirty, dangerous jobs to be done. She wondered how grossly she might have misjudged him. What of her reason for her leaving him? Because he had always left her. But perhaps not always for the lure of excitement and danger, flags flying in stiff breezes. Maybe he had left her in the past as he had left her tonight, to do something that other men ordered him to do, something essential and perilous. But in this moment of terror, she was desperately grateful to him for leaving her. She was given annealment and hope because it was her husband, Luther Boyd, who was searching for Kate. And with that thought came a guilty conviction that hundreds, maybe thousands of soldiers had been given hope, as she was given hope now, because there was a Colonel Luther Boyd to lead them into battle.

But it was too much to ask of any one man. Or any one woman, she realized miserably.

To question his judgment and appraisal of the situation might be fatal, but after an agonizing moment of indecision Barbara picked up the phone and with trembling fingers rapidly dialed the New York police department.

She was transferred from Central to a switchboard and within seconds was answering questions in response to the impersonal but strangely reassuring voice of a Lieutenant Vincent Tonnelli.

After logging the time of Mrs. Luther Boyd's call (six fifty-eight P.M.), Lieutenant Gypsy Tonnelli had ordered into action fifty percent of the provisional equipment and personnel assigned to his task force and had notified Manhattan borough commanders, North and South, Chiefs Slocum and Larkin, that he had placed the remainder of his forces on a standby Red Alert status.

This might have been considered an overreaction to the report of a missing child, but both chiefs had agreed with the Gypsy's decision. Because there was something strange and dangerous about the times. . . . The child had gone into the park about six P.M. The parents had learned of her disappearance at approximately six thirty but had waited another half hour to notify the police. Which meant the child had been in the park almost an hour by the time Mrs. Boyd's call came in. In addition, the department had had a probable visual "make" on the Juggler at five forty-eight at Eighty-third and Lexington, not more than six or eight minutes from where Kate Boyd had gone into the park.

It was the killing day, the killing hour, and they had certain knowledge the Juggler was in a fateful radius of Central Park and Kate Boyd.

In the conference call with the chiefs, Chip Larkin had concluded by saying quietly, "Say a Hail Mary and pour it on, Lieutenant."

And Chief Slocum had added, "Put a frigging noose around the park, Gypsy, and we'll pull it up hard and tight."

At Tonnelli's headquarters, Sokolsky had dispatched squads and patrolmen from standby pools to the east and west perimeters of Central Park, sealing it off from

Seventy-eighth Street north to the borders of Harlem. The squads were to be parked at hundred-yard intervals with dome lights flashing, while the patrolmen would maintain surveillance on sidewalks at fifty-yard intervals until further notice.

Dispatcher Ed Maurer on the switchboard at Sergeant Boyle's headquarters had dispatched similar units to establish identical cordons from Seventy-seventh Street south to Fifty-ninth and across Fifty-ninth from Fifth Avenue to Central Park West.

Thus, within fifteen minutes of Mrs. Boyd's call to Lieutenant Tonnelli, these units had been deployed, and from an aerial view, Central Park would appear as a huge black rectangle with its four sides defined by mile-long lines of flashing red dome lights.

Tonnelli said to Sokolsky, "Send the child's description to the local radio stations. White, blond, age eleven, wearing a red ski jacket." He had got these details from the child's mother.

"How about TV?" Sokolsky asked him.

"They'll pick it up anyway," Tonnelli said.

"Then why give it to radio?"

"It's a thousand-to-one chance, but I'm taking it. Some guy driving in the park might just spot the girl. I'd rather keep a lid on it, but we've got to give the Boyd child every break we can."

Lieutenant Tonnelli told Sokolsky to notify Deputy Chief of Detectives Walter Greene that he was leaving headquarters and would be at the Boyds' apartment within minutes.

She was an attractive lady with style. Lean, rangy body, tawny hair, college, of course, and money—these

164

were Gypsy Tonnelli's first impressions of Barbara Boyd, who stood waiting for him with Mr. Brennan under the canopy at the entrance of their building.

After introducing himself, Tonnelli checked the line of squad cars bordering the eastern edge of the park on Fifth Avenue.

"Your daughter went into the park about six? Is that right?"

"She may have fallen or sprained her ankle," Barbara said. "Or she might have got turned around, lost her way."

"Yes, of course. Something like that probably happened. But about the time. You said you learned she had gone into the park about six thirty."

"Make that six thirty-five," Mr. Brennan said.

"Thank you." Gypsy Tonnelli looked steadily at Barbara Boyd. "But you didn't call the police until six fifty-eight, Mrs. Boyd. Which means we're starting twenty-three minutes late. Mind telling me why?"

After a brief pause, Barbara moistened her lips and said, "Because my husband told me not to call the police."

"Why would he tell you a thing like that?"

"He simply thought it best we didn't."

"He went after your daughter?"

When Barbara nodded, Gypsy Tonnelli felt a stab of exasperation and anger. Civilians, he thought. Fucking civilians. The last thing they needed right now was a hysterical father running around the park, bawling out his kid's name.

Barbara correctly interpreted his expression and said, "You'll send your men after him, is that right?"

Sprained her ankle. . . . Lost her way. . . . Of

course they had no way of knowing that the Juggler might have his hands on their daughter, but he couldn't control an illogical anger at their innocence.

"Yes, we'll pick up your husband, Mrs. Boyd. For his sake and the sake of your daughter. If he got in our way, he could be hurt."

Tonnelli gave her a soft salute and turned toward his car, but she grabbed the sleeve of his topcoat and pulled him about with surprising strength.

"Then take me with you. *Please.*"

"I can't do that, ma'am. We've closed off the park. Now we're going to search it, tree by tree, bush by bush until we find—"

She interrupted him with a frantic headshake. "*Listen.* That's our child out there. And there's something else you should know. My husband has a gun. I might be able to persuade him to cooperate with you. But I doubt if you can."

Sweet Jesus Christ, Tonnelli thought wearily. All his Sicilian demons told him that they at last had the Juggler in a trap, but their chances of springing it could be destroyed by this gun-waving hysteric who might fire at shadows, could conceivably wound or kill police officers, but whose actions would surely and certainly warn the Juggler that the police were closing in on him, and with this in mind, he made a quick but reluctant decision.

"Get in the car," he said to Mrs. Boyd.

166

14

KATE BOYD stopped in the middle of a silent glade glowing softly with moonlight and made a practical attempt to assess and try to find some solution to her problems. She hadn't heard her Scottie barking for the last several minutes and was praying fervently that he had tired of romping about the park and was now trotting back to Fifth Avenue, where Mr. Brennan would find him and take him up to their apartment.

But Kate, in running after the elusive sound of her Scottie's barks and yelps, had managed to get herself hopelessly lost; she had the worrisome notion that she had been traveling in a wide circle for at least the last five minutes. If she walked east, that would take her back to Fifth Avenue. If she went south, that would bring her out on Fifty-ninth Street, and from there she could walk to her apartment. But the difficulty was, she wasn't sure which way was east and which was south. Once on a camping trip, her father had taught her how to find the north star by using the Big Dipper; the handle pointed to it, or the tip of the bowl, she couldn't remember which. In any event, the information wouldn't help, because while the pale sky was full of stars, she couldn't seem to find the Big Dipper.

Then there was something about Orion the Giant. His sword—did it point south? Or was it his belt?

In the distance, but quite a way off, she could see an occasional flash of headlights, car curving through the park's traffic system. She turned in a slow, full circle, hoping to find a building on the skyline she could identify. But she was too close to the trees for an unbroken view, and the odd spires and lights she could make out were indefinite patterns against the darkness.

And so she stood uncertainly in the moonlit glade, glancing again at the sky but finding no help or reassurance from the stars. . . .

Gus Soltik stood in the shadows of a huge oak tree and watched her. . . . She was lost. He knew that. It gave him a strange sense of superiority, because he was never lost. He didn't need street names and numbers. He could go anywhere he wanted, guided by subtle instincts, along alleys and docks, across tenement roofs, aware of every smell and stir within range of his acute senses, moving always with relentless but unconscious precision.

His huge hands tightened on the flight bag, and he could feel the strong, hot rush of blood in his body. Now, he thought.

Now. . . .

Kate heard the approach of his pounding footsteps. She turned and saw a big man in a brown turtleneck sweater and yellow leather cap rushing toward her, and something familiar about him made her wonder if she had met or seen him before.

"Excuse me, sir," she said, but then she became aware

of his slack lips and glazed eyes, and she knew the look of him was wrong, dreadfully wrong, and when his huge hands reached for her, Kate Boyd began to scream for her life.

Rudi Zahn heard her screams. He was about fifty yards away, striding along in his vigorous fashion, when Kate's first screams destroyed the night's silence.

Luther Boyd, south and east of the glade by several hundred yards, sensed the merest whisper of that scream and wondered if it had been the cawing of a nocturnal bird or branches of trees twisting against each other in freshening winds.

But he zeroed on that sound like the needle of a radar screen, orienting himself to its location by a stand of *Styrax japonica* to the left of it and ,an outcropping of natural rock directly in line with it. And then he began to run.

Rudi Zahn's first reaction to those screams was a sickening indecision; his fears were so deeply rooted that it was almost physically impossible to take a step toward danger. His instinct was to run in the opposite direction, with the solacing lie in his throat that this was the best thing to do, to find a phone or police officer, professional aid. Then the screaming stopped abruptly, replaced by an even more terrible silence.

His body was trembling with fear, but some emotion kept him rooted to the ground, and that was the rekindled memories of Ilana, whose pale face blazed in his mind like a star. He had watched from a basement window of the priest's house while soldiers dragged her to the trucks. She had fought like a hellcat, but no one in the village had raised a hand to save her. The others

169

were willing victims, going to slaughter like cattle, but Ilana had fought back, which hadn't angered the soldiers, of course; they savored resistance, it added spice to their dreary brutality.

Against his will, against everything he was trying to safeguard for himself and Crescent Holloway, Rudi Zahn ran in the direction of those now-silent screams.

He came into a clearing filled with moonlight and saw a huge man in a brown sweater running toward the shadows of trees with a young child in his arms. The girl's white legs were thrashing helplessly, but the big man had locked her arms with one arm and had stifled her screams with a huge hand across her mouth.

"Stop!" Zahn shouted, and ran after the man and the struggling little girl.

Gus Soltik wheeled around, his heavy, smudged features working with terror and rage.

"No!" he shouted at the man. "No!" he cried again, his voice high and shrill, almost strangled against the pressures of his corded neck muscles.

"Let her alone!" Zahn screamed the words at him.

Gus Soltik threw the girl aside and ran at Rudi Zahn, his mouth twisting spasmodically, his body feverish at this dreadful, frustrating intervention; his excitement had been so intensified by the girl's struggles that he felt as if his blood were boiling.

Zahn avoided Soltik's first lunging charge, leaping to one side and kicking at Gus Soltik's legs, which sent the huge man sprawling to the ground.

"Run!" he shouted to the girl. He might take the beating he had always dreaded, but that might buy enough time for the girl to get away. "Run!" he shouted again, as Gus Soltik scrambled to his feet, his breathing heavy, eyes dilated with rage.

170

But Kate Boyd didn't run; she stood her ground. She wasn't sure why, but some deep instinct of survival told her that was the wise thing to do. She would fight back her fear and stand fast because she believed she knew what excited this big man, and that was her screams, her struggles; she had already felt what they did to his body.

Rudi Zahn swung a fist at Gus Soltik's face, and while the blow landed, it had no more effect than if it had struck a mountainside. Soltik bellowed hoarsely and with the back of his huge hand struck Zahn across the side of his head and sent him reeling to the ground, his skull exploding with roaring flashes of pain.

Gus Soltik kicked him in the ribs with his heavy, thick Wellingtons, and Zahn groaned in agony. The powerful kick struck Zahn in the face, laying bare his cheek to the bone, but after that searing torment came merciful oblivion.

Gus Soltik stared at Kate, puzzled and vaguely fearful. Why didn't she run? You couldn't chase them if they didn't run. Then his big body became tense once more with fear and anger. Someone else was coming after him. . . . Silent, so silent that the girl hadn't heard the whispering sounds in the underbrush beyond the black trees. Picking up his flight bag, he grabbed the fabric of Kate's ski jacket, twisting it sharply at the collar line, so powerfully that it strangled the scream rising in her throat. With long strides which forced Kate into a stumbling run, Gus Soltik vanished from the clearing, losing himself with the girl in the shadows of big trees.

It was only seconds after this that Luther Boyd came on the body of Kate's little Scottie, its head twisted sideways at a grotesque angle, its black body pitifully small in death, looking somehow lonely and discarded and forgotten on the ground in a tangle of wood ivy. But Harry Lauder's death had not been without point, for it gave Boyd a direct bearing on the course of the man who wore those huge Wellingtons. He had no longer needed the dog's barking to lure Kate toward him; from this exact geographical fix, he obviously had a visual make on Kate Boyd.

Without fully regaining consciousness, Rudi Zahn stirred reflexively against the pain in his face and stomach. When he tried to rise, placing his palms against the ground and pushing down hard, his ribs reacted in an agonized spasm, and a groan forced itself past the constricted muscles of his throat.

Boyd, coursing warily through the trees a dozen yards away, heard the sound and ran toward it, his right hand whipping the Browning from beneath his belt and flipping it off the safety in a fluid gesture that was as effortless and reflexive as the beat of his heart. He ran into the moonlit glade and saw a man with thinning hair lying motionless on the ground. One side of his face was chopped up like raw meat, the cheekbone pale and clean in the soft yellow light.

Boyd checked the perimeter of the clearing with alert eyes. A mugging, that was a first thought. As he walked to the figure on the ground, his eyes checking the black honey locusts circling the glade, he spotted something that caused anger to surge through his veins, but it was anger tinged with hope, for in several areas near the unconscious man were the familiar imprints of big Wellington boots, their stacked heels creating indentations an inch deep in the damp earth.

Boyd checked the clearing in an ever-widening circle

172

until he came to footprints he knew had been made by Kate's small black boots.

Running back to the unconscious man, Luther Boyd gripped his shoulders and turned him as gently as he could onto his back. Nevertheless, a groan of pain burst from the man's lips, and Boyd then saw the muddy imprint of a boot against the tattersall vest under the man's gray flannel jacket. The jagged flap of flesh hanging away from his cheekbone was probably the result of another blow from those Wellingtons. Boyd checked the man's wallet: Rudi Zahn was the name on his driver's license, and his address was in Beverly Hills, California.

Luther Boyd had spent his adult life in practicing and teaching martial arts and as a military historian had professionally examined terrain long after the cannon had faded into the silence of history.

And now he stared about this open stretch of moonlit ground and studied it as he would a battlefield.

Kate had screamed; no cawing bird or rustling tree, but his daughter, Kate, screaming. This man, Rudi Zahn, had heard her, had gone to her aid and had taken a brutal battering from the man who wore the Wellingtons. The question he couldn't answer was this: Why hadn't Kate made a run for it? Maybe she believed she had no chance of getting away. But possibly, and this gave him a certain hope, she had been shrewd enough to do something so unpredictable that it might jar a psycho off balance.

It was then, with his exceptional peripheral vision, that Boyd noted a movement among the trees, and when Patrolman Prima came running into the glade, the Browning in Boyd's hand was pointed squarely at

Prima's head. Prima's own police special was in his hand, but it was pointed fifteen degrees off target from Boyd, and instinct told Prima with chilling force that he couldn't move it fast enough to turn the situation at least into a stalemate. Something in the way that big, rangy man held the gun warned Prima that he knew how to use it.

"Holster your weapon, son," Boyd said quietly, and turned back to look for signs of consciousness in Rudi Zahn.

"On your feet," Prima said, swinging his gun around on the man crouched in the middle of the clearing.

"I told you, put that gun away," Boyd said without looking at Prima. "I'm Colonel Boyd."

"And I'm telling you—" Prima stopped abruptly in mid-sentence, swallowing with difficulty, reacting then to Boyd's name. "Jesus Christ," he said softly. "You're the kid's father."

Boyd looked at him intently. "How would you know that?"

"Well, your wife called it in."

"Goddamn her," Boyd said bitterly. And now, he thought, the park would be crawling with cops, rookies like this one blundering through the woods with drawn guns, and he had to stay here until he asked Rudi Zahn one vital question. No, he thought, and checked his wristwatch. I'll waste just thirty more seconds.

"Sir, she did the right thing," Prima said. "Lieutenant Tonnelli's already got the park sealed off with squads."

Still eyeing his watch, Boyd said, "Then tell your lieutenant to set up an east-west skirmish line between Sixty-ninth and Seventieth Streets, from Fifth Avenue to Central Park West. Some psycho—and my daughter —are traveling north and they've crossed Seventieth."

174

Rudi Zahn moaned and opened his eyes.

"Ilana," he said. "He took Ilana."

The man was in shock, Boyd knew. Maybe he'd wasted a precious moment after all.

"Why didn't my daughter try to run?" he asked Zahn, his voice low and intense.

"I couldn't help her," Zahn said. "He was too big, too crazy. He took her away."

Patrolman Prima removed the police artist's sketch of the Juggler from his tunic, quickly opened it, and held it in front of Zahn.

"This the guy grabbed the kid?"

Zahn's eyes narrowed, and he nodded.

"Brown sweater, maniac."

"Was my daughter tied up?" Boyd asked him sharply.

Zahn shook his head wearily. "I told her to run. I shouted at her to run. But she didn't."

"Get a medic for him," Boyd said to Prima, and while Prime was debating with himself just how many orders he should take from this civilian, Boyd leaped to his feet and within seconds was lost among the dark trees, running north after the imprints of the big Wellingtons.

Patrolman Prima snapped a switch on his two-way radio and spoke into it.

"This is Patrolman Prima. About twenty yards east of the Mall, between Sixty-ninth and Seventieth. We got action here. Lieutenant Tonnelli? Lieutenant Tonnelli?"

"Give me what you got," Rusty Boyle answered him. "He's on wheels. I'll patch it to him through Central. . . ."

Within minutes after receiving a positive make on the Juggler and the confirmation that he had crossed

175

Seventieth Street and was traveling north, Lieutenant Gypsy Tonnelli's unmarked car turned off the Mall and drove at speed through a formal stand of red maples toward the glade where Prima was administering rudimentary first aid to Rudi Zahn.

More equipment had already been dispatched to the scene: light trucks, an ambulance with police medics, communications units and emergency service vans equipped with shotguns and snipers' rifles, and two teams of expert marksmen. The caliber of the ammo used in the sniper's rifle was incredibly low, almost a third less than a .22, but with a muzzle velocity so fast that its striking power was such that a human target would go down no matter where the bullet struck it. The scopes on the rifles were powerful enough to bring targets to the cross hairs that would be invisible to the naked eye.

And from the first radio broadcast ordered by Lieutenant Tonnelli, the print and electronic media had been gathering pools of photographers, reporters, TV and radio staffs to monitor the remote-control units already on their way to cover still another of the Juggler's grisly escapades.

While from opposite ends of the borough, Commanders Slocum and Larkin, in their limousines with sirens wailing, were on their way to give the public what it seemed to want and need: the drama of the human chase, the exhilaration of a televised scrutiny of the police running a monster to ground under the direction and scenario of borough commanders in uniform, twin silver stars gleaming on their shoulders.

15

LUTHER BOYD followed the track of the Wellingtons and his daughter's boots through stands of cut-leaf beech trees which made his task laborious and difficult because a luxuriance of foliage fell to the ground from masses of horizontal branches, and Boyd had to sweep them aside like coarse curtains to find the sign he was searching for. But when he reached the band shell, an open-air theater at the head of the Mall—he was north of Seventieth Street now—he came on a narrow, spongy strip of ground which circled the theater, and it was here, traveling east, that he again found sign of the Wellingtons and Kate's small boots. Following their trail, he turned north at the eastern end of the theater and made his way past the Mall and band shell through heavy stands of giant sycamores, with mottled gray-white trunks, and huge exposed roots. There were heaps of fallen branches and scattered stacks of underbrush left by the park's cleanup crews.

He ran a zigzag course, steadily extending its perimeters, but the exposed roots and heaps of windfall timber made an impossible tracking surface; the wood, hard as iron, would require an ax to so much as dent it. And here Boyd lost the Wellingtons.

Instinct told Boyd his quarry hadn't doubled back on him, so he continued on a northern line until he came to the barrier of Seventy-second Street, brilliant and noisy with traffic. He looked toward Fifth Avenue and saw that the light had turned red against the east-west flow of cars. In seconds, he could cross this conduit and try to pick up the Wellingtons on the turf he could see on the opposite side of the street.

But while he was waiting, his muscles tensed and ready to run, a black sedan pulled up and parked directly in front of him, and from the front passenger seat a man with a huge chest and a vivid scar along his cheek stepped out and said, "I'm Lieutenant Tonnelli, Colonel Boyd."

At the wheel of the car was the young patrolman, Max Prima, whom Boyd had encountered only minutes before in the park. In the rear of the car was Boyd's wife, Barbara, and he could see the tears in her eyes and the ravaged lines of fear in her face.

"I did what I thought best, Luther," she said. "You must believe that."

Recriminations were irrelevant now. She had cast the die, and he would have to live with it. Whether Kate would or not was another matter. She had added chaos to his simple strategy, and that might destroy their daughter. Like most civilians, Barbara lacked control of her emotions, but none of these bitter thoughts was reflected in Boyd's manner or expression.

"I know you did what you thought best," he said. And because he knew Barbara, he added, "I think you did right."

He could give her that. Maybe not Kate, but a sustaining lie at least.

178

Gypsy Tonnelli was not a notably tactful or patient man, but something about Luther Boyd, the clean, powerful lines of his body, the tough, cold intelligence in his eyes and face, warned him to proceed discreetly. He wanted and needed his cooperation, which meant he wanted him back in his apartment with his wife, out of the park, out of the search for the Juggler.

"Colonel Boyd, believe me. The best chance of getting your daughter back is to let the police handle it," he said. "We've got the equipment, the manpower—"

Boyd cut him off with a headshake. "You've got work to do, and I expect you'll do it. But I've also got a job, which is saving my daughter's life."

Tonnelli glanced at the Browning beneath Boyd's waistband, then looked steadily at Boyd. "You got a permit for that?"

"Lieutenant, I'm not being hard-nosed, but I can't waste any more time. I have a permit for this particular weapon, and every weapon issued by the United States Army up to and including AR-21's. I'll talk fast now—"

"Your wife told me about Fort Benning and the Rangers and —"

"Please give me the courtesy of listening, Lieutenant. I tracked my daughter from where she was grabbed by what I presume to be a psychopath. . . ."

"Don't presume, he *is*."

"I've tracked him and my daughter this far, to Seventy-second Street." Boyd pointed north past the streams of traffic. "He's only a couple of minutes ahead of me. You want to help me take him, fine. Say no, I'm gone."

There was a new element in Boyd's tone and manner, and it sent a tiny chill down Tonnelli's spine.

179

Luther Boyd's spirit had been hardened and tempered by the habit of command; it had been drilled into him by his superiors and, more significantly, by the necessity of saving lives, including his own, in combat. It was elemental to the construct of his character; it was not that he was convinced of the inevitable rectitude of his decisions, but he knew that any decision was preferable to indecision in warfare, and he believed this so strongly that it never occurred to him, even fleetingly, that anyone in his command would disobey his orders.

It was this projection of granitic authority that struck Gypsy Tonnelli with the impact of a fist.

The Gypsy traced the vivid scar on his cheek with a fingertip. "Let's take him," he said.

Pulling a police whistle and red-beamed flashlight from the pocket of his topcoat, Tonnelli ran to the middle of Seventy-second Street, leaping nimbly from the path of a station wagon of blacks who left streams of curses trailing on the air with their exhaust fumes.

Tonnelli blew a half dozen piercing blasts while the red beams of his flashlight cut wide and brilliant arcs through the darkness.

"Police! Hit your brakes! Halt!" he shouted at the on-rushing streams of traffic.

Luther Boyd went to Tonnelli's car and put his hand on Barbara's cheek.

"I'll get her back. That's a promise. Hang in there."

And then he was gone, running through a corridor formed by stopped cars to join Tonnelli on spongy ground north of Seventy-second Street.

In less than a minute, Boyd had once again picked up the prints of the Wellingtons and his daughter's small boots.

He asked Lieutenant Tonnelli, "Did you post a skirmish line across the park between Sixty-ninth and Seventieth?"

"That was done five minutes after your wife called us. Except that I put them on Transverse One at Sixty-sixth Street. It's a wall of cops. I figured the Juggler had to be on one side or the other of it."

Tonnelli flicked the switch on his two-way radio. "This is Tonnelli. I want Rusty Boyle."

After a few seconds, Boyle's miniature voice sounded from Tonnelli's radio.

"Ten-four, Lieutenant."

"Rusty? I want you to move our line from Sixty-sixth up to Seventy-second Street. Make damn sure the men are in voice contact with each other. Make *goddamn* sure nobody goes south through that line without being stopped and questioned."

"Roger, Lieutenant."

"Then let's move out," Luther Boyd said.

Searching the ground with narrowed eyes, he went off at a pace which forced Tonnelli to break into a half run to keep up with him.

"We've got to take the north end of the park away from him," Luther Boyd said.

"Any idea how we do that?"

"Yes," Luther Boyd said. Then: "You call him the Juggler. Why?"

"You'd be better off not knowing, Colonel."

"It's not what I want to know. It's what I *need* to know, Lieutenant. . . ."

They were moving swiftly through a shadowed meadow on which the first traces of hoarfrost were gleaming under the moonlight, an expanse bordered with the dramatic green of Austrian pines, and it was against this background of fairy-tale beauty and tranquillity that Gypsy Tonnelli told Luther Boyd what he knew of the creature the New York police called the Juggler.

"To win battles, you do not need weapons, you beat the soul of the enemy. . . ."

Patton was more often right than wrong, Luther Boyd believed, and believed from his own experience that to know the enemy was half of victory.

He had seen the man they called the Juggler, he realized, standing stock-still in nighttime traffic on Fifth Avenue, staring up at their apartment. That fact was no help to him, but knowing who and what the Juggler was did give him a certain hope. A psychopath, corroded with guilt and fear. They could use that to their advantage. . . .

To confuse him without frightening him, that was essential, so that his panic would be tinged with uncertainty rather than defensive anger. Destroy his orientation, but without threatening him. Make him believe he had lost direction or taken a wrong turning; never make him feel cornered or trapped.

Kate must have sensed what he was. . . . At eleven, she was a highly perceptive and intelligent child. She might well have realized that if she could summon up the nerve to conceal her fears and stand her ground, this could conceivably deflect and disrupt the Juggler's monstrous needs.

She was walking beside him, and that fact gave him additional hope. As long as she was not under physical restraint, it could be inferred that the Juggler had a destination in mind and was heading for it.

And where would that be? Far north of here, beyond the Receiving Reservoir, beyond the upper Nineties, where Central Park became a true jungle, an area where not only the laws of the city but the laws of humanity had long since been suspended.

Luther Boyd stopped and checked Tonnelli with a hand on his arm.

"Hold it a minute," Boyd said.

"What is it?" Tonnelli asked him quietly.

Boyd stared ahead into the darkness and listened to the sounds of winds in the crowns of giant oak trees.

"A hunch. He knows we're after him."

"What makes you think so?"

Boyd thought fleetingly of classrooms at Fort Benning where he might have answered Tonnelli's question in some detail. . . . He would have explained intangibles, such as the inferences to be drawn from the sounds and smells and "feels" of battlegrounds. He might advise him of Mao Tse-tung's famous Three Rules and Eight Remarks, a code of military and civilian principles adopted by the Red Army, whose applications had broken the combined might of the Japanese imperial forces and the U.S.-bolstered troops of Generalissimo Chiang Kai-shek. Arise in the east, but attack from the west . . . destroy confidence in terrain . . . confuse the enemy's rear . . . feint reserves into chaos.

He couldn't pin down what was alerting him now. It was pure instinct, and he couldn't explain that to the lieutenant any more than he could explain why soldiers were comfortable with the expected sounds of combat, but that something unexpected like screaming banzai charges or the wild, thrilling music the North Koreans

183

had used so effectively could turn seasoned troops into disorderly mobs.

It was hard to explain things like that unless you'd experienced them.

"For one thing, his strides are longer now," Boyd said.

Then he noticed something that gave support to his previous instinctive anxiety. He moved swiftly but silently to a twisted thorn-studded Japanese angelica tree and from one of its spikes picked off a strand of coarse brown wool. Even though the cluster of threads was small, no larger than a fingertip, they exuded a rank, animallike odor.

"Brown sweater," Boyd said.

"The Juggler," Tonnelli said.

"And one other thing," Boyd said. "He wouldn't have walked into that tree, unless he was looking over his shoulder, worried about something behind him."

"What could have stirred him up?"

"Psychopaths usually have physical compensations."

"Better eyes, better ears?"

"Right. So far, he's made only one mistake. When I found my daughter's Scottie, that gave me a direct fix on him. When I heard Kate scream, I ran toward the sound. But I could have missed it by a hundred yards or more if the dog's body hadn't given me the line."

"Jesus Christ," Gypsy Tonnelli said softly. "Colonel, compared to you, an iceberg would look like a blast furnace. How can you just stand here?"

"Because I must," Luther Boyd said. "Let him calm down. I want my daughter alive."

Boyd began to consider options, a tactical administration of his simple strategy. They stood presently on the east-west line of Seventy-third Street. Transverse Three

184

to the north ran a curving course from Fifth Avenue at Eighty-fourth Street to Central Park West, Eighty-sixth Street.

"Lieutenant, do you have fifty officers in your reserve?"

"We got a hell of a lot more than that, and I'm taking a hell of a responsibility not committing them."

Central Park was about a half mile wide. Fifty times fifty would cover it.

"Then commit fifty patrolmen to Transverse Three with transistor radios. Post them at fifty-foot intervals. Tell them to take positions north of the transverse, to take cover in shrubbery or shadows, and to turn their radios onto rock stations at full volume."

"That going to stop the Juggler?"

"Lieutenant, we learned a bitter lesson from North Koreans on the psychology of sound in combat. We paid a stiff price for not doing enough research into troop response to unexpected audio impacts. A soldier expects artillery fire, braces himself for it. But if silence is broken by something unexpected, laughter or singing, for instance, it can bring a column of troops to a full halt.

"You used the phrase 'a wall of cops.' I'm proposing a wall of music. It may not stop him, but it will confuse him. He's bracing himself for sirens, flashing dome lights, police whistles. Not music. It's a chance to destroy his game plan, take away the north end of the park. Then we've got him in a box. And when we make visual contact, you can take him out with one shot."

Tonnelli made up his mind with a figurative finger snap. Putting the two-way radio to his lips, he flipped the switch and asked quietly for Sergeant Rusty Boyle.

185

16

KATE BOYD was half running to keep up with Gus Soltik's long strides. His huge hand was tight on the collar of her ski jacket and her breathing was labored and difficult. With a flex of his thick wrist, he could strangle her or break her neck, she knew, but an instinct for survival and the genetic temper of her father strengthened her conviction that to show signs of panic and terror or to make any attempt to struggle against him would again create that dreadful response in his body.

They must be close to Seventy-fifth Street, she thought, trying to anesthetize her torturing fear with distracting considerations. They had already passed the Bethesda Fountain in one of the southern coves of the lake. She had walked the steps to the water there many times and had had ice cream in the fountain café, with the smell of the fresh lake around them and the sun shining on bronze statues. Somewhere off to their right was the Conservatory Pond. She remembered a story about it. Stuart Little had won a race there at the helm of the *Wasp*. . . . It was a dear book, and she kept it in a drawer beside her bed with the Hobbitt books and the

187

story of Jay Trump, the lovely steeplechaser who had won the Maryland Hunt twice and the Grand National at Aintree, and thinking about this and her room and talking to Tish on the phone brought stinging tears to her eyes.

Luther Boyd's estimate of the Juggler's line of march and his eventual destination had been on the mark; the Juggler was heading north with Kate Boyd, following the East Drive toward the Receiving Reservoir, which was still almost two miles ahead of them. There he planned to swing east to avoid the precinct on Transverse Number Three, skirting the reservoir and continuing on toward the trackless sanctuaries in the jungle above Ninety-seventh Street.

But a word was forming in Gus Soltik's mind, a word symbolizing a dangerous, frightening concept. The word that blazed now in the darkness of his mind was "coldness." It was his surrogate for a dread expection of shame and punishment. By people angry and loud. He couldn't always remember who the people were, but he sensed that they were after him now.

The messages drumming on all of Gus Soltik's physical receptors warned him that the men who would hurt him were close behind him. Above the sound of sporadic, spiraling winds he had heard someone shouting at the cars on Seventy-second Street, and that voice brought frightening memories of a powerful man with a scarred face who hated him and wanted to make him cry out in pain for mercy.

This was Gus Soltik's deepest fear. He knew he deserved to be hurt. (His mother and Mrs. Schultz had told him this, and they wouldn't lie to him.) But the conditions of that punishment, consisting of relentless and endless torments whose nature he could only guess at, on occasion would pull him sharply from sleep, a moan in his throat, icy sweat on his trembling body.

He knew that he deserved to be beaten unconscious, then revived and hurt still more, but the cruelest terror was that this torture would never end, that there was no way he could be forgiven and allowed to die.

He stopped, tightening his grip on the collar of the young girl's ski jacket and looked back through the darkness toward Seventy-second Street.

Shadows drifted, and moonlight lay in silver patches on the ground. When he saw his big footprints in one of these pools of light and beside them the impress of the girl's boots, he nodded then, knowing. . . .

Gus Soltik steered Kate through a thicket of trees at a right angle to his previous course until he came to a path formed of shale and rock. He went north for another fifty yards, dragging the girl along behind him, leaving no trail on the hard surface of the path. The sound of their footsteps was covered by the traffic on the East Drive, which was twenty or thirty yards to their right, with automobile headlights flashing against the trees.

He was too close to the drive to feel safe. When they stopped following him, he would go back through the trees toward the lake and go north again past the boathouse to the big reservoir.

Gus Soltik sat in the shadow formed by a thicket of trees and pulled the girl down beside him. He put his airlines bag on the ground and looked at the girl.

Kate had been trying hard to control her emotions,

but the effort was so physically draining that she felt faint and exhausted. There was an aching tension in her stomach, and she was afraid that at any instant she might burst into tears and begin to scream. But she knew that would be dangerous for her; she knew what that would do to him. That was one thing she was certain of.

She did not know specifically what he wanted to do to her, but her maturing sexual instincts warned her it would be agonizing and obscene.

She knew nothing about him, his fears, his torments, his rages. She did not know he had never been to a dentist, had never been treated by doctors or psychiatrists with shock therapy or tranquilizers. She did not know that he had dislocated a girl's shoulder in a playground because she had grinned at him and that as a result he had been thrashed mercilessly by the athletic director of the school while two older boys had held his arms.

And that girl's father had come to Mrs. Schultz's home that night, and Gus, hiding in the basement, had heard the man's wild, screaming voice declaring that he would kill him like a savage dog if he ever so much as looked at his daughter again.

As punishment his mother had made Gus Soltik stay outside all night in the muddy backyard of Mrs. Schultz's home, wearing only sneakers, jeans, and a thin shirt, with the temperatures dropping below freezing. That was why cold and coldness had become to him surrogates of shame and punishment. The coldness and the shame and that girl's father and the punishment had been forged into a single mnemonic unit in his brain.

190

At the age of eleven Kate Boyd knew the only way she could save her life was to analyze and attempt to apply a diverting therapy to this man who wanted to hurt and kill her.

Partly by luck and partly by virtue of shrewd female instinct, Kate Boyd composed a question which probed like a lance at a core of fear in Gus Soltik's dreadfully twisted nature. She managed a tremulous smile and said in a practical voice, "If you wanted a date with me, why didn't you just call me on the phone?"

The concept of the word "date" confused Gus Soltik. He felt a warmth in his cheeks. Her question made him uncomfortable. In his dim mind he knew what dating was. He had seen boys and girls, young men and young women, walking with their arms about each other's waists. Their smiles confused him. He saw them going into movie houses, laughing and talking easily, and he couldn't understand it. The girls had razors and bottles of acid in their purses. They would hurt you if you touched them. He felt sorry for the boys, the young ones. He had wanted to be with a boy, he liked to look at them, an inchoate impulse he did not comprehend; but there was only Lanny, and he was different, he was old.

Suddenly he saw with a twist of fear that "white legs" carried a green suede purse on a leather strap over her shoulder. With a quick move he snatched it from her, dizzy with relief, convinced he had saved himself from pain and humiliation.

Kate's fiercely held composure almost cracked then; she fought back the scream rising in her throat as she felt the awesome power in the hand that ripped the purse from her shoulder.

Gus Soltik opened it and anxiously inspected its

contents in the thin moonlight. He found a clean, neatly folded handkerchief, two pencils and a book with names in it, a wallet with a single dollar in the bill compartment, and a photograph of a little black dog. He had seen the dog before. He had done something to the dog, he remembered vaguely. It was over, and now no one cared. He tore the snapshot of the small black dog into several pieces and dropped them on the ground. But it was bad of her to make him think about it. It was over, and he could forget about it. But she had the picture of the dog. Maybe it wasn't razors or acid; maybe there were other ways they hurt you. But he wasn't angry with her. The word "date" had started a slow but tantalizing tremor in the sludge of his mind. He wanted to know about dates. She knew about them. His helplessness made him sullen. This time was different from the others. Before, it had been him, and the lessons. And anger.

Always before, the ferocious exhilaration, the riotous, clamorous release linked to his rage. But now there was an anxiety about what to say. How to ask.

"Date," he said, blurting the word out. "Where?"

She tried very hard not to blink, for she knew that would bring the tears. She could only guess at what his sullen anger at the picture of Harry Lauder had meant and pray that her guess was wrong. She tried to make her mind a blank, attempting with her tone and manner to strike a casual, impersonal note; she realized that she was walking a dangerous tightrope and that any mistake in judgment might be fatal. But even more difficult was finding the will not to think of Harry Lauder.

"Well, it would depend on whether someone was going out at night or in the daytime," Kate said. There

192

she stopped, and while she weighed her next words, she felt a cold and painful knot of fear gripping her stomach.

Kate Boyd knew who and what she was, and liked what she was, with the result that her ego structure was as solid as might be expected in a young and healthy girl who had been exposed to the molding influence of intelligent teachers and parents and to the company of companions whose emotional values were approximately as sane and practical as her own. She and her friends had not been taught that their desires were tainted and evil.

But there were areas of sexual maturity where Kate had no explicit experience. And this was what frightened her now. In their apartments, with Cokes and bowls of popcorn, she and her friends might talk and laugh about their awareness of one another's sexuality, making titillating jokes and naughty plays on words. But it was innocent and fun, while this was ghastly and fearful. She felt lost and desperate because she knew of no way to talk about dates with this man. She had no way of knowing how this perverted creature would react to what she might say. To talk about dates meant touching on sexual potentials, and she realized that her life would literally hang in the balance if she said anything that stirred or angered him in ways she couldn't control.

"We might just go for a walk and stop somewhere for hot chocolate," she said.

His face was sullen, impassive, his eyes glazing as he watched her moving lips, the animation in her expression. He was waiting for her to lie.

She breathed through her open mouth. This was

something her father had taught her once when they were backpacking through a forest where a skunk had laid down his scent. If she breathed through her mouth, she avoided his terrible smell.

"Would you like that?" she asked him.

He looked away from her, confused and angry, not at her but at himself. He should say yes or no. But they had told him to say nothing to them. And in his tortured mind there were no words at all. His eyes looked dimly at the dark trees and the glimpse of moonlight he could see on the lake, while that part of him that was pure animal listened for the footsteps he knew were not too far behind. . . .

Why had he looked away from her? What did that mean?

"There's a place on Park called Armand's," she said tentatively, while studying his blunted face, the muddy eyes staring off toward the lake.

"In the window, there's trays of cookies and cakes and little figures made of marzipan."

She sensed a tension in his manner as he looked off into the trees. Her purse fell from his limp hand to the ground. She picked it up slowly, carefully, and looped it over her shoulder.

"Or we could take a boat ride around the island," she said.

He saw the word "lake"; he understood "boat," but he said nothing and did not look at her. How did they know? Boats and water. Places to buy cakes. . . .

For Gus Soltik's ignorance of the commonplace was as vast as it was frustrating to him. He did not now why some people wore glasses and others didn't. He had never fathomed why in the winter men in red suits and

194

white beards stood on street corners ringing bells. He did not know where the people on the screen went when Mrs. Schultz turned the TV off. He had looked behind the set many times but had never found any of them. He did not know where his mother was.

The word "cold" was blazing again in Gus Soltik's mind. The wind was rising in the tops of the trees, diminishing what he could hear, and this made him feel tense and vulnerable. In spite of her fear and terror, Kate felt a tiny stab of compassion as she saw the lonely agony in his expression. But as she watched him scenting the wind like a frightened animal, she felt a sudden stir of confidence. Perhaps she could manipulate him now. Perhaps she could even make him take her home. She might convince him he hadn't done anything really bad yet. He had hit the man who tried to help her, but that was all. No, there was another thing, but she had willed herself not to think of it.

"I've got an idea," Kate said, smiling to complement what she hoped was a tone of surprise and enthusiasm in her voice. "We could go to my apartment and listen to records. I'd make sandwiches, and there's Cokes."

With growing assurance, she added, "And there's cold beer, too."

Gus Soltik turned to look at her, and there was something blurred and smudged in his expression now; it was as if a huge, flat thumb had exerted pressure against a malleable nose and cheekbones. His shadowed eyes, which gave the haunted impression that if he ever saw clearly it might be unbearable, were suddenly alert.

"My father wouldn't mind, really he wouldn't. And once you met him you could ask him if you could take me out on a real date. . . ."

195

Father and shame and punishment. The coldness was a torturing demon in his skull.

"My father is—"

Gus Soltik's hand moved with blurring speed, flexed powerfully; the collar of Kate's ski jacket tightened cruelly across her throat, cutting off her words in mid-sentence, and the echo of her single strangled sob faded swiftly in the rising winds. . . .

17

THE New York police department command post had been established at the head of the Mall in the cruciform esplanade bordering the open-air theater, and the scene now was one of disciplined chaos.

Remote units from the TV networks had flooded the area with their arc lights. Patrolmen Sokolsky and Maurer had been moved to the CP to man portable switchboards. Ambulances with crews at the ready were on the scene.

Detectives Corbell, Karp, and Fee were standing by for orders, while Sergeant Boyle and Detective Tebbet had proceeded north with fifty-odd patrolmen and a van of transistor radios.

From Gypsy Tonnelli's unit Carmine Garbalotto and August Brohan were also standing by, while Detectives Scott and Taylor had joined the skirmish file of uniformed patrolmen who were advancing north to Seventy-second Street at ten-foot intervals, their powerful torchlights probing into every shadow and gully and every pocket of darkness on their line of march. Present also were a hundred-odd patrolmen in uniform. The sniper teams were in cars with motors turning over softly.

In the northwest corner of the esplanade there was a huge contour map of Central Park so large, in fact, that it was supported on sawhorses placed at six-foot intervals.

Deputy Chief of Detectives Walter Greene stood studying this immense map, which featured all of the park's terrain and buildings and grottoes. Flanking the deputy chief were Detectives Scott and Taylor. They had all been dubious about Tonnelli's orders to Boyle. But Borough Commander South Chief Larkin had overruled them; the chief knew of Luther Boyd, had heard him speak at a police convention in Cincinnati only the year before, and Chief Larkin realized not only that the tactic made sense, but that it stemmed from Luther Boyd rather than Tonnelli.

Rudi Zahn sat in the rear of a squad car with Barbara Boyd. The medics had taped his ribs and applied a bandage to his slashed cheek and had given him an injection to ease the pain temporarily. This sedation, plus his agitated emotional state, had led him into a dark fantasy in which he imagined himself failing again to try to save Ilana.

"You were so brave," Barbara had told him at least a half dozen times, but he had shaken his head and said in a low, discouraged voice, "I didn't help her."

"No one could have done more."

Paul Wayne of the *Times* had recognized Zahn and was presently on his way to the Plaza Hotel to try to get a story from Crescent Holloway.

Meanwhile, TV cameras were relentlessly probing the expressions and reactions of Borough Commanders Larkin and Slocum, who was an oak of a man, the highest-ranking black in the New York police department, and who held a degree in criminalistics from Stanford University. The commanders were in uniform, their two stars gleaming under the glaring lights and reflectors of the cameras. Reporters held microphones in front of the chiefs and asked them rapid, insistent questions.

"Commander Larkin, can you give us a yes or no on this: Is the girl still alive?"

"We believe that she is."

"Is that a positive affirmative?"

"Of course it isn't," Commander Slocum said. "We've got reason to think she's alive, but we aren't commenting on those reasons."

While the questioning went on, Chief Larkin was thinking of that stretch of the park bordered by Seventy-second Street, Transverse Number Three, Fifth Avenue and Central Park West. It was a corridor a dozen street blocks wide and a half mile long, but if they could trap the Juggler in that area, huge as it was, they'd have a chance.

"Commander, if you've got a fix on this psycho, why aren't you using helicopters?"

"At this point, I won't comment on that," Chief Larkin said.

"Every year the police budget gets bigger. Isn't this the time to put the taxpayer's money to work?"

Chief Slocum was not a political man.

"We'll spend every goddamn dime of his money if we have to," he said. "But not till the time is right."

"You'll have to excuse us now, gentlemen," Chip Larkin said, and turned from the mikes and walked through hurrying streams of police personnel to join Deputy Chief Greene at the contour map of Central

Park. Chalk marks had been drawn across the map on east-west lines at Seventy-second Street and Transverse Three, which curved from Eighty-fourth Street at Fifth Avenue to Eighty-sixth Street at Central Park West.

Commander Larkin's mind was like a gridiron with each square flashing its own particular warning lights. The Juggler would be only one of his problems on this particular night. He was presently awaiting reports on the following events: a murder in Greenwich Village; a bank robbery in progress in the financial district; nineteen hostages held by a gunman in an all-night supermarket; a French delegate to the UN and his wife, bound and gagged in their St. Regis suite, a quarter of a million in jewels stolen, the contessa raped; a five-car collision in the Lincoln Tunnel which had backed up traffic for miles on the New Jersey Turnpike in addition to claiming six lives.

There would be, and this was a statistical certitude, more than one hundred stickups and armed robberies throughout Manhattan that night. The police had a profile of the criminals: They were poor, they wore sneakers, could run fast, sixty-two percent of them were black, and most of them used cheap handguns (so-called Saturday Night Specials which frequently exploded upon firing, occasionally killing the would-be robbers as well as their victims).

Deputy Chief Greene glanced toward Chief Larkin and said in his low, growling voice, "The Gypsy just called in. They lost the track of the Juggler."

"Then dispatch a dozen squads to Fifth Avenue north of Seventy-fourth and a dozen more to strengthen the line from the Seventies to the Eighties on Central Park West. The Juggler may know he's in a trap. . . ."

Mrs. Schultz was watching the action at the command post on her television set. They didn't know who he was, but she did. Things were gone from his room. The knife and the rope. She wondered if she had always known, all these years.

It was good they didn't know who he was. They couldn't come here with questions.

Sixty-two years ago her father and mother had brought her from Canada to Minnesota without papers. How they had got from Germany to Canada, she never knew. But it was the terror of their lives. No papers. They dreaded signing things. For ration books in the war. For getting gas lines connected. There was always fear they'd ask for papers.

But it wasn't fair. There were so many of them after him, with speeding police cars and men at switchboards. And the girl. Maybe she was no better than she should be. Why would a girl go into the park after dark? Where was her mother?

In halting English she had been taught by nuns, Mrs. Schultz began to say a Hail Mary for Gus.

At approximately the same time John Ransom sat huddled despondently on a bench in a subway station in the borough of Brooklyn. He had thought it would be so simple and gratifying just to close his eyes and step into triumphant oblivion under the wheels of a hurtling train.

He had planned it with such painstaking care. For one thing, no note. He had called a friend in Brooklyn to tell him he'd like to stop by for a visit, assuring his wife he'd be home within an hour or so. It would have to be presumed an accident, and all his dreams and the dreams of his wife and daughter would be fulfilled then, paid for by only a split second of pain and the cessation of pain for all eternity. But that thought had raised the specter of his Catholic background. No suicide was welcome in the presence of God.

In his anguish and terror Ransom had stopped a portly middle-aged black man and confessed his torments to him. The black man had been sympathetic, had clucked his tongue, had spoken words of comfort and compassion, but when he realized what Ransom was begging him to do, which was to push him from behind into the path of a speeding train, the big black had reacted at first with astonishment and then with swift, hot anger.

"You think because I'm black that I'd commit a murder just like it was no more than spitting on the sidewalk. You think I'm a dumb nigger without feelings or values. Grab him by the arm and tell him to kill or mug somebody or shoot up a liquor store, and he'll do it because he's nothin' but an animal anyway. Well, you want to die, you jump in front of that train your ownself, you damn honkie bastard."

The black man strode toward the turnstiles, muttering to himself in tones of outrage and indignation while Ransom slumped in shamed dejection on the wooden bench, tears welling in his pain-haunted eyes and the rank taste of bile rising from his condemned and corroded stomach.

There seemed no strength or purpose in the world, no sanity or kindness now, except the unexpected warmth and compassion that had been tendered him by a complete stranger, the big red-haired cop Sergeant Rusty Boyle.

18

ON that same night Joe Stegg was working alone in the Loeb boathouse a hundred yards or so north of Seventy-fourth Street. During the working day, from nine A.M. to sunset, Joe Stegg and his staff were often too busy supervising the rental of aluminum and wooden boats to keep their books on an hourly basis, and that was why Joe Stegg was still on the job, totaling the last of the day's receipts.

All in all, however, he savored his work, even the extra time, because he enjoyed instructing the youngsters who rented boats from the park. They were a good bunch of kids for the most part. They loved the park and took care of it, and it was the rare boy or girl who would throw candy wrappers or orange peels or soft drink cans into the lake.

Stegg had no children himself, and by now—since he was forty-nine—he had grown used to the idea that he and Madge would have to Darby and Joan it alone in some upstate trailer camp when he retired from the park service.

His thoughts were running to children, he surmised, because there was a kid missing in the park tonight, a little girl. Somebody had got hold of her, and by now cops were swarming all over the place.

It was something he couldn't understand, that anyone would relish hurting a child. But such devils existed, no doubt of it. And appearances told you nothing. They could be men in business suits with briefcases, construction workers in hard hats, or the character with the duck-tailed haircut who parked cars in basements beneath the big office buildings. Any of them could have a devil inside him where you couldn't see it.

Sometimes when he read of murders and rapes in the city, he was almost glad he didn't have kids. How could he stand it if it were his daughter missing out there? Or if his son walked home past leather bars and gay joints and got seduced into that scene of perversion and drugs? He could imagine how Madge would crawl the walls if someone tried to hurt a kid of theirs. When their niece came to visit them from Scranton, Madge didn't let her out of sight unless she was taking a bath or something.

Joe Stegg put his pencil down and closed the ledger he had been posting figures in and at the same time turned and frowned at the closed and locked door of the boathouse.

Joe Stegg switched off the radio, and when the last rock beat faded into silence, he heard it again, the sound which had alerted him, a child's voice rising in a thin cry of protest or anger.

Stegg rose swiftly, took a .38 Colt revolver from a drawer, snapped off his desk light, and ran through the darkness to the door of the boathouse. Opening it a cautious inch, he saw nothing but black trees streaked by headlights. But then he heard the girl cry out again, and when he flung the door open, he saw them, traveling north on the path, twenty yards from him, a huge, hulking figure of a man in a brown sweater and a girl he was dragging along by the collar of her red jacket.

"Hold it, damn you!" Joe Stegg shouted at the man. He ran along the pathway, the gun steady in his hand. "Let her go, damn you, or I'll put a hole in your head."

Gus Soltik screamed in anger and frustration, his voice raging like some primitive, terrified animal. And with that primal bellow, he hurled Kate Boyd aside as effortlessly as he would a rag doll, and when she struck the ground, stars exploding in her head, Gus Soltik rushed at Stegg, taking a bullet in the upper flesh of his left arm, but before Stegg could fire again, Gus Soltik's fist had crashed into his face, shattering his nose and cheekbones and slamming him with stunning impact against the wooden planks of the boathouse.

Gus Soltik took the gun away from Stegg's limp hand and beat him across the head with it until splinters of bone pierced Joe Stegg's brain, ending forever his errant and mortal thoughts of a sheltered trailer camp and the best ways to teach youngsters about currents and winds and weather. . . .

Gus Soltik lifted Stegg's lifeless body high above his head and hurled him with all his strength over a link-chain fence into the shallow water near the pier flanking the boathouse. Then, trembling with fear, his mind in a turmoil of terror, he ran to Kate, who lay dazed on the ground, scooped her up in his arms, and ran north toward his sanctuary, the jungles above the immense reservoir.

The echoes of the shot which Joe Stegg had fired at Gus Soltik reverberated south to where Luther Boyd had been traveling in wide circles to pick up a sign of the Wellingtons. Boyd estimated the sound due north of them, and within a minute or so, running hard, he and Tonnelli arrived at the boathouse, where the Gypsy's flashlight, after a rapid, circular probe, found and focused on the lifeless body of Joe Stegg, drifting with the sluggish current against the pilings of the pier.

While Boyd circled the area in front of the boathouse, bending to inspect the ground, Lieutenant Tonnelli spoke rapidly into his two-way radio.

"Tonnelli here, Sokolsky. I want Garbalotto."

Within seconds, the detective's miniature voice was sounding from Tonnelli's speaker.

"Ten-four, Lieutenant."

"Garb, we got a dead one, male Caucasian at the Loeb boathouse. That's where I am. Here's what I want, and fast. Scramble our helicopters in Brooklyn, tell them to fly north-south patterns, at treetop height, with ground beams at full power, starting at Seventy-third Street and crisscrossing the park all the way up to Harlem. I want Patrolman Branch and his crew to bring their dogs up to the boathouse. Make sure everybody snaps ass, Garb. We got him in the cross hairs now."

Luther Boyd spun around and stared with cold anger at Tonnelli. "Lieutenant, are you out of your goddamn mind? Countermand those orders and countermand them *now*."

Tonnelli shook his head with hard finality. "This is police business from now on in, Mr. Boyd."

"You will countermand those orders, Lieutenant," Boyd said quietly, and with the words, the Browning automatic came smoothly into his hand in one fluid, disciplined gesture.

Tonnelli looked at the gun, then stared steadily into Boyd's eyes. "That's real stupid, Mr. Boyd," he said.

"My daughter and that psycho can't be more than a block or two north of here. You churn the air with choppers, set packs of dogs howling through these woods, he'll panic. He'll break my daughter's neck like a stalk of celery and run for it."

"I'll say it once more," Tonnelli said, his voice rising angrily. "This is a police show, and I'm running it."

"Then you'll become a statistic, Lieutenant. One more backfire in Central Park."

"You'd waste me?" Tonnelli was trembling with fury. "Because I'm doing my job?"

"Countermand those orders, Lieutenant."

Tonnelli's heart was pounding like a hammer against his massive rib cage, but there was confusion mingling and tempering his rage because his Sicilian instincts warned him there was logic in Boyd's thinking. And he had to buy that thinking for another reason because he realized that his grip on life was at this instant slippery and tentative. It wasn't the gun alone that swayed him, but something in Boyd's eyes and the way he handled that gun.

The gun appeared to be an extension of Luther Boyd's character, and Tonnelli knew that no one developed that identity with a weapon, that projection of functional authority, by firing for scores on pistol ranges. You acquired it by drawing guns and pointing them at people and killing them, not once or twice, but so often that it became as reflexive as breathing.

"You know I'm right, Lieutenant," Boyd said. "I'll settle for one half hour. On my own. And I want your word on it. But not at gunpoint."

207

To Tonnelli's total surprise Boyd replaced the Browning beneath the waistband of his slacks, then turned his palms upward in a gesture of powerful supplication.

Gypsy Tonnelli grew a fingernail slowly down the scar that cut across his cheek. "Jesus Christ, you are something else," he said.

"Just remember, she's our only child. Do I have your word?"

"Deal," Tonnelli said, and spoke again into his two-way radio. "Garbalotto?"

"Right here, Lieutenant."

"Cancel those last orders. Hold the choppers and dogs."

"Any reason? In case the chiefs ask?"

"Yes. The girl's safety," Tonnelli said, and broke the connection.

"Thank you," Boyd said.

"I hope to God you're as good as you think you are," Tonnelli said. "We just turned off a ton of professional help."

"Come over here," Boyd said, and walked north along the path. When he stopped and pointed at the ground, Tonnelli saw imprints in the soggy ground of the Juggler's Wellingtons and near them, like rubies in moonlight, drops of blood in stark relief against hoarfrost gleaming on the grass. Boyd bent over and picked from the ground a tuft of brown woolen shreds, darkened with blood.

"There was only one shot fired," Boyd said. He looked at the bloody twist of wool in his hand, then threw it aside. "He's wounded, which could slow him down," he said. "And since I haven't been able to find the gun, we can assume he's armed."

"Two things," Tonnelli said, speaking rapidly and insistently because he knew that Boyd was tensed to run. "You got my word for that half hour. But we got two borough commanders, two-star cops at the command post. They're in charge; they could countermand me with a finger snap. This is a chance to show taxpayers how their money's spent. Helicopters, Dobermans, squads racing in and out of that CP with dome lights flashing. So you may not get that full half hour, Colonel.

"And the last thing. We don't take prisoners tonight. That's my side of the deal. Whoever finds that bastard wastes him. I don't have your word on that, you don't have *my* word on anything."

Boyd bitterly remembered Isaiah: "We have made a covenant with death, and with hell are we at agreement."

"You have my word," Luther Boyd said.

"Then let's go," Tonnelli said.

Boyd was off immediately with long, smooth strides, his body merging and disappearing in the shadows of big trees, but before the Gypsy had covered a dozen yards, the growling voice of Deputy Chief of Detectives Walter Greene sounded from his radio, jerking him to a stop like a dog on a taut leash.

"Tonnelli?"

"Ten-four, Chief."

"Why did you countermand those orders to Garbalotto?"

Tonnelli swallowed a dryness in his throat. "Colonel

Luther Boyd, the girl's father, believes the Juggler is only a couple of minutes ahead of us."

"And since when the fuck is Colonel Luther Boyd running the New York police department!" The chief's voice was rising in a blend of exasperation and anger. "We got a skirmish line moving north past Seventy-second. We got guys in blue stretched all across Transverse Three. I told you once before I don't like my lieutenants out on these Dick Tracy hero bullshit deals. We got a hairy night, Gypsy. So get your ass back to the command post. I want you to take the chiefs off my back and run this show you put your neck on the line for. That's an order. You got it?"

Tonnelli felt that his heart might literally explode with frustration. He said bitterly, "Yes, Chief. Tell Garb to send a car for me at Seventy-second Street and the Bethesda Fountain."

"One more thing. Bring that goddamn Luther Boyd in with you. I want him out of the park, permanent."

"Too late, sir. He's gone."

Retired Detective Samuel "Babe" Fritzel stood in shadows on a serpentine pathway that followed a curving course through Central Park's forty-odd-acre bird and animal sanctuary. Babe Fritzel had entered the park on Central Park West between Seventy-first and Seventy-second streets. After striking up a pointedly casual conversation with a veteran patrolman named John Moody, Fritzel had shown him his gold badge and mentioned that Lieutenant Tonnelli had asked to meet him at the PD command post.

It had been that simple. Moody hadn't known

anything about Howard Unruh, and it had been the Babe's pleasure to brief him on that particular case. ("You guys'll probably never see anything like it. Man walking down a street with a rifle, blasting people every which way. Thirteen of them in all. Just as cool as if he was in a shooting gallery. Even got an old lady parked at a stoplight. It was an honor, I tell you, like a medal, to be the cop that put the cuffs on Unruh that day.")

Now Babe Fritzel stood with a hand on the butt of his gun, eyes narrowed to catch anything moving in the shadows. He could still show them a thing or two. These young cops thought a guy of seventy-four should be in a cemetery or on display like a freak. He might not make the kill tonight, but he'd be close to it. And that would be like another medal, Babe Fritzel was thinking, and would add a luster to fresh stories he could tell while working the bar in the Elks' Club.

At the intersection of Eighth Avenue and Forty-ninth Street, Tonnelli told Prima to stop and pull over to the curb; he had spotted Coke Roosevelt standing on a corner talking with a group of young black studs.

Tonnelli climbed from the squad and walked across the sidewalk to Coke, who greeted him by touching his fingers to the wide brim of his digger's hat, a mocking little salute. In the patrol car Prima unholstered his gun and held it just below the window of the passenger seat.

Tonnelli's smile was as cold and insincere as Coke's.

"Got anything for us, gold-nose?"

The soft glow of yellow and green fluorescent lights seemed to intensify a jungle tone in these car-infested Manhattan trails. Soul rock blared from music shops,

211

angry and defiant like tribal drums. Tonnelli glanced at Coke Roosevelt and the dark, impassive faces of the young men circling him, the odd gold tooth gleaming against red lips and black skins. The city was turning into a nightmare you couldn't wake up from, he thought, not with rancor but with regret. It was the Gypsy's city, his fierce Camelot, and he loved it. But the relentless competition for clean space and air and silence was transforming its people into a breed crazed for the simple fundamentals of existence.

"We got a name," Coke said. "Like Gus Soltik."

"Got an address to go with it?"

"No, and we ain't got his Social Security number or his fingerprints," Coke Roosevelt said dryly.

Tonnelli looked up and down the street. "Don't press it, gold-nose. Where'd you get the name?"

"Sam spread two big ones in the street. Some dude pinned the description to the name. He seen him once up in the Bronx. Remembered his name."

"Not that I care, but I'm curious," Tonnelli said. "Where'd he get the description? It wasn't on the air, and it's not in the papers."

"Maybe one of your boys in blue talked in his sleep."

"One of the black boys in blue?"

"Now you said that, Lieutenant." Coke grinned at the young blacks who were watching his performance with wide smiles. "You cats hear me say anything like that?"

They shook their heads, and one of them said, "Naw, no way," in a soft, drawling voice.

"I told you, it didn't matter," Tonnelli said. "Tell Samantha thanks."

"Why don't you tell her your own self, Lieutenant?"

As the squad car rolled south again Tonnelli checked his watch, then asked for Garbalotto on his radio.

When Garbalotto came in Tonnelli said, "Garb, I got a name for you. Gus Soltik. Could be the Juggler. Start checking Motors, phone books in all boroughs, the FBI, Social Security, criminal records, everything we've got."

"Right, Lieutenant." Garbalotto lowered his voice. "Something you should know, Gypsy. Your last orders to me got tipped over by the chiefs. They've scrambled the choppers and sent dog teams up to Seventy-fifth Street."

"All right," Tonnelli said, and with a weary sigh broke the connection. Glancing at his watch, he saw that Luther Boyd hadn't got his half hour after all. Just seventeen minutes to be exact, and if Boyd was right, the little girl didn't have a prayer in hell now.

19

HE had been moving slowly and cautiously through a grove of white trees, his big hand tight on the collar of her ski jacket, when he first heard the strange music on the horizon. It confused and hurt him because its rhythm matched the throbbing pain in his left arm. It had made him anxious and fearful because where he expected comforting silence there was instead a relentless barrier of noise.

He stopped and listened, his senses alert to danger. Kate twisted her head to look up at him, trying to learn something from the fear and confusion in his face.

Gus Soltik, still clutching the girl's collar, made his way west, trying to turn the corner of that sound. Then he retraced his steps, pulling Kate behind him. But there was no break in the wall. The rhythm was relentless, blocking his way and matching the pulsing pain in his arm. The sound made him think, or try to think, which was worse. The security beyond the reservoir, the dark paths, the silent stretch of trees, that was denied to him now, taken from him by the music.

Music frightened and angered Gus Soltik because he didn't understand it. Even at the Delacorte clock with

Lanny he was puzzled and sometimes angered by people who smiled and snapped their fingers to the music of the prancing little animals. He had never known the thrill of a marching band. He had never shared a song with a girl. He had never been sung to sleep. Thus the sounds that other men smiled at were frightening assaults on his senses. At work, pushing refuse into heaps, browned cabbage leaves, bruised and rotting fruit, he would hear noise from the radio, and one clerk might nod to another and say something like, "*Compadre,* remember where we go after that night at Joselita's?" And the reply would be equally unintelligible to Gus Soltik. Perhaps: "Ah, she was *bonita,* you lucky *pavo.*" Music evoked a world which Gus Soltik had been forbidden to enter.

He was like a trapped animal. Something was behind him, the "coldness," and the frightening noise sounded all around him. If he could make them stop. But they wouldn't stop hurting him. And they wouldn't let him die. His mother had told him that.

"Listen to me," Kate Boyd said, the words a whisper on the winds.

She didn't scream. He felt no fear in her body.

"You're hurt," she said. "Blood is soaking through the sleeve of your sweater. We should go to a hospital."

Kate knew there was some kind of trap ahead of them. The loud music stretching the width of the park was no coincidence. Without realizing it, she had become his conspirator. The soft, vulnerable warmth she felt for puppies and kittens made her sorry for this dumb wounded creature and made her hope he might escape. But this hope was more than a budding maternal instinct. It was based on the practical realization that unless both escaped, both would die.

216

"I know someone who can help you," she said.

He looked down at her, squinting in the darkness, to peer into her eyes. She knew that the mention of the word "dog" had triggered sullenness in him and the word "father" had evoked a dangerous rage. Her throat was dry with fear as she sought a safe way to manipulate him.

"He's kind and strong. And he'd be good to you," she said.

Gus Soltik scratched the thick blond hair at the base of his broad neck. How did she know?

"Lanny?" he asked her, the word squeezed with an effort from his corded throat muscles.

Now she could only guess. "Well, he's like Lanny."

But Gus Soltik wasn't listening to her then. Another sound distracted him. He looked up and saw three helicopters flying toward them, motors thundering, giant beams of light covering the ground, flashing through the tree like brilliant lances.

His heart pounded with fear and rage. He clamped a hand across Kate's mouth, and it was then he felt her fear, her terror. As she fought against him, he was shaken by a savage joy. But he must hide now, and he knew where to hide. He set off at a run, sweeping Kate off the ground with his uninjured arm, traveling toward the middle of the park to the Ramble.

Gus Soltik, with animal instinct, had chosen his terrain with savage, tactical brilliance. In that expanse of gullies and caves and grottoes, all of it hidden by massive trees and choked with foliage, they would never find him and never hear her. . . .

Sergeant Boyle stood in the shadows of a grove of trees a dozen yards south of Transverse Number

217

Three. He was the point of a skirmish line of patrolmen stretching across the transverse from Fifth Avenue to Central Park West.

Rock music blasted to the right and left of him, but his eyes were keyed to something several hundred feet away. In a broad meadow dappled with moonlight, the most obvious cover was a towering stand of silver linden trees, ghostly and white in the darkness. Rusty Boyle had thought he had detected someone moving in those trees. But it might have been shadows or tree limbs moving in the wind. Or for that matter, his imagination, his nerves. It was hard to wait. It was easier in action when adrenaline flowed to add power and speed to your reflexes and muscles. But waiting was wearing him down. And John Ransom's call, patched through to him by Sokolsky, hadn't helped much. . . . Couldn't kill himself . . . but grateful to Boyle for caring . . . must thank him . . . must see him. . . .

Something moved behind the sergeant.

Rusty Boyle spun around, dropping into a crouch, while his hand moved with blurring speed toward the butt of his gun, but he froze when he saw that the tall man who faced him had extended both hands to indicate that they were empty.

Sergeant Boyle had an impression of rangy strength, dark hair, and cold, chiseled features that reminded him of portraits he had seen as a boy of Indian scouts.

"Luther Boyd," the man said.

"Boyd? The girl's father?"

Boyd was staring with bitter eyes at the helicopters crisscrossing the northern end of the park.

"Sergeant Rusty Boyle here, sir."

"I lost him when your people sent up those goddamn

218

firecrackers," Boyd said. There was no place in his strategy for anger, but he couldn't stifle all of it. "Ten minutes more and I'd have had the bastard," he said. "He doubled on me somewhere in those lindens."

"Hold it," Sergeant Boyle said, his voice suddenly tense with excitement. "I thought I spotted something moving west over there just a minute or so ago."

"Give me the line," Boyd said. "Use your arm as a pointer."

Boyle turned and extended his hand toward the tree, then moved it to the right about a dozen inches. "About there, sir."

Boyd moved behind the sergeant and took a bearing along his rigidly extended arm. He charted his course on the tallest of the silver lindens, a giant of a tree several degrees to the left of the line Boyd was indicating.

Boyd dropped to a crouch in a single fluid motion and with the flat of his hand wiped a square of earth free of leaves and twigs. Taking a key ring from his pocket, he used the tip of a key to draw a furrow in the earth eighteen inches long on the east-west line of Transverse Three.

Puzzled, Rusty Boyle knelt beside him and glanced from Boyd's lean profile to the mark he had drawn in the ground. Sergeant Boyle believed in this man; there was a rocklike quality about him, a projection of authority you could depend on. He had been impressed by the concept of a wall of music, not only because Chief Larkin had endorsed it, but because it appealed to something mystical in his Celtic spirit.

Boyd, in turn, liked what he had seen of this sergeant, a tall and resolute man with alert, intelligent eyes.

219

"Sergeant, where is the southern line of patrolmen now?"

"They're at about Seventy-sixth Street, sir."

"Then here's what we'll do," Boyd said, and pointed to the furrow he had drawn in the earth. "Equate that line with your troops along the transverse. Think of that line as three mobile units, a middle and two flanks. Order the middle to move out south on a straight line, while your east and west flanks move forward at a fifty-five-degree angle toward the middle line. This is a simple enfolding operation. Your east and west wings will eventually link with the line moving north from Seventy-sixth. It's the fastest, simplest way to take terrain away from that psycho."

Never mentions his daughter, just the Juggler, Boyle thought. But it probably wasn't lack of emotion; it was probably the only way to stay functioning and sane, think of an exercise in tactics, not a small girl screaming in agony. . . .

"When I move my men out, I'll follow your line, sir."

"Welcome aboard," Boyd said. "But let's not have any surprises out there. If I hear you or anyone else, I'll say one word: 'bullet.' Your countersign is 'trigger.'"

"I use it the same way? I say 'bullet' and you bounce a 'trigger' off me?"

Boyd simply nodded and was gone toward the stand of silver lindens in long, loping strides, but silent as a cat stalking prey across the mossy floor of a jungle.

The three Bell helicopters flew crisscrossing patterns above the middle and northern areas of Central Park. The downdraft from their rotary blades lashed at treetops like blasts from miniature hurricanes; their powerful searchlights probed at pathways and stands of trees, brilliant as columns of fire, and the thunder of their engines beat on the ground like flails, and those explosions raced in trembling, diminishing waves along the length and breadth of the park.

The crews of the helicopters were scanning the grounds rushing beneath them with high-power binoculars. From their vantage point, despite the dizzying, erratic patterns they were flying, they could see the line of police pressing steadily north, individual officers defined by the powerful torchlights they carried. And they could see the east and west flanks of Sergeant Boyle's troops closing in like great wings on the middle of their own line, slowly but inevitably narrowing the distance between the formations advancing from the opposite directions.

Police officers in Central Park had already stopped and interrogated dozens of men and women. Prostitutes of both sexes, winos, couples making love in shadows and a half dozen or more types who had managed to slip past police cordons to savor personally the action and excitement in the park and at the command post.

Another problem confronted New York police that night, an unnecessary problem, although a real and ugly one. That problem was rooted in the human need to witness tragedy, to examine, if possible, the mother's ravaged face, to speculate with other voyeurs on what peculiar torments might already have been inflicted on the missing child. Instead of following the story on radio and television, there were New Yorkers from all

221

five boroughs converging on Central Park to the disgust and wrath of patrolmen assigned to traffic control. Their job was complicated enormously by carloads of flushed and noisy people turned on by the prospect of tragedy unfolding before their very eyes.

Some of the questions shouted at traffic cops angered and sickened them in almost equal proportions.

"She dead yet?"

"The weirdo, Officer. He's a nigger, right?"

"Is it true he cut something off her already?"

"It wouldn't have happened if she was a God-fearing child."

But there were moments of sanity.

"I'm a doctor, Officer. Any way I can help?"

"Look, Mac, I'm on my way home. I'm not rubbernecking. But if you want, I'll stall this rig right here and block all those crazies behind me."

"Thanks, pal, but keep it moving."

Old John Brennan stood with his arms crossed and looked with sadness and anger at the streams of cars flowing down Fifth Avenue, circling the park like effing vultures, he thought, adding to the cops' problems, just for the thrill of seeing somebody shot or killed or a little girl (he crossed himself at the thought) lying dead and bloody somewhere out there in the park's trees and meadows.

During a rare break in the traffic John Brennan saw a kitten creeping along on the opposite side of Fifth Avenue. As he walked swiftly across the street, he wondered if this was what had drawn Kate toward the park earlier that evening.

The little kitten cringed away from John Brennan's

222

hands but didn't attempt to run off, and he was able to pick it up and cuddle it against the warmth of the rough fabric of his doorman's coat.

As he started back across the street, his way was blocked momentarily by a car halted in the traffic. The driver was a beefy young man with small, lively eyes. He wore a scarf knotted high about his throat, and this gave his narrow head a curious but definite resemblance to that of a turtle.

"Hey, Pop. You're a doorman. Can you get me up to the roof of your building for a better look? I got binoculars. I ain't asking favors . . . there's ten bucks in it for you."

With distant memories of the roars of St. Nick's Arena stirring in his mind and the cheers for a gamecock dubbed Kid Irish, John Brennan's left hand moved with professional speed and power, flattening the young man's nose and causing twin jets of blood to spurt from each of his splayed nostrils.

"There's your ten dollars," John Brennan said, and returned to his post under the awning of the apartment building.

20

MANOLO crossed the East Drive and walked through stands of dark trees until he came to the eastern boundary of the Ramble, where he stopped at the edge of a clearing, a frost-bright expanse sparkling with moonlight.

It was pretty, and Manolo smiled at it. The gleaming frost made him think of the cookies his mother used to make for him, the tang of lemon, the icings of sugar.

Manolo still needed two hundred and ninety dollars for Samantha. He was frightened by the presence of so many cops in the park, but he knew the park like the palms of his pretty pink hands and so far had had no trouble slipping through their ranks and avoiding their flashlights. What frightened him was they would probably scare off his customers. And even more frightening was what Samantha would do to him if he came up short. Not that she'd do anything herself; she'd just turn his sweet ass over to Coke and Biggie. But she had been good to him yesterday, arousing him so effortlessly and excitingly that the memory now made his cheeks grow warm. *Malo,* he thought. How could he hustle the streets if he started making it with chicks?

His emotions were a nerve-racking blend of anger, frustration, and fear. Manolo had turned a trick about forty minutes ago on a park bench, like a rough-trade freak. But he was desperate for the money the man had offered him, forty-five dollars, but when it was over and after he rinsed his mouth out at a water fountain, he checked his pocket and found that the forty-five dollars was gone. The fink had picked his pocket, and Manolo had got nothing for his efforts but a sour stench in his mouth. He prided himself on being street-smart, and it enraged him to be taken like that. Fortunately he had lost only the forty-five dollars and not the nearly four hundred taped inside the arm of his white fur jacket.

He took some satisfaction in knowing that he still looked exciting and desirable, with gracefully teased black curls and midnight blue suede pants which fitted his rounded buttocks and slim thighs as if the material had been applied with a spray gun.

He had been lucky on more than one time in the Ramble. Once he had made almost four hundred dollars from three big Texans. The Ramble was a kinky, dangerous place, and something feverish in its menacing atmosphere stirred the blood of transvestites and the leather boys.

What were they looking for? All those cops and those noisy helicopters? He'd give it just fifteen minutes, Manolo thought, try his luck that long and then split and work the lobby of the St. Regis and the Plaza again.

Gus Soltik had heard Manolo coming through the woods. Alarmed, he had turned from "white legs" and climbed silently down the side of a knoll. Now, drawn by compulsions and feelings he didn't understand, he stepped into the clearing to stare at the slim young man.

226

Manolo turned to him, a teasing, professional smile on his lips, but his heart thudded with panic because he smelled weirdo. The man was huge, wore a dirty brown sweater and a small leather cap, and his forehead bulged wide above muddy, puzzled eyes.

Maybe not, Manolo thought, and wet his lips with the tip of his pink tongue. The crazies who wanted to twist your arms or burn your belly with cigarettes usually came on fast and violent. But this big stud, ugly as he was, didn't look like that kind of trouble. But the man's rank odor disgusted Manolo and he decided to trust his first instincts: weirdo.

They stood looking at each other in the little glade with moonlight on the hoarfrost and the winds now soft but cold in the big oak trees.

The word forming in Gus Soltik's mind as clearly as if it were written there in bold letters was "black-sweet." This mnemonic unit equated with a concept of "safe" in Gus Soltik's peculiar lexicon. In blackness he would not be seen and therefore felt safe. And sweet things of all kinds, jellies, sugars, candies, made him feel warm and secure. *This,* which looked at him with eyes outlined by curling dark lashes, was "safe." Gus Soltik experienced a strange excitement. He was confused but not angered by a physical sensation he hadn't known before, or, at least, never so acutely. It was blended of the silence, the moonlight, the soft swell of sexual organ he saw molded by tight blue trousers and a fragrance like that of cherries when they broke in his hands in the store, and he knew that clean, cloying scent came from the boy's dark, curling hair.

In damp, silent woods about fifty yards from that clearing, Kate Boyd lay helpless on slick, mossy ground, wrists and ankles bound excruciatingly tight with thin nylon rope. A broad patch of adhesive tape was plastered across her lips. She was crying now, trying desperately but vainly to free herself from the cruelly knotted ropes. Within a foot of her eyes Gus Soltik's airlines bag lay on its side, and she could see the big hunting knife near a cigarette lighter and a gun.

Drifting casually toward Kate Boyd at this time were a pair of black teen-agers, whose names were Billy Smith and Hugo Thomas.

They were in a lighthearted and light-headed mood, larking their way through the Ramble, sucking on joints, and occasionally breaking into pointless but helpless giggles. They weren't out for trouble, although they might have rolled a drunk if they had lucked on to one. They weren't pushing anything; they weren't looking to hurt anyone; they were simply young and turned on and curious to find out what all the cops were doing in Central Park that night.

"Please," Gus Soltik said. He was terribly confused, but excited; he felt as if his whole body were glowing pleasantly and warmly, but it was a sensation he relished, "black-sweet," for he realized there was no need to create that dreadful, guilty exhilaration by teaching him lessons. And he realized again, though very dimly, that no one would hurt him or beat him for the rush of emotion now surging through his veins. "Please," he said again.

Manolo knew this big man could break his back with those huge hands. But he hadn't survived the streets and alleys of New York for five years without learning how to take care of himself.

"You got any money?" Manolo asked him with a teasing little smile.

Gus Soltik shook his head slowly.

"Can you get some?" This worked sometimes, Manolo knew; a freak would go off to find bread, whip-dick dumb enough to expect you to wait for him.

Gus Soltik was thinking about money. He knew the coins in the heels of his boots wouldn't . . . and he thought of Lanny then. He began to hope. Lanny would help him. Give him some money. Lanny talked slow and soft to him. And that was why he always knew what Lanny meant.

Billy Smith and Hugo Thomas stood stock-still, smoke from their joints curling up around their startled, incredulous eyes, staring in fear and bewilderment at the little white girl lying gagged and trussed on the ground.

"God *damn!*" Hugo said, his voice tense and anxious.

"We caught here, we get blamed," Billy Smith said. "Cops'll be whipping our heads till hell dries up. We split this mothering scene, Hugo."

"No, wait." Hugo moved closer to Kate Boyd, looking into her tear-bright, hysterical eyes. "It's the honkie chick Sam put out the word on."

"You gonna be a hero?"

"Well, I ain't gonna leave a little kid like this. See, she's scared simple."

He knew from the store how to say it.

"How much?" Gus Soltik asked Manolo, blurting out the words, his excitement frenzied now.

This was the tough, the dangerous part of it. Name a price too high, you ran the risk the weirdo might take you right on the ground, probably rip hell out of your fancy gear and all of it for free. Manolo moved slowly away from Gus Soltik, smiling at him over his shoulder, trying to increase his advantage without making the big man suspicious.

"Ten dollars," he said.

Lanny would give him ten dollars, Gus Soltik thought. Yes, ten dollars. "Yes," he said. "Yes."

Manolo smiled. "Go get it, lover man."

"Wait?"

"Why, sure. Think I'd skip this kind of action? You'll see." Manolo's pink tongue moved slowly between his full, wet lips.

From somewhere deep in the woods came the hideous sound of a child's screams.

Gus Soltik wheeled with amazing speed for his great bulk and ran across the clearing, but suddenly he stopped as if he had collided with a physical obstacle and turned and looked desperately at the slim figure of Manolo. Gus Soltik was like a giant racked by forces of tremendous and almost equal strength; one half of him was pulled agonizingly toward the sound of Kate's screams, while another part of him was torn with the need to be with this smiling boy.

"Come back?" he cried to Manolo.

"Sure," Manolo called to him, and ran with relief into the shadows of the trees.

Hugo and Billy had pulled the adhesive tape from Kate's mouth. And that was when she had screamed. But she wasn't screaming now, for they were working feverishly and rapidly to untie the knots which fastened the ropes searingly about her slim wrists and ankles.

230

"Hurry," she cried softly. "Use the knife."

They heard him coming then, smashing and clawing his way through underbrush like a wild beast, and before they could finish untying the intricate knots, he burst into sight among the trees and charged at the terrified black boys.

Gus Soltik struck Hugo across the side of the head and knocked him sprawling, but Billy dodged behind Soltik and hit the back of his legs with a rotting tree limb he had scooped up from the ground. The blow sent Gus staggering to his knees. To break his fall, he braced his weight with both hands on the ground, and the sudden, excruciating pressure on the wound in his upper arm made him bellow with pain. Before he could regain his feet, the two black boys were running off through the trees, insubstantial as a pair of midnight shadows.

Gus Soltik plastered the tape again across Kate's mouth, scooped up his airlines bag, but then stood perfectly still, testing the night and the winds for movement or sounds, knowing now that he was surrounded by danger, that the girl's screams would have been a magnet to all those men who wanted to hunt him down and hurt him. . . .

But an area of his tortured mind was concentrated on the slim "black-sweet" he had met tonight. Gus Soltik was struggling to understand a concept he was totally without words or metaphors to define or analyze. For the first time in his waking life he had known a sexual arousal that for him was truly normal and innocent. His desires had not been stimulated by the thought of hurting him or watching his blood flow or listening to his screams.

Tears stung his eyes, and when he blinked, they ran

231

down the rough, unshaved skin of his cheeks. "Green-ropes," he thought. If he let her go, they wouldn't hurt him. No lessons for "white legs." But she would tell, as someone had told on him tonight. But if they didn't find her, no. In the ground, under rocks. Then he shook his head. Not to her.

She watched his tears, her own eyes bright with hysteria.

Maybe his mother had lied to him. There were no razor blades in her handbag, and she knew he was hurt. She said hospital. She knew he could be hurt. Others didn't know that.

Since Gus Soltik had no way to understand the thoughts that were flashing through his mind like random electric sparks, he groaned aloud in a torture of self-loathing and frustration, and then, with no plans and no clear purpose, he scooped up the little girl and ran off into the trees.

The NYPD command post was charged with boiling excitement now, but the accelerating energies were held in disciplined harmony by Borough Commanders Larkin and Slocum. The TV and newspaper coverage had intensified, and the cameras were now focused at Sokolsky and Maurer's switchboards, where a semicircle of top-ranking police brass, including the borough commanders, Deputy Chief of Detectives Greene, and Lieutenant Gypsy Tonnelli were listening to the amplified voice of Sergeant Rusty Boyle coming over the police speakers.

" . . . and my suggestion is we move that line to the southern edge of the Ramble. I'm moving my people to surround it. I'm going in west on a line with Seventy-seventh."

"You got a fix, Rusty?" Tonnelli said.

The connection was broken then, a dry final click that told Gypsy Tonnelli Boyle believed he was close to the Juggler.

Their problem, as the chiefs and Gypsy Tonnelli fully understood, was that pinpointing the Juggler within the forty-odd acres of the Ramble intensifed the danger to Kate Boyd, if in fact she was still alive. They could not flood the area with police. There were literally thousands of hiding places in the rocky grottoes and gullies of the Ramble. It could not be attacked like a fortress. If they invaded it (the Gypsy was now in agreement with Luther Boyd), the Juggler would break the child's neck or bury her under a heap of rocks.

Chief Larkin, as if reading the Gypsy's mind, said, "Lieutenant, send in a small task force on Sergeant Boyle's line. Five of your best, Gypsy."

From his own unit, Tonnelli chose Detectives Scott, Brohan, and Garbalotto and from Boyle's unit, Detectives Miles Tebbet and Ray Karp.

In unmarked cars with dome lights dark, that group was dispatched at speed to the Ramble.

Standing inconspicuously on the outskirts of these scenes of orderly tension, the arrival and departure of squads, the exploding flashbulbs, the noontime brilliance of the TV lights and reflectors, aching with the cancer he knew was soon to devour him, was John Ransom. He had got into the park by telling an earnest young rookie at Fifty-ninth Street that Sergeant Boyle had given him a verbal message for Dispatcher Sokolsky.

In life, generosity is not only possible but gratifying because of the benison of tomorrow, but in the certain expectation of death, the corollary to life, there is only selfishness. And now John Ransom was selfishly determined to find and speak again to the one man who had given him not only compassion and kindness in his ordeal but the courage to bear it.

Within minutes of hearing his daughter's screams, Luther Boyd had found the mossy area where she had lain bound and gagged on the ground. He noted several footprints, probably made by tennis sneakers, and then he found the prints of the dreadfully familiar Wellingtons.

When Boyd traced the heel marks away from the mossy grove, he found no sign of Kate's boots. But now the prints of the Wellingtons were deeper in the ground, and he presumed the big man had slung her over his shoulder, which could mean that she was bound and gagged or was unconscious or dead.

Sergeant Boyle, however, was closer to the Juggler than Luther Boyd was. He was traveling in the shadows of big corkscrew willows, their frantically contorted silhouettes outlined in movement and moonlight. These trees bordered three sides of a clearing which abutted against a towering wall of rock, whose jagged surface was scarred and pitted with fissures from which grew a dense maze of thornbushes.

Approximately five minutes earlier, Rusty Boyle had spotted two drops of blood gleaming and wet on a leaf fallen from a paper birch tree. This wasn't conclusive in itself, but he knew the man they were after was wounded. The fact, and that his name was Gus Soltik, had been crackling from radios in the park for an hour or more. It was the evidence of the blood which had prompted his call to the CP. And the screams that he'd heard.

From that moment he had proceeded on a western line, and he now stood in the shadows of the willow trees, studying with narrowing eyes the massive escarpment of rock rising dramatically at the edge of the clearing. Could a wounded man climb it? Alone, perhaps, but not with the girl. So if the Juggler had got up there, there must be an easier route. The back or sides of the rock might be more sloping, providing a practical angle of ascent.

Boyle considered the prospects of scaling the face of the rock. He could use the roots of thick thornbushes for handholds. The risk was that he would need both hands to do that, and if the Juggler heard him coming, Boyle's gun would be useless in its holster. But on the plus side, if he could make it, he'd have the tremendous advantage of speed and surprise.

But at the instant he made up his mind to take the chance a slender man walked into the clearing and said to him, "Sergeant Boyle, I had to come here. . . . I had to thank you."

Boyle spun around, his gun covering the man. When he recognized John Ransom with a start of shock, he said in a low, insistent voice, "For God's sake, take cover."

But Ransom had already lost touch with the practical world. He didn't know he was endangering himself and

235

the big redhead who had befriended him. He didn't know he was recklessly intruding into a police operation where a child's life was at stake. He knew only the needs of his selfish gratitude.

"You will never know what your help meant to me," he said, stopping and speaking the words simply and quietly in the silence of the glade.

Jesus *Christ*, Boyle thought. I've got to get the poor sick bastard out of here.

"Sergeant, I'll write down what you've done for me. So my wife and daughter will know. . . ."

Boyle came out of the shadows like a sprinter from starting blocks, driving fast for Ransom, with the thought of dragging him into the cover of trees. But at that instant Ransom, looking past Boyle, saw the silhouette of a huge man with a gun in his hand standing high above them on the facing of rock, a spectral, terrifying figure against moon-bright skies.

Ransom shouted a warning at Boyle, and that sound caused Gus Soltik to change aim. Instead of cutting down the red-haired man who had tried to hurt him in a dark basement, Soltik swung his gun left and squeezed off two shots, which struck John Ransom in the face and killed him instantly.

Instantly in a temporal sense, but in a different calibration of time, there was a unit of eternity in which John Ransom had a last memory of his daughter, a moment to realize he had given her this final gift, and thus that last memory was free of guilt or shame, charged instead with shimmering pride.

Instinctively, Boyle had gone to the ground at the first shot, rolling over twice, then swinging his gun rapidly toward the towering figure above him, the butt

236

locked tightly in both of his big hands. But before he could squeeze off a round, Soltik fired two more shots, one of which went cleanly through Boyle's left thigh and a second which drew a scalding line of pain across his rib cage, smashing through his radio, finally spending itself in earth already darkening with his blood.

Gus Soltik pulled the trigger again, but the hammer fell on an empty chamber. With a sob of fear, he threw the gun aside and ran toward the shallow cave where he had left Kate Boyd, gagged and helplessly bound, but now mercifully insensate from the enduring terrors of her ordeal.

. . . didn't get one shot off, Rusty Boyle thought, fighting down his nausea but feeling the dizzying surge of blood through his veins. Not one shot. Turning with an effort, he looked at the body of John Ransom. Poor bastard, he thought. No, this was what he wanted. Curtains. It wrapped everything up for him. College, his wife, a certain honor. But, Christ, I'll bet he wouldn't have wanted it at my expense. He wouldn't have wanted to take me with him.

Fighting back gasps of pain, Rusty Boyle pushed himself to a sitting position, bracing his back against a tree trunk. Blood was pumping evenly and rhythmically from the wound in his thigh. His head felt light. His thoughts were already blurred. Even if he could use the broken radio, it probably wouldn't help. He was close to shock now. Losing too much blood. They hadn't shared that steak and wine and made love tonight. And now they never would.

While he was thinking of Joyce, resigned to never

knowing her beauty and grace again, he heard a single word, an urgent whisper against the dark silence. One word.

"Bullet!"

For an instant, Rusty Boyle didn't believe it. Then, relief choking his voice, he gave the countersign to Luther Boyd. Again one word.

"Trigger."

Triage, from the French, is a word defining the process of grading marketable produce. The word is also used on the battlefield and defines a similar process, except it involves the grading of wounds inflicted on human beings rather than foodstuffs destined for the marketplace. Thus, the dead are ignored as dysfunctional; the grievously wounded receive a low priority; terminally wounded soldiers are given the lowest rating of all; those with superficial wounds are treated first because they can be swiftly returned to their units or to battlefronts.

Thus, when Luther Boyd hurried through the trees toward Sergeant Boyle, he noted Ransom's body but dismissed it with that single, disinterested glance. The man was dead, but Sergeant Boyle was alive, and in the process of triage that earned him a top priority.

"Where are you hit?" Boyd asked as he knelt beside the big sergeant.

"Left leg, up high."

Boyd cradled the sergeant in his arms and gently stretched him full length on the ground. Then he unsnapped the small leather medical kit from his belt, removed a slender pair of scissors, and cut the blood-soaked fabric of Boyle's trousers away from the

238

gaping wound. Breaking open the plastic cover of a surgical bandage, he placed the thick antiseptic wad on the bullet hole in Boyle's thigh, fixing it in place with adhesive tape. Boyd took off his belt and buckled it loosely around the sergeant's thigh above the wound. He found a fallen tree limb from which he broke off a foot-long branch to use as a lever for the tourniquet.

"Hang on now," he said while he eased the thick piece of wood beneath the belt circling the sergeant's leg.

Boyd twisted the wood in a circular motion until Boyle said, softly, "That's about it, Mr. Boyd." Boyd took the sergeant's hands and placed them on the piece of wood that had driven the belt deep into the muscles of Boyle's thigh.

"Can you hold onto it? Maintain the pressure?"

"Sure. Thanks."

Boyd searched gently through the sergeant's pockets and found the smashed two-way radio and realized there was no way he could report the sergeant's condition and position to the CP.

"I'll try to get aid to you," he said.

"Listen. I just saw him, not your daughter. And unless he's got another gun, he's out of ammo. Don't worry about me. Go get the bastard."

Luther Boyd gave the sergeant a soft pat on the shoulder and then sprang to his feet and ran swiftly into the shadows of the trees beside the massive wall of rock.

21

THEY traveled south on Central Park West in the long green Cadillac, Samantha and Coke Roosevelt in a leather cocoon of luxury in the rear seat with Samantha's chauffeur, Doc Logan, at the wheel. Samantha put her head back and closed her eyes and rested her legs on one of the jump seats. She wore purple suede boots, a darker purple suede pants suit, with a jacket which flared at the hips and whose color was in brilliant contrast with her flaming red cashmere sweater.

Coke put a hand on the back of her shoulders and neck and began to massage her muscles, which under his probing fingers felt stiff as boards. She sat silently with her eyes closed, but he could feel some of the tension easing in her body.

"What else you prescribe, Coke?"

Coke fished a pillbox from the pocket of his leather jacket, opened it with a flick of his thumb, and held it out to Samantha.

"Come on," he said, and removed a flask from an inner pocket of his jacket. She opened her eyes and looked down at the box of pills.

241

"Pop a couple of these and have a taste," he said.

"Think that's all I need?" But she took two of the pills and swallowed them with a sip of whiskey. Then she said, "Where's Manolo and them black kids now?"

"Biggie collected them twenty minutes ago; they're probably at that circus the cops are staging for the boob-tube set. What's in this for us, Sam? She's a white kid. Snow-white, the magic princess. What's that got to do with our brothers and sisters?"

"I told the Gypsy I'd help him," Samantha said, and winced as needles of pain pierced her temples.

"You need more than pills and booze to stop those ice picks punching your eardrums," Coke said, looking at her clenched jaws and flaring nostrils. "You're rippin' yourself off, Sam, helping Whitey. And what's worse, helpin' honkie cops."

"You're a dumb nigger," she said. "How come you're talking like a headshrink?"

"Don't take an Einstein to dig it. Look. You and me travel first-class. But most of the brothers have to kiss white-fuzz ass, grin, and bob their heads at 'em, hoping, just hoping, they won't ram their nightsticks up their butts. So when you help cops who do that to your people, then you put your head in a vise and crank the handle to hurt yourself as bad as you can."

Samantha sighed and looked down at the backs of her hands. They were a nice color, she thought. There were places in the world men would write poetry about them. Places she could take Manolo.

"Lemme say something, Coke," she said. "I can't help the way I feel. I wish I could. God, how I wish I could! But something inside me won't let me hate like you do."

Coke smiled and took a swig of whiskey. "Let's keep that our secret, Sam," he said.

Her mother did not think that white people were devils. Neither did her grandmother. Nor had Emma and Missoura, who from faded photographs she knew as large, cowlike girls, her great-great-aunts and the daughters of slaves. They all had kind words for white folks, because a white man had once been kind to Emma and Missoura at a time when kindness to blacks had a high price tag on it.

But what a cruel kindness it had been, Samantha thought.

Emma and Missoura had worked for a white family, the Meltons, in the twenties in Mobile, Alabama. They lived in the black community on the outskirts of town, without heat, light, or plumbing facilities on meadows that were churned frequently into nightmarish quagmires by seasonal rains and hurricanes that swept across them from the Florida coastlines. But Emma and Missoura shared a comparative comfort with their elderly mother, subsisting on toting privileges and what money the Meltons paid them.

It had been on one of those rainy nights when Mr. Melton committed that act of kindness which sang down the filaments of time and caused Samantha's throbbing headaches when the Gypsy asked her for official favors.

One night Mr. Melton had told his black chauffeur, Abraham, to drive the girls home during a rainstorm. Abraham had been frightened and had made some excuse. No chauffeur drove dumb black maids around in those days. So Mr. Melton drove the girls home himself. He had done the same thing on numerous other occasions. He had been warned by white friends that he was making a mistake; he was ridiculed for it. And he was threatened because of it.

But Mr. Melton hadn't budged, had driven the girls home whenever the weather was too bad for the five-mile walk. If he'd done it just once, Samantha thought, she could write it off as just plain damn foolishness. But he had done it for the three and a half years the girls had worked for the Melton family.

The stories of Mr. Melton, sagas more like it, had come down to Maybelle Cooper like tales from King Arthur's Court.

On one occasion when a pack of red-neck white trash had circled the shanty town, screaming filth at Mr. Melton and the coloreds huddling in their cold shacks, Mr. Melton had leaped from his car and had shouted songs of freedom and glory at them in a fine, vigorous voice and the red-neck pack had slunk off into the shadows.

When she was a little girl, it had amused Samantha to hear her grandmother talk about Mr. Melton and croak off-key phrases from songs like "The West's Awake" and "Kelly, the Boy from Killan," and to listen to her re-create the picture of that big Irishman standing in driving rains and chasing away yellow bastards with his powerful voice and songs of freedom. When Samantha went to school in New York, she found some of the songs in an old sheet-music shop and had picked out the tunes with one finger on an upright piano in the school gym.

One line she had never forgot: "The harp he loved, ne'er spoke again, for he tore its chords asunder. And said 'No chains shall sully thee, the soul of love and liberty. Thy songs were made for the pure and free, they shall never sound in slavery.'"

During her adolescence, Samantha had tried to convince herself that Mr. Melton had done only what any decent man would do; he had done what only a courageous, sensitive, and feeling man would have done, and the worm in Samantha's soul was that she hated him for it.

Mrs. Schultz stood behind the police lines, so swaddled in sweaters under her bulky cloth coat that she looked almost as wide as she was tall. Mrs. Schultz had asked the policeman if she could go into the park. In her worried old head was the thought that she might find Gus and talk some sense to him before he hurt the girl. But when the policeman asked her why, she didn't tell him because that would only lead to other questions. About Gus and other nights. And why their family had no records when they came from Canada into the United States.

She told him she wanted to use a toilet, and he told her there was one off the lobby of the Plaza. She nodded and went off into the crowd. Imagine her in the Plaza in her old cotton stockings and worn coat.

She watched a tall man approach the police line, accompanied by a slim girl with a scarf knotted about her blond hair. She heard him say to a policeman, "Wayne, the New York *Times*. This is Crescent Holloway. She's with me."

The patrolman nodded and waved them past the barriers into the park.

Watch him, his mother had said, Mrs. Schultz

thought bitterly and wearily, but how could she help him if no one would let her? Her lips moved in prayer. In her halting English she said, "Holy Mary, Mother of God, pray for us sinners, now and forever . . . amen."

Barbara Boyd was alone in the rear of a police squad when Paul Wayne stopped beside the car and spoke to her.

"Mrs. Boyd? Paul Wayne, the *Times.*"

"Yes," she said.

A strikingly beautiful girl stood with Paul Wayne, and her face was vaguely familiar to Barbara.

"Crescent Holloway, Mrs. Boyd. She's a friend of Rudi Zahn's."

What did they want from her? Barbara wondered, because she could see questions in their eyes, in their expressions. But she couldn't help them. She couldn't think of anything but a desperate black terror that was like a physical presence inside her body. She sat hugging her arms across her breasts, numb and isolated in the orderly turmoil of the command post. This concentration of equipment and manpower didn't touch Barbara Boyd; nothing existed for her but the terrible certainty that her daughter was dead. Not taken away with a merciful illness, not dying in a split-second fall from a horse, but taken away—Christ, no! she pleaded silently, but the dreadful thought could not be exorcised—taken away by a sadistic monster who would torture and terrify her before finally killing her.

Her only hope was contained in a cruel paradox. The facets of her husband's character that she hadn't understood, that she had been critical of were the only strengths that might save their daughter's life tonight.

She wasn't afraid for him, but she longed to be with him.

"I'm really terribly sorry, Mrs. Boyd," Crescent Holloway said. "Words are pretty stupid now. I'll just say some prayers."

"Thank you," Barbara said.

"Mrs. Boyd, do you know where Mr. Zahn is?" Wayne asked her.

"He was so brave," Barbara said. "He tried to save my child."

She was in shock, Crescent realized; her eyes were glazed, and a tiny tic pulled rhythmically at the corner of her lips.

"Did he say where he was going?"

"He just went away. He said he hadn't done enough. He said he'd never done enough."

Ilana, Crescent thought, while an anxious fear stirred in her heart. Was that where Rudi had gone? Into this dark and dangerous park to look for a lost little girl who had disappeared from his life but never his memories almost three decades ago?

Paul Wayne took Crescent's arm and led her away from the squad car.

"We can check with Lieutenant Tonnelli," he said.

They found the Gypsy standing with a cluster of detectives and patrolmen studying the brilliantly illuminated contour map of the park.

But Tonnelli had no news of Rudi Zahn. "Thought he was with Mrs. Boyd," he said, and beckoned to one of the detectives of his unit, Jim Taylor. He told Taylor to pick a detail of men and start looking for Rudi Zahn.

As Taylor went off, Max Prima came hurrying up to Gypsy Tonnelli.

"Got a message from that black lady that shylocks up in Harlem. She wants to talk to you, says it's important."

"Where is she?"

"Parked due east of here, on the drive."

There were two cars parked on the East Drive, Samantha's green Cadillac and Biggie Lewis' white Imperial. As Tonnelli crossed the brightly lighted CP with Max Prima, he saw that Biggie, Coke, and Samantha were standing on the lawn beside the cars, and beside them were Manolo Ramos, a faggot hustler, and a pair of young black boys he didn't recognize.

Prima and Gypsy Tonnelli stopped, and Tonnelli looked at Samantha and drew a thumbnail down the length of his scar.

"What you got?" he asked her.

"Tell him, Hugo."

"Well, me and Billy were cruising through the Ramble, and we saw this little white girl lying there on the ground all tied up with ropes and a piece of tape over her mouth."

"When and where was this, son?"

"I'll wrap it up," Samantha said. "About thirty minutes ago, east side of the Ramble. About Seventy-fifth, Seventy-sixth. Hugo and Billy here pulled the tape off the little kid's mouth, and she began to scream, and who could blame her?"

"And that's the last I saw of the big horse who wants to trick with me," Manolo said. "We hear somebody screaming and he—"

Tonnelli cut in. "Let's sort this out," he said. "You first, Manolo."

"I'm hustling the park, this big stud comes out of the

woods. He don't talk much, but I know he wants to mess around. He got no money, but I don't like his looks. So I tell him I'll meet him later to get rid of him. He says he could get some money, but then we heard her yelling."

"Big bastard chased us away before we could untie her," Hugo said, excitement threading his voice.

Tonnelli was staring intently at Manolo. "You said you'd meet him later?"

"Don't cost me nothing to say that."

"You could find where you said you'd meet him?"

Manolo was savoring his moment of importance, enjoying Lieutenant Tonnelli's attention.

"The place, I can find it easy."

Gypsy Tonnelli glanced at Prima, beckoned to him, and the two officers moved away from the group in front of the big cars. It was worth a try, he thought.

The emotional profile which department psychiatrists had constructed of the Juggler over the past few years placed a primary emphasis on the fact that he was driven by feelings of psychopathic inferiority, but they had also concluded that his compulsions were deeply rooted in latent homosexuality.

"Report to Deputy Chief Greene," Tonnelli said to Prima. "Tell him we may have a geographical fix on the Juggler. And that I'm alerting our marksmen."

When Prima went off, Tonnelli walked back to Samantha, who was watching him with cold, suspicious eyes.

"What you setting up, Gypsy?"

"Manolo's got a date," Tonnelli said. "Naturally, he's gonna keep it."

"No way, unless he wants to."

"I think he'll want to," Tonnelli said. "Otherwise, I know a dozen interesting ways to kick his little ass clear out of New York City."

"Will you kindly shut up, Pope?" and there was a mix of anger and fear in her voice. She knelt so that her great white-rimmed eyes were on a level with Manolo's and put her hands gently on his slim shoulders.

"What about it, Manolo. Want to help the Man?"

Manolo looked sullenly at Tonnelli. "What's he talking about kicking my ass out of New York for?"

"That's the way Italians talk," Samantha said. "They don't know any better."

"Think I should, Sam?"

"It's up to you, Manolo." He was so pretty, she thought, fragile and delicate as a flower. "You could get hurt, and that's the truth."

"I'm still short about three hundred, Sam."

"Do what the lieutenant wants, if *you* want to, then you don't owe us nothing."

Tonnelli looked appraisingly at Manolo. "You're sure this bad-ass will keep this date with you?"

"No way he won't," Manolo said.

"I'm asking again. How do you know?"

"I turn on a stud, Lieutenant, he stays turned on," Manolo said, and gave him a smile of such piercing sweetness and intimacy that Tonnelli experienced an involuntary spasm in his loins and realized guiltily that a tide of color was rising in his cheeks.

Sweet Jesus, not *me!* But the reflection was touched with only a wry amusement, for he had no confusion about his sexual identity. Nonetheless, Samantha's needling smile both irritated and embarrassed him.

Well, who could blame anybody, he thought, because

250

this beautiful youngster seemed able to flick a switch that caused an explosion of sensual excitement? This was quality merchandise, a choice package, the white fur jacket and the blue suede skintight trousers, the curly black hair oiled and perfumed, and those eyes like velvet flowers, these were major-league, high hard ones, and the Gypsy was thinking, if we've got to bait a trap for a faggot, we're in luck, because we got a prime piece of ass to do it with.

22

GUS SOLTIK stood motionless on a rocky hill, his huge figure merging with the shadows of trees. His heart was pounding, and his dim thoughts were streaked with panic and confusion. The word forming torturously in his mind charged him with frustration and helplessness. "Walls . . . walls."

The hammer and thunder of the police helicopters were gone from the skies above Central Park. The blaring music had faded away, and the sound of yelping dogs had disappeared into the strange and ominous silence that lay with a smothering weight on Gus Soltik's angry fears and confusions.

He felt at the exact center of that silence, walls. . . . It was difficult and dangerous to move. They would hear. And he knew that "coldness" was close behind.

Not hurt. He hadn't wanted to hurt him. He was too old, not like Lanny, but he wasn't good like Lanny. He had a gun and yelled at him. Then he had to hurt him.

He tried to control his growing excitement because he could go to find "black-sweet" now. His mother got angry when he was excited. Because it led to his rages.

But he felt no rage at "black-sweet." It was a relief, a happiness. And he had money. From the old like Mrs. Schultz that he had hurt.

Even if they caught him now, they would never see "white legs." He would never tell them where she was, because if he didn't tell them, no one would ever find her. And so they wouldn't hurt him.

But Gus Soltik's dim brain was troubled. Not by the pain in his shoulder or whether they would find "greenropes." It was the dread of the beginning of pain that tortured this thoughts. Once it was present, wild and living in his body, he could accept it. It wasn't even the fear of "coldness" that troubled him.

It was the silence. . . .

And it was because of that strange silence that had settled over the park that Luther Boyd made an almost fatal mistake. At that instant he was very close to the Juggler. Boyd was, in fact, slowly and with infinite care, climbing the escarpment of rock on which Gus Soltik was standing.

For the last twenty minutes, Boyd had been trailing the Juggler and Kate across acres of rocky ground, topped with a thick cover of thornbush and gorse.

In three separate places he had found flecks and threads of red nylon from Kate's ski jacket snagged on spiky underbrush. The last had been impaled on the broken limb of a stunted horse chestnut which was growing out of such a tight crevice of rock that Boyd surmised it has been planted there by a squirrel or blue jay.

Since all those tiny bits of fabric had been snagged approximately six feet above the ground, Boyd knew that the Juggler was still carrying his daughter over his shoulder.

But now Boyd was deeply troubled because sounds he had heard only seconds earlier told him that the Juggler was retracing his original route, which could mean he had abandoned or destroyed Kate at the terminus of that line and was now doubling back in an attempt to slip past the police and out of the park. But now those sounds of his passage through heavy brush had merged into the eerie silence.

The man had stopped moving, was standing above him. Why? Was the psycho stalking him now?

And it was at that instant, climbing the steep angle of the escarpment, that Boyd made a miscalculation. Testing a knoblike tree root for a handhold, he judged it to be strong enough to support his weight, but when he pulled himself up, the rotting wood splintered in his fist, and he slipped a dozen feet down the facing of rock, the sprawling descent of his body creating a miniature avalanche of loose shale and twigs that shattered the silence as dramatically as rifle fire.

Boyd froze his body against the cliff, knowing that any motion would betray him to the man on top of the hill. But his right hand moved silently toward the Browning, which was pressed hard against his stomach by the weight of his own body.

In the shifting shadows created by moonlight and swaying trees, he saw the figure of a huge man high above him on the crest of the hill. The man raised both hands in the air and hurled a large jagged rock at Luther Boyd. The rock struck the side of the hill four feet above Boyd and sent a spray of flintlike splinters into his face and eyes. He threw himself sideways, but not in time; the caroming rock slammed into his left shoulder and knocked him in a breathless, flailing heap to the foot of the cliff.

He bounced from the ground like something made of steel and rubber and dived full length behind the mass of a pair of tangled wild holly bushes. Boyd worked the Browning free from beneath his belt. His mouth and nostrils were full of dust, and he knew his face had been nicked and bloodied by the shower of rock fragments. But it was the shoulder that worried him; if it were broken, the Juggler would have an overwhelming advantage.

Moving with gingerly caution, Boyd climbed to his feet and peered across the tops of the holly bushes. The man was gone. Boyd tested his left arm and shoulder and to his relief felt only the pain of bruised muscles, not the crunch of broken bones.

Then far away to his north and east, Boyd heard someone calling Gus Soltik's name, the sound high and sweet in the silence, as pretty as circles of silver against the darkness.

Above him and to his right, he heard the pound of distant footsteps, the passage of a big body through grass and bushes. It was the Juggler, he knew, and by the length and speed of those strides, Boyd knew the Juggler was now traveling alone. . . .

With nothing to be gained by silence, Boyd rapidly climbed the escarpment of rock, but when he reached the small clearing on top of the hill, the footsteps of the Juggler had faded off on an eastern line into dark stands of trees.

Luther Boyd stood still for a moment, massaging and kneading the muscles of his left shoulder, while testing freshening winds and the unnatural silence with the antennae of his probing senses. The police tactics had been radically changed, he realized then. They weren't trying to run the Juggler to the ground. They were setting a different kind of trap for him. And there was a sickening implication there which made it imperative for Boyd to change his own plans. He had been determined to go after Kate because as long as there was a chance she was alive, that was his only priority. She might be bound and gagged in a way that would strangle her unless he got to her in time. Or she might be confined somewhere, smothering for lack of air. Or bleeding. . . .

But he couldn't go after her now. He had to find the Juggler first because the police might waste him on sight and that psycho was the only person in the world who knew where Kate Boyd was now.

Boyd swept the ground with his flashlight to find the Wellingtons, but something else caught his eye, a large, jagged rock gleaming with blood and a cluster of white hairs. Not Kate's blond hair, he realized with exquisite relief, but coarse white hair in lacy relief against the shining blood.

He followed drops of blood and the Wellington prints a dozen yards to a mossy ravine, where he found the sprawled body of a white-haired man with a Colt diamond-back .38 revolver lying near his right hand. The right cheeks and skull of the old man had been crushed and bloodied by brutal blows. A wallet lay beside the body. There was no money in it, but the ID revealed the man's name to be Samuel Fritzel, with an address in Teaneck, New Jersey.

Protruding from a pocket of Fritzel's topcoat was a

narrow leather case with a carrying strap and Boyd saw that it encased a two-way radio. He pulled it from Fritzel's pocket, flipped a switch, and spoke urgently into the microphone.

"Lieutenant Tonnelli!"

"Tonnelli here."

"This is Luther Boyd."

"I leveled with you, Colonel. The chiefs scrambled those choppers."

"Why did you discontinue the aerial surveillance?"

"We've set a trap for him. We've cooled everything, hoping he'll relax and fall into it."

"Then goddamn it, listen to me, Lieutenant. The Juggler's alone, traveling east. Do you understand what that means? He's either killed my daughter or hidden her someplace where she's helpless. I'm heading west, on a line with Seventy-seventh Street, trying to find her. But I want your word that you take that bastard alive, Lieutenant. Because he's the only one who know where Kate is."

"You've got it, Colonel. We may waste his kneecaps, but he'll be alive."

"Two things," Boyd said, bitter at each wasted second. "Sergeant Boyle's in the Ramble with a bullet through his thigh. Between Seventy-seventh and Seventy-eighth, a hundred yards from the eastern border, near a grove of corkscrew willows. Now does this mean anything? I'm using the radio of a dead one, name of Samuel Fritzel."

"Jesus!" There was weariness in Tonnelli's voice. "An old bull from New Jersey. Wanted to help us out because—"

Boyd cut the lieutenant's voice in mid-sentence and

258

was off at a fast tracking gait to find sign of his daughter.

Within twenty yards of the facing of rock, after running a relentless zigzagging course, Boyd found a fleck of red fabric on the limb of thornbush, threads snatched in passage from Kate's ski jacket. It was still six feet above the ground, so at that time she was still slung over the psycho's shoulder. Within another few yards he found prints of the Wellingtons, which he followed into a clearing, moving faster now, running very nearly in a straight line, picking up prints by a flicking left-right movement of his flashlight, tracking them easily across the wide lea of rough moist grassland to where they stopped at an immense sentinel of a tree which loomed ghostlike in the darkness, its bark whitened and deadened by some lost-past bolt of lightning. The trunk of the tree, which Boyd identified as a swamp oak, had been splintered and breached ten or eleven feet above the ground, and the dead wood around the black, gaping hole was brightened by a few tiny clusters of stubbornly clinging twigs and a feathery tracing of frost-tinged autumn leaves.

The Juggler had stopped here, and Boyd guessed that he had done so to check the clearing he had just crossed to see if there was any sign of pursuit.

Then the Wellingtons resumed their western line, but Boyd lost them within a dozen yards because the terrain changed from spongy grassland to jagged sheets of shale and granite.

Ahead of Boyd were walls of rock rising in irregular contours against the horizon, and as he made his way toward these natural barriers, assaying their obvious capacity for concealment or imprisonment, he began to experience a touch of hope.

For this was a logical and strategic goal for the Juggler: a maze of gullies, caves, and potholes, dank and fearsome as dungeons, natural oubliettes a deranged mind would choose for the confinement of a small, helpless child.

If Kate was dead, he thought, there was nothing but heaven for her beyond tonight, because as a marine epitaph he had seen on Guadalcanal put it, she'd already served her time in hell.

Lieutenant Gypsy Tonnelli was waiting for the Juggler. He stood with Samantha in the shadows of a grove of colossal male cork trees, with heavily corded bark and wide, speading limbs. The Gypsy and Samantha were concealed five yards behind a ten-man formation of marksmen, who were also covered completely by the shadows and trunks of the giant trees.

Every pair of eyes was fixed on Manolo, who strolled through a moonlight glade, softly calling Gus Soltik's name, his sweet voice threaded with suggestions of intimate excitement.

The marksmen were in uniform, rifles at the ready. The eyelets of their boots and their belt buckles were painted black. The buttons of their uniforms were covered with black suede. Each man wore a helmet of tight black knit. No man was wearing a ring, a wristwatch, or an identification bracelet. Nothing on their persons could create betraying reflection of moonlight.

Everyone was scanning the opposite side of the glade toward which Manolo was casually sauntering.

Lieutenant Tonnelli had in effect given the western side of the glade to the Juggler. At the opposite end of this open clearing there were no police officers. All potential firepower had been concentrated on the eastern side of the field, while the western area had been left enticingly empty for the Juggler.

But Tonnelli's conscience was uneasy. As a police officer he knew he had made the right decision and therefore could live with it. But it had been hard to lie to Luther Boyd. The marksmen were not going to take the Juggler alive. Their orders from Tonnelli had been cold and classic: shoot to kill. There was simply no alternative. They had to kill him now while they had the chance. If they failed, where would he sur-face next October 15? How many tender, young victims might he claim in the coming years if they lost him tonight?

That was their job as cops, to waste him the instant he appeared on the cross hairs of the marksmen's scopes, the instant he moved into Manolo's moonlit terrain.

Then, with the Juggler dead, Tonnelli could send a thousand cops into the park to search every square foot of it. They could illuminate shadows with the brilliance of light trucks and helicopters, and each cop could work with the confidence that there was no madman running loose to blow his brains out with a gun or drive a knife between his shoulder blades.

Luther Boyd had himself confused with Daniel Boone and God, Tonnelli thought bitterly. But the Gypsy's attempt to assuage his conscience was not wholly successful. Because it wasn't his daughter's life at balance in the golden scales of Libra; it wasn't his blood and kin.

261

"The little bastard's showing off," Samantha said tensely.

"He's doing fine."

They spoke in whispers.

"Well, I'm scared for him," she said. "I'm scared for him, you hear me, Gypsy? He's a smart butt. A showboat."

And indeed, Manolo was showing off, converting his slow and sensual passage across the glade into an amusing and outrageous ego trip. Laughing softly, he patted his pretty curls and called to Gus Soltik in tones that quivered with sexual promise.

Manolo felt lucky and happy. On a practical note, he was out of hock to Sam, and when you did a favor for a police lieutenant, you just might get one in return, and that was a nice thing to have going for you when you sold your ass for a living in the streets and alleys of New York.

Manolo lit a joint and sucked smoke slowly and deeply into his lungs, holding it there for a pleasurable, dizzying moment before exhaling it through the perfect circle formed by his soft red lips.

"Come on, Gus. No need for a big stud like you to be afraid. Big lover stud, we'll trick up a storm."

In the grove of cork trees, Samantha said tensely to Tonnelli, "What's he using that psycho's name for? You told him not to."

"It's all right, Maybelle," the Gypsy said, but he had also felt a stir of anxiety. Manolo was taking a long and unnecessary gamble using Gus Soltik's name.

They had told him to stay in plain view in the

moonlight, to keep out of shadows. But Manolo wasn't afraid of Gus Soltik. He was supremely confident of his ability to manage and manipulate faggots. He was always in charge there, literally in the saddle. He was the candy they drooled for, and unless they were good little boys, they'd never get their hot fingers on it.

23

PRECONCEPTIONS of the human mind and eye are the prime hazards in aerial reconnaisance: Airfields are expected to be long and narrow; military units in barracks are formed in squares; cannon revetments, with circles of sandbags, appear as doughnuts from the sky; and their supply roads, unless artfully camouflaged, are arrows that reveal their existence by pointing straight at their hearts. Nature is haphazard, careless, disorganized; man's inevitable tendency is to make his environment conform to orderly and discernible patterns.

Luther Boyd was searching acres of rock and underbrush for the sign of man. He was seeking evidence of someone's need to alter the natural disorder of environment.

The night was colder, and the wind was rising, stirring dry leaves on rock-studded sheets of ground. Rain was in the freshening air, and above him the sudden gusts and squalls drove tatters of clouds across the waning moon.

It was then he found what he had been searching for. Before that moment his frustration had deepened into despair. He remembered the quotation from Von Moltke which had been stressed at the Point: "First ponder, then dare." But what to dare? What to dare *with?* he had been thinking helplessly.

But now his flashlight revealed a heap of stones stacked against a wall of rock in an orderly fashion, and this was what he had been seeking, not the casual formations of nature but the defining work of human hands.

He hurled the rocks aside, breathing hard after the first minutes of work, because the stones were large and heavy and packed tightly against the mouth of a tunnel. But when he forced an opening and poured light from his flashlight into a small cave, he found himself staring at a dusty stack of empty wine bottles. He read labels with listless interest, his eyes helpless and despairing, realizing that each passing second might be ticking off his daughter's life. Wine-Apple, Muscatel. . . . Suddenly, and for reasons he didn't understand, he was warned and alerted by a leaf on the ground. It was flecked with mud, but beautiful with the autumn colors of yellow and scarlet. His heart began to pound. He knew then he must have made a dreadful error. A mistake of miscalculation. First ponder, then dare. He had dared, in a sense, to outguess the Juggler, but had he pondered, had he *thought?* He had misread signs, he was sure of it. A clue, an arrow pointing to his daughter, had escaped his trained eyes.

This conviction of failure was a special torture to Luther Boyd because he had failed Kate where he shouldn't have failed her, in the area of his own professional strengths and skills.

Boyd picked up the mud-flecked red-and-yellow maple leaf and stared at it, demanding an answer from it.

From behind the shadows that Manolo was approaching, Gus Soltik was crouched close to the ground, concealed by dense underbrush and the low black limbs of trees. His body was responding with almost agonizing excitement to Manolo's presence and beauty. But some primal fear warned Gus Soltik against revealing himself. It was the man in black climbing the rocky hill to get him. That was what had been behind him all night. The "coldness."

Deflecting that primitive terror was the thought that they would never punish him because they would never find her.

He was blinded by lust. His eyes saw nothing but Manolo, the black, curly hair and the soft, smoothly vulnerable throat.

Manolo was only twenty feet from the Juggler now, standing in moonlight, blending with shadows, and Gus Soltik was achingly ready for him.

In an urgent whisper Samantha said to Tonnelli, "Get him the fuck out of there, Gypsy."

"Don't worry, we got him covered."

"But not if you can't see him."

It had amused Manolo to drift at last into the shadows of the big trees. It amused and excited him because he thought (or hoped, at least) that it would frighten Samantha. It made him feel important to know he could do that to her. She had some kinky thing going for him, the way she had hugged and patted him in the police

267

car that brought them up to this area of the park.

He stood shrouded in darkness, laughing and softly calling Gus Soltik's name.

When Manolo disappeared from view, Samantha tried to scream a warning at him, but Tonnelli saw the tightening cords of her throat and swiftly clamped a hand across her mouth, stifling the sound into a strangled sob. Several of the police marksmen turned, reflexes instinctively triggered by the silent struggle between Samantha and Lieutenant Tonnelli.

The Juggler spotted movement in the trees at the east side of the glade. Frowning lines formed on his wide, rounded forehead. At first only a dim curiosity stirred in his mind. Somebody . . . somebody else wanted the boy.

But after that first jealous thought, which made him wince like the cut of a whip, other thoughts formed in his mind, ugly and dangerous. His animal instincts were suddenly aroused. He listened, and he sniffed the air, and his small, muddy eyes focused on the trees on the other side of the clearing. The shadows there were merging into patterns. He saw the shapes of men. While numbers confused him, he singled out four shapes, counting them on the fingers of his massive right hand. He saw more shapes, but trying to count them deepened the texture of his confusion and anger. The shapes stood still, like people waiting. He could smell the essence of cherries in the oil glistening on Manolo's curly black hair; but the word "wall" had appeared in his mind, and his hands were beginning to tremble with fury.

He knew why those men were waiting. They were

here to hurt him, using the boy to trap him inside walls. His name. Sometimes he forgot his own name. But the boy knew his name. Someone had told him.

They always said calm down. Stay calm. His mother, Mrs. Schultz, Lanny at the zoo. They said it was the other thing, the anger, that caused the trouble. Always. But Gus Soltik couldn't fight the rage that gripped him now. It was like an animal inside him, a snarling that roared in his head, claws slashing at his heart and lungs, screaming for release.

Resisting a compulsion to bellow his rage at this betrayal, Gus Soltik opened the flight bag and removed his heavy hunting knife. Then he ran silently into the shadows behind Manolo, and before Manolo could scream even once, the Juggler's knife had flashed across his throat, opening an inch-deep of furrow in that soft, vulnerable flesh, the flesh he had wanted only to touch, he thought, as he sobbed and lifted Manolo's body high above him and hurled it like a broken doll into the moonlight of the glade.

And then, while rifle fire erupted and muzzle blasts glowed in the night like angry, flaming eyes, Gus Soltik fled in terror toward the sanctuary of the trees.

Luther Boyd threw aside the scarlet-yellow leaf he had been examining and wheeled in the direction of the fusillade of gunfire that was exploding through the dark trees on a line far to the east of him. He experienced a sick and savage anger at Tonnelli's betrayal, for these were not the precise and meticulously squeezed-off shots of marksmen aiming only to wound. No, this was barrage fire, random and reckless and murderous, and he knew from its volume and

269

intensity that it was designed not to disable the Juggler, but to execute him.

Tonnelli might believe this was a first priority, a cop's duty, in fact, but if they killed the Juggler, his daughter might also die, because only that psycho knew where in the vastness of this park Kate Boyd was held captive.

In his anger, Luther Boyd felt in his gut that Gypsy Tonnelli didn't give a good goddamn about that. He wanted only this dramatic, crowd-pleasing performance, that notch on his gun. . . .

Gypsy Tonnelli ran across the glade to Manolo's lifeless body, laboring for breath and feeling despair in the uneven stroke of his heart. Ahead of him the line of marksmen were fanning out through the woods where the Juggler had disappeared, like a figure of myth, vanishing into the mystery of the night after wielding the savage, sacrificial knife.

Tonnelli was screaming into his two-way radio, "Command! Command!"

To responses he cried, "Scramble our choppers. The Juggler's about two hundred yards west of the drive, between Seventy-seventh and Seventy-eighth." Breathing hard, his mouth open, the Gypsy stopped running and looked down at Manolo's small, slack body, the white fur jacket stained scarlet with his blood.

Samantha knelt beside Manolo and put a hand out toward him but didn't touch him. Then she looked up at Tonnelli with tears glistening in her enormous white-rimmed eyes.

"I told you I was scared for him," she said.

Close to hysteria, she repeated herself, but now her

voice was shrill and ugly. "I told you I was scared for him."

"We didn't want this to happen," Tonnelli said. There was naked anguish in his face. "Jesus, we didn't want this to happen."

"No, you didn't want it to happen," Samantha said, "but you made it happen, Gypsy. And if you'd made the bust, you wouldn't give a shit one way or the other, would you?"

Gypsy Tonnelli ran the tip of his thumbnail slowly and painfully down the length of his disfiguring scar and looked from her accusing eyes toward the black trees.

Detectives Carmine Garbalotto and Clem Scott hurried into the clearing where Sergeant Rusty Boyle lay on the ground, hands gripping the wooden lever of the tourniquet fashioned by Luther Boyd. The big redhead was pale, and despite the cold wind blowing in eddying gusts across the glade, there were blisters of perspiration on his upper lip and forehead. The helicopters were flying again, and the sound of their blades and the powerful lights from their fusilage hurt his ears and eyes.

Carmine Garbalotto flipped the switch on his two-way radio and called the CP. He gave the approximate grid coordinates of their position and yelled for an ambulance. Clem Scott knelt beside Sergeant Boyle and took over the task of maintaining the pressure on his thigh above the wound.

"You'll be fine," Scott said.

"Sure. Got it stopped in time."

"Who's the dead one?" Scott said, glancing at Ransom's body.

"Funny," Rusty Boyle said, in a voice weary with pain. "I mean, he's fine, too. Just fine."

Out of his skull, Scott thought.

"They find the girl?" Boyle asked him.

"Not yet, Sarge."

"The Juggler?"

"No. But some clown who drove in to look at the action was found lying with his head busted in a gutter on the East Drive. Said a guy that could be the Juggler pulled him out of his car about twenty minutes ago."

"So the bastard's on wheels now."

Luther Boyd now knew that the Juggler was alive. On Babe Fritzel's radio he had monitored Lieutenant Tonnelli's screamed orders to the command post, and while he knew that Rusty Boyle was also alive, he didn't as yet know the Juggler was on wheels, for that exchange between Scott and Sergeant Boyle hadn't been on the police channel.

Boyd felt a stir of hope. He had, in a sense, infiltrated the police positions and had access to their movements and intelligence reports through Babe Fritzel's two-way radio.

Boyd felt secure behind enemy lines; in classic guerrilla tactics, attack from the rear inevitably offered the promise of ferocity and surprise.

But there was a dreadful irony in the fact that now Boyd must save the Juggler before Tonnelli's units could trap and destroy him.

Checking his watch and with the radio an aural spy at his ear, Boyd ran east. . . .

272

24

THE Arsenal is situated at Sixty-fourth Street and Fifth Avenue, south and east of the Mall. Constructed in the middle of the nineteenth century for the function its name suggests, at various times in its existence it has also been used as a police station and a weather laboratory. Presently this four-story edifice with crenellated towers is the headquarters for Central Park's recreation and cultural affairs administration. Its rear abuts on a quad formed by the animal and bird houses, the rows of bear caves, and the park's cafeteria. In the middle of the quad is the seal pond, guarded or decorated on all four corners by the figures of giant stone eagles.

There are no guards or attendants inside the animal and bird houses at night. There is no external security, except for random checks by pairs of policemen on bicycles and the occasional cruising squad car from the 22d Precinct on Transverse Three.

The Arsenal is locked at the close of the business day, and only one man remains on duty, a night watchman whose presence is required by insurance regulations.

Lanny Gruber, on duty that particular night, sat in his small office on the first floor just off the main entrance preparing to enjoy his supper. Lanny, a middle-aged man with kind and thoughtful eyes, had poured coffee from a thermos and was in the act of unwrapping a ham sandwich when something made him pause and glance toward the open door of his office. Was it a sound or simply his nerves? Glass breaking in the basement? Couldn't be. . . . It had been a dreadful and disturbing night for him because he had seen the police artist's sketch of Gus Soltik on television and had recognized it. He had called the 22d Precinct, but they already had his name. And there had been another brutal and senseless tragedy in the park. A young Puerto Rican boy, to judge from his name.

But Lanny felt a reluctant compassion for Gus Soltik. In Lanny's view, Gus had made a pathetic attempt to understand a world that for the most part ridiculed and despised him.

Then he heard another sound, a footstep in the corridor. He felt his heart lurch with fear. There was a gun in the locker across the room, but before he could rise, Gus Soltik, his face haggard with confusion and pain, limped into his office. He stopped at Lanny's desk, blood dripping from the fingers of his left hand. The single word he spoke came with a gasp of anguish.

"Help," he said to Lanny Gruber.

"Yes, I'll help you, Gus," Gruber said, speaking slowly and quietly, using the warmth of his voice as he might use a gentle hand to stroke a frightened animal. He was a realistic man and was keenly aware of his own danger. He fully understood that whether he lived or died would depend on whether or not he could exert a

274

calming effect on Gus Soltik and make him understand that he must call the police.

"Help," Gus Soltik said, and extended his right hand to Lanny. Then he spoke again, another single word which Lanny didn't understand. "Cage."

A certain expectancy in Gus Soltik's manner gave Lanny confidence.

"There is only one way I can help you, Gus," Lanny said, again slowly and quietly. "We've been friends, and you can trust me."

Gus Soltik continued to stare dumbly and hopefully at Lanny.

He's always done everything I've asked him to, Lanny was thinking, and encouraged by the expression on Gus Soltik's face, he decided to chance it. He casually lifted the phone from its cradle and smiled at Gus as he began to dial the police emergency number.

"Since you need help, Gus, we might as well get it. It's the best way, believe me."

But Lanny Gruber had fatally misjudged the hope and expectation in Gus Soltik's muddy eyes and twisted features. He couldn't know what powerful elements had been churning in Gus Soltik's psyche tonight. There could no longer be times without anger for Gus Soltik.

Lanny Gruber, smiling and dialing at a deliberate pace, couldn't know that blazing in Gus Soltik's mind was the concept "white legs" and a twisted and frenzied compulsion for revenge.

"Cages," he said again, but insistently now. What Gus Soltik wanted were the thin metal things that opened doors. In his feverishly tortured mind he believed that if he released a cage, the great, roaring cages that were strong as he was strong but helpless as he was in their barred boxes, when it was free the cage would help. Kill them. All. And the coldness. . . .

"Twenty-second Precinct, Sergeant Dorman."

Lanny Gruber said, "Officer, this is—"

Gus Soltik's hand moved with blinding speed, his fist closing on the telephone cord and ripping it from its base in a floorboard wall socket.

"No, please!" Gruber cried, knowing this was a mistake but unable to control the hysteria in his voice, for Gus Soltik was lunging toward him, his hands forming a loop with the length of plastic telephone cord.

Gus was thinking dimly as he looked down at Gruber's body of the time he had brought the week-old produce here and how nice Lanny had been to him, and these memories merged with memories of his mother and Mrs. Schultz and the young boy whose curly hair smelled of cherries, and tears began to well in his eyes.

Brushing them from his cheek with the back of his hand, he removed three rings of keys from a drawer in Lanny's desk.

Male Caucasian, age twenty-nine, name, George Cobb, address, the 300 block of East Fifty-fourth Street, Manhattan. Aproximately 5 feet 9 inches in height, weight 200 pounds. Brown hair, blue eyes. No distinguishing scars. Small mustache.

That was the police description of the man who had been assaulted by Gus Soltik. George Cobb was presently being interrogated by Lieutenant Tonnelli at the CP. Crews of television and press reporters were gathered in a semicircle about Cobb, their silhouettes thrown into grotesque shadows by batteries of brilliant camera lights backed by huge aluminum reflectors.

Cobb was speaking hesitantly, almost timorously, avoiding the baleful glare of the powerfully muscled detective with the hideous scar on his left cheek.

"Well, I was watching it on television, and when I saw the dogs and the helicopters, I just decided to come over and take a look-see," Cobb said. "Just for—"

"All right." Tonnelli cut him off and glanced at the notes he'd taken. Yellow leather hat, brown turtleneck sweater, six-two or -three. "He say anything to you, anything at all?"

"Well, he just made some noises," Cobb said. "They weren't words."

Patrolman Prima pushed his way through the crowd and caught the lieutenant's eye. "We got the heap, Lieutenant." Prima looked at George Cobb. "Sixty-nine Pontiac, maroon with black stripes, needs some work on the front fender?"

"That's my car," Cobb said.

"Where did you find it?" Tonnelli asked Prima.

"In the woods, east of the Mall, on a line with Sixty-sixth Street," Prima said.

Gus Soltik ran with lumbering strides from the Arsenal, past the seal pond, and under the Delacorte clock to the double doors of the animal house. Unlocking them, he pushed them back until metal spring plungers dropped into slots in the tile floor. His nostrils flared, and his senses were aroused by the strong smell of cat urine and disinfectant.

This narrow wing of the zoo was dark, as were all the

277

others. Some moonlight fell in through the arched and barred windows at the back of the cages, shining on dull yellow brick walls and the black tile flooring.

Most of the animals were asleep, and at this time of the year all were quartered inside the building. In warmer seasons the big cats were allowed to prowl into the rows of outside cages which faced the greenery of the park.

Gus Soltik stepped over the wooden barrier that kept visitors a safe distance from the bars and unlocked the door of a cage which confined a black-maned African lion, the great male whose name was Garland.

The lion was lying on a thick wooden shelf built four feet above the concrete floor of its cage. The big cat was awake, yellow eyes glowing in the darkness, but it indicated no interest in the door which Gus Soltik had opened.

Gus Soltik made a clucking noise with his tongue. The big cat put its massive head on its paws and closed its eyes.

Gus stood in the darkness for what seemed a long time, feeling confusion and frustration and feeling too the pain in his left arm and the sluggish flow of blood down his wrist and fingers.

Then he remembered something Lanny had told him about animals. Animals in forests. Animals in barns. Gus Soltik stepped back over the barrier and left the animal house and went to where there were rows of trash cans waiting a morning collection.

He ignited a newspaper with his cigarette lighter and pushed it deep into the can. Soon the brisk night wind whipped the blaze into roaring flames.

Gus Soltik put the can on his shoulder, grunting

harshly at the pain in his arm, and stumbled back into the lion house.

Sparks trailed brilliantly in his passage; smoke and fire gusted toward the tiled ceiling.

Gus Soltik hurled the can of blazing trash through the open door of Garland's cage. The heavy container fell with a metallic crash on the concrete floor, its contents scattering across the concrete floor in flaming heaps.

While Garland raced from one barred wall to another, whining at the searing barrier of fire, and other big cats began roaring in panic, Gus Soltik ran through the double doors of the lion house and out into the night.

Garland, roaring with pain and fear, leaped across the blazing trash through the door of the open cage. By then Gus Soltik was running toward a parks department vehicle and thinking with savage anticipation of "white legs."

Uncaged for the first time in seven years, Garland faced the open double doors of the lion house and the black night beyond them. Belly close to the ground, trembling with fear and excitement at this new experience, Garland padded through the open doors and into the darkness of Central Park.

Twenty minutes later, Tonnelli was giving urgent orders to Sokolsky on the switchboard in the Central Park command post. The Gypsy himself had just received a tense report from patrolmen in a cruising squad car operating out of the 22d Precinct on Transverse Three. The report had created a reaction like a spasm in the orderly and disciplined chaos at the

CP. Squad cars had been sent streaking toward the Arsenal from all areas of the park, their revolving dome lights flashing like giant fireflies against the black trees.

Gus Soltik drove north on the East Drive, traveling at a conservative speed which in no way reflected the thoughts storming at gale force within his tortured head. The interior of the cab was dark, and his face was only a blur behind the windshield, and this, plus the parks department legend on the doors of the truck, gave him safe-conduct past clusters of uniformed patrolmen who stood with red flashlights at hundred-yard intervals along the drive.

He would leave the truck in the parking lot off the drive. Then he could hide in the darkness and make his way to her.

The headlights of oncoming traffic struck at his face like angry lances, and their glaring attacks intensified his rage and his hungers.

Tonnelli had said to Sokolsky, "First, send a homicide detail to the Arsenal. Lanny Gruger is dead. Then alert every cop and detective in this area that there's a lion, that's right, Sokolsky, a *lion,* and it's loose in the park. The chiefs have dispatched three armored jeeps with marksmen and tranquilizer bullets. Don't anybody try to stop him with a police special. It won't."

After Sokolsky had transmitted these messages to all patrolmen and squads in and around the park, he flicked his receiving switch and gestured to Tonnelli.

"Something else is coming in, Lieutenant." Sokolsky listened for a few seconds, nodded, then glanced up at

Tonnelli. "The same guys from the Twenty-second. They've been checking around, found a parks department truck missing. Seems Lanny Gruber usually took a swing through the zoo area around midnight. Then he parked the truck on the south side of the Arsenal, you know, after making sure there was nobody loitering—"

Tonnelli cut him off with chopping gesture of his hand.

"When did they find it missing?"

"Couple of minutes ago, I guess."

Potentials and timetables and routes began to form patterns into the Gypsy's intricate perceptions. Not south but north. He wouldn't drive south toward that barrier of squad cars on Fifty-ninth Street. North then. At least twenty minutes ago, possibly more. And the Juggler's destination? Boyd had given him an answer to that.

West across the Ramble on a line with Seventy-seventh Street. If Kate Boyd was alive, that's where the Juggler was heading. If she were dead, he would travel north inevitably, hoping to escape from the park through the trackless areas that merged with Meer Lake and the edges of Harlem.

Sokolsky flipped a switch and spoke into his mike. "Code Three, all units. . . ." Tonnelli cut him off with an angry headshake.

"Hold it!" Tonnelli said.

Sokolsky looked at him with puzzled eyes. "Sure, Lieutenant. But I thought—"

"We'll finesse this one," Tonnelli said. The Gypsy turned and stared north at black stands of trees on the horizon. His expression was hard and cold, and his eyes

281

were narrowing as if he had already caught sight of his quarry.

"Forget the report on that missing truck, Sokolsky. That's an order."

"Check, Lieutenant."

"One more thing. I want every cop and detective out of the Ramble. Instruct them to report to the reserve unit in the Sheep Meadow. Put that signal on the air right now."

"Check, Lieutenant."

Tonnelli walked with long, deliberate strides, not to his unmarked sedan, but to a row of pool squad cars which were equipped with standard dome lights and whose interior arsenals included bullhorns and riot guns. Tonnelli jerked a thumb at a young uniformed officer behind the wheel of one of these reserve squad cars. The patrolman slipped hastily from the car, and within seconds Gypsy Tonnelli was driving across the meadow that would lead him to the East Drive.

Gus Soltik crouched low in the dark, warm cab of the parks department truck and watched two young patrolmen crossing the lot in his direction, their red flashlights cutting rhythmic swaths across the paved surface of the parking area. Gus Soltik sat very quietly, but his right hand gripped the handle of his knife with painful intensity. His thoughts were chaotic, and his body was hot and trembling with his needs.

The red beam of a flashlight flicked across the windshield of the truck; but Gus Soltik's head was below the dashboard, and the officers continued on toward East Drive, their lights eventually winking out in the darkness.

With an animallike moan Gus Soltik climbed from the truck and ran swiftly and silently into trees bordering the parking lot.

25

LUTHER BOYD stopped in the darkness near a massive facing of rock. From Babe Fritzel's two-way radio he was monitoring a conversation between Assistant Chief Inspector Taylor "Chip" Larkin and Dispatcher Sokolsky, who manned the switchboard at the command post in Central Park.

Commander Larkin was driving north in his chauffeured sedan from the supermarket in Greenwich Village where the gunman, after improbable intercessions from a pair of street people, had released nineteen hostages unharmed and surrendered himself in tears to the police.

Boyd's reaction to the following exchanges was tense and expectant, but there was something else in his expression, a challenge to the gods, the sacrilege of hope.

"Sokolsky? I've had a report from the Twenty-second that a parks department truck was stolen from the Arsenal approximately the time the super was murdered. Did you have that, Sokolsky?"

"Yes, Chief. I had it."

There was something close to anger in Larkin's musical Irish voice. "Why didn't you notify all units?"

285

"Lieutenant Tonnelli gave me a negative on that, Chief. The lieutenant made it a direct order, sir."

"Is Lieutenant Tonnelli at the CP?"

"No, Chief. He left here a few minutes ago in one of the pool squads."

"Alone?"

"Yes, sir."

The chief's voice rose sharply. "Central, this is Borough Commander South. Patch me through to Lieutenant Tonnelli, and don't waste time about it."

Boyd stood perfectly still, controlling his emotions with a discipline acquired from years of training, while listening to Central's operator ordering Lieutenant Tonnelli to report his position and destination immediately to Chief Larkin.

There was no answer from the Gypsy. Boyd could envision the situation as clearly as if it were flashing before his eyes on a screen. The Juggler was in that stolen truck, and Tonnelli was after him.

But Boyd knew what the Juggler wanted, and he knew why. Only one question demanded an answer now: Where would he leave the truck?

With animal cunning, the Juggler might instinctively realize it would point after him like an arrow if he abandoned it near his eventual destination.

So where would be the most obvious and innocent place to hide a truck? Ideally, a gas station or a used-car lot. But the plain fact was there were no such facilities in Central Park. Then the answer hit Boyd so abruptly that it sent a shock wave of hope and excitement through his body.

And considering that Boyd had an almost certain fix on where the Juggler was heading, he could make a shrewd guess at where he would leave the truck, the

286

parking lot closest to the Ramble, that oblong stretch of pavement that abutted the Loeb boathouse just north of the East Drive.

Tonnelli angled his pool squad car toward the curb and stopped near Max Prima and another patrolman who were in position at the East Drive on a line with Sixty-eighth Street.

When he rolled down the window of the car and looked up at Prima, the faint light from a streetlamp ran like quicksilver up and down the scar that streaked across the Gypsy's cheek.

"You men spot a parks department truck traveling north fifteen or twenty minutes ago?"

Max Prima hesitated a fractional instant. As in any other tightly interwoven organization, gossip and rumor spread like storm fires through the police department. And there was a rumor, an ugly one, that Lieutenant Gypsy Tonnelli had gone shut-eye, had cut off his radio, and was deliberately refusing to report to Chief Larkin. Sokolsky had asked all units for a make on that particular truck, but almost twenty-odd minutes after it had first been reported missing by officers from the 22d. It could be out on Long Island by now.

But Max Prima was not staring into the eyes of just another cop, not just a lieutenant in the New York police department. He was looking at a scarred man who was a legend in all five boroughs of the city, and so he said simply, "Yes, Lieutenant. We spotted it. About eighteen minutes ago, heading north."

"Still got that good pair of eyes, Max," the Gypsy said.

The parks department truck was at the far end of the boathouse lot, its shiny surfaces partially obscured

287

by the overhanging limbs of immense willow trees.

Luther Boyd approached the truck with the Browning in his hand. He jerked open the door and smelled the rank, fetid odor of the Juggler and saw—as he had guessed—that the cab was empty. There were bloodstains on the leather of the passenger seat.

After checking the rear of the truck and finding it empty, Boyd ran across the pavement of the parking lot to open ground that led toward the Ramble. He came to a thick tangle of hawthorn hedges, stopping at an area which looked ragged and torn, as if a wild animal had charged through it. And as he forced his way through this ragged passage, his flashlight picked up the distinctive prints of the Juggler's Wellingtons.

Attack now, he thought, and as he bent low and ran swiftly along the line of those tracks, an irrelevant but annealing maxim of war came to his mind: "My center is giving way, my right flank is crushed, situation excellent, I am attacking." That was Marshal Foch to Paris Headquarters, Second Battle of the Marne.

Within minutes, he spotted a movement far ahead of him in the shadows created by the tossing crowns of great trees. Then Boyd saw him clearly, still hundreds of yards ahead of him, a huge figure lurching across a moonlit meadow. And Boyd could see, even at this distance, the Juggler's yellow cap and the light flickering on the blade of the knife in his right hand.

Luther Boyd flicked off the beam of his flashlight and ran silently at speed after his quarry.

Lieutenant Tonnelli drove slowly into the boathouse parking lot, and his headlights bathed the sides of the parks department truck in brilliant illumination. The front door of the truck was open, and the cab was empty, and this confirmed the first estimate of the Juggler's route: into the Ramble west on a line with Seventy-seventh Street. That was the fix that Luther Boyd had given him. Gypsy Tonnelli didn't need to track the prints of those Wellingtons, even if he had had the skill to do it. Cutting the headlights of his squad car, Tonnelli drove slowly from the parking lot across a meadow that was flanked by a tangled thicket of low hawthorns. He rounded this hedgerow, which had been torn apart in one area, and drove slowly onto the flatlands of the park, the squad car merging slowly and silently with the shadows of huge trees.

26

HIS odor was rank on the air now, and when Luther Boyd stepped from shadows into a moonlit grove, the movement froze Gus Soltik into immobility, and he stared at Boyd in terror, his body trembling and his breath coming so rapidly and harshly that saliva churned into froth on his lips. This was what he had feared this night, the "coldness" that had stalked him so cruelly and relentlessly. His thoughts were like splinters of steel piercing his tormented mind, bringing the redness there, the agonizing memories of the father's threats and his mother's punishment, the way they had held him and beat him, and his terrifying conviction that he knew no words to make them stop.

With an inarticulate scream of rage and fear, he jerked the hunting knife from his belt and rushed at Luther Boyd. He raised the knife high in the air, plunging it toward Boyd's face, but Boyd trapped his wrist in a powerful Y formed by his own crossed forearms. The tip of the blade glittered inches from his eyes, but it was held there finally and forever by the strength of Boyd's tempered muscle, and when Soltik tried to free himself, Boyd swiftly went to attack, the palm of his right hand going behind Soltik's neck and the full swing of his arm sending the big man sprawling to the ground.

When Gus Soltik tried to rise to his feet, Boyd kicked him in the stomach with a lightning-fast blow, and an instant later, he broke Gus Soltik's right wrist with a chop of his hand that sent the hunting knife flying into thick underbrush.

Sobbing with pain, Gus Soltik stumbled backward and collapsed on the ground against the bole of a tree.

He longed for his pain and torments to cease. He wanted it to be over forever. Why was it always like this? Going on and on. While his eyes filled with tears, he looked up and saw that the man standing above him held a gun pointed at his forehead, and the hand holding that gun was like something carved from rock.

Luther Boyd stared at Gus Soltik's swollen features, noting narrow eyes the color of mud, slack lips and bad teeth, the bulging forehead behind which stretched the festering swamp of mind. There was nothing there to salvage; this was human refuse. It was so often like this when you had slain your enemy on the battlefield; there was little cause for triumph because what you had destroyed was only another miserable and suffering human being, a youth whose mother went to sleep praying for him or something black and charred in the wreckage of a war machine.

He asked one question in a voice an inquisitor might have applied to a man stretched on a rack.

"Is she alive?"

Gus Soltik nodded dumbly, eagerly, filled with a desperate need somehow to soften the hatred and contempt he saw blazing in the eyes of the man who held the gun in his face.

"Date," he said, in a hoarse, choked voice.

Luther Boyd put a hand on the man's shoulder and jerked him to his feet, spinning him around and ramming the muzzle of the Browning against his spine. "Take me there," Boyd said in the same voice he had used before.

Gus Soltik nodded quickly, almost happily and lurched forward, the gun at this back prodding him into a stumbling run.

The direction the Juggler had chosen coincided exactly with Boyd's earlier estimate of where his daughter might be, and with the realization that this dreadful night might finally end with Kate alive and warm in his arms, he felt a surge of relief flowing through his veins.

"Hot chocolate," Gus Soltik said, and his voice was soft and gentle and questing. "Boats to ride around the water."

"Shut up!" Luther Boyd said, speaking quietly and ramming the barrel of the gun harder into the big man's spine, increasing their speed until they were devouring ground with long, running strides.

Boyd flicked a glance over his shoulder. He couldn't see him yet, but he could hear the soft purr of the motor on the night winds. Earlier he had monitored Sokolsky's orders to all forces in the Ramble to return to the reserve unit in the Sheep Meadow. And so this could only be Tonnelli coming after him, stalking him in a police squad car, his Sicilian passions aroused to destroy the Juggler at any cost, including Kate Boyd's life.

293

Tonnelli quietly braked the squad car to a complete stop and cut the engine. As silence settled around him, he carefully opened the door and stepped frm the car, his eyes tracking back and forth across the darkness of the Ramble. Nothing stirred in that black expanse but the silhouettes of moving trees against a clear sky, and the only sounds he heard were occasional gusting winds that created a delicate rustle among the fallen autumn leaves.

Tonnelli's hand was on the butt of his gun. He knew that Boyd had a two-way radio, and without any doubt Boyd would know the Ramble had been emptied of all police officers. And would know of the missing parks department truck, of course.

Tonnelli stood quiet and motionless in the darkness for at least thirty seconds, straining for a glimpse of Boyd or the Juggler, testing an almost unnatural silence by turning his head from side to side, trying to track sound and motion like a human radar screen.

At last the Gypsy moved carefully behind the wheel of the car, settled his powerful torso silently into the leather seat, and then turned the ignition and allowed the motor to idle softly before touching the accelerator and letting the car inch slowly toward a tunnel formed by towering fir trees.

Luther Boyd had checked the Juggler with a grip on his arm, and they had stood stock-still after Boyd had heard the sound of the squad car's engines fade away into the silence of the night. He turned and stared over his shoulder at tangles of underbrush and the slowly swaying crowns of tall trees, trying to analyze Tonnelli's tactics. Why had he stopped? Was he tracking him on foot now?

Then, after an interval of almost a minute, Boyd heard the squad car's motor cough softly to life, and he tried to judge whether Tonnelli had got a fix on his position during that beat of silence.

He pushed Gus Soltik forward, prodding him with the barrel of the Browning.

"Faster," he said, his voice as soft as the whispering winds in the trees.

Gus felt blood welling from the wound in his shoulder, and a sobbing moan grew helplessly in his throat.

"Quiet!" Boyd said, again speaking softly.

Tears were blinding Gus. Each time his heavy boots struck the ground, hot pain streaked through his body. His great chest heaved in spasms, but the air gave him no relief; it was scorching his lungs like the fires he dreaded at the dead mass. He was close to exhaustion, eyes blurred with helpless, agonized tears, when his swinging foot collided abruptly with the gnarled root of a tree, and he pitched forward to the ground, his great weight crashing down against the bullet wound in his shoulder. An involuntary scream was torn from the corded muscles of his throat, and he bellowed in pain again as Luther Boyd seized his arms and jerked him back to his feet.

Boyd clamped a hand with savage strength across Gus Soltik's mouth, cutting off his screams.

"There's a cop behind us," he said, staring into the Juggler's glazed, terrified eyes. "He wants to kill you."

Gus Soltik fought back the scream that was trying to

explode from his throat, for he realized in the depths of his shredded mind that this "coldness" would stop hurting him while the man with the scar he remembered so fearfully would never. . . .

Tonnelli hit the brakes of the squad car and quickly rolled down the window. There was silence now, but he had heard those screams and he knew he was on line with them. Removing his .38 from its holster, he took the bullhorn from the dashboard and put it on the passenger seat, and then, his mood blackly triumphant, he floored the accelerator of the squad car and it raced ahead under a surge of power as if flung into the darkness by a giant catapult.

Boyd heard the sudden, accelerating roar of the squad car's motor, and simultaneously he was blinded by the brilliant radiance of the car's headlights. When Boyd spun to face the onrushing car, Gus Soltik collapsed to the ground, now attempting to stifle his screams by pressing the knuckles of his huge hands into his mouth.

Tonnelli slammed a foot against the brakes and pulled down powerfully on the steering wheel, bringing the car to a stop in a four-wheel drag, ten yards from the .38 in his hand, the bullhorn at his lips.

"Get out of my way, Boyd," Tonnelli said.

"Kiss off, Tonnelli. You promised me you'd take him alive, but you tried to slaughter him."

"Goddamn you to hell," Tonnelli said, and his amplified voice was hoarse with anger and frustration. "We waste the psycho. Then I'll flood this park with a thousand cops to find your daughter. He's first priority.

That's police business. Don't make me waste you too, Boyd."

"Our covenant did not include sacrificing my daughter," Luther Boyd said, his voice cold.

"You're the bleeding-heart civilian after all," Tonnelli said, naked contempt in his voice.

"He'll lead me to my daughter. That's what matters. Nothing else."

"You're wrong, Boyd. There's more at stake."

"I'm taking him out of here *now*," Boyd said.

"God*damn* you!" Tonnelli shouted at him. "They'll plea bargain him into five years at some mental country club. Then he's out on the streets with that knife again. How many kids does he get on the next go-round? We got him now, Boyd. I want him dead. Can't I get through to you?"

"On your feet," Boyd said to the Juggler.

"One last time!" Tonnelli said furiously. "Out of my way."

"Try me," Boyd said quietly. And there was an edge to his tone that had brought battle-weary soldiers to attention in dozens of combat areas throughout the world, but Tonnelli either didn't recognize it or chose to ignore it.

He nodded grimly. "Right," he said.

Tonnelli put the car into reverse, slammed his big foot down on accelerator. As the car leaped backward, he spun the steering wheel until the grill of the car pointed directly at Boyd and the huddled body of Gus Soltik.

"I'm coming," Tonnelli shouted and floored the accelerator, but as the car leaped forward under

297

maximum power, Boyd whipped the Browning up with practiced speed and fired a shot that smashed through the passenger side of the windshield.

Firing two more shots so rapidly that the sounds merged into a single explosion, Boyd shattered both of the car's blinding headlights, plunging this mad arena into total darkness.

Inside the car, Tonnelli had flung an arm across his face to block the stinging fragments of glass that were ricocheting from the roof and windows. Blinded by the sudden darkness, he heard two more shots, and his car went suddenly out of control as his front tires exploded. While he fought the wheel to stabilize his direction, the crazily angling front wheels turned the car onto a collision course with a giant elm tree.

It was at that exact instant in this terrifying eruption of noises that the pain in Gus Soltik's mind became intolerable. With a scream of anguish that was smothered by the crash of Tonnelli's car against the trunk of the elm tree, Gus Soltik scuttled like a giant crab into the shadows of the Ramble.

Boyd listened to the sound of his passage through heavy underbrush. He hesitated only long enough to make sure that Tonnelli was conscious and could summon aid from his radio if he needed it.

Then he ran west after the Juggler. Within a dozen yards, he heard the big man trip and fall, heard his body sprawling and crashing down a long escarpment of rock, his descent creating a noisy cascade of loose shale and stones.

And when the Juggler struck the ground at the foot of that long slope, he screamed in agony, and after that rending cry of anguish, his screaming stopped, and his pain was over.

Luther Boyd stood at the top of the escarpment and looked down at Gus Soltik's body impaled on a triangular-shaped shard of black lava rock, the characteristic ribbing of the park, an impersonal, arbitrary instrument of execution, without judgment or reason, whose knife-sharp tip had plunged through Gus Soltik's chest and now gleamed with his blood where it had broken through his spine.

There were flecks of blood on Gus Soltik's big hand which was extended before him, pointing toward the immense sentinel of a tree where Luther Boyd had stopped earlier that night while tracking the Juggler and his daughter.

It was the tree that had been blasted dead-white by some long-past bolt of lightning and whose trunk had been splintered and breached ten or eleven feet above the ground, and it was there he had seen the dead wood around the black gaping hole brightened by clusters of clinging twigs and a line of frost-turned autumn leaves.

That had been the mistake he had made, and now he prayed to God and cursed himself without mercy that he hadn't discovered this error too late to save Kate's life. Traveling at a pace he no longer thought he was capable of, he ran toward that ghostly oak tree, shouting his daughter's name but hearing only echoes sounding in pulsating rhythms through the darkness.

Not bright fall leaves growing improbably in dead wood ten feet above the ground, not the vivid fleck of berries, not the breast feathers of a robin or cardinal ringing the gaping hole in that lightning-blasted swamp oak. But red silk threads from Kate's ski jacket. . . .

Boyd stopped at the trunk of the tree and murmured a prayer while crouching and leaping high enough to gain handholds in the lower half of the great gaping hole. Swinging his legs up and propping his feet flat against the tree trunk, he hung there, suspended in midair, straining against the wood with all his strength, using the muscles of his thighs and back as well as his shoulders and arms. How long Boyd remained in that position he would never know, but after what seemed an eternity, when the great resilient muscles of his body were at their breaking point, he heard a rending, grinding sound, and then, inch by agonizing inch, a wide section of the rotting trunk began to separate from the tree, bending away with Boyd's weight until finally it snapped well below his feet. And as he hurtled backward, the rotting wood clutched to his chest, he saw—a second before crashing to the ground—the bound and gagged figure of his daughter inside the hollow bole of the tree, the tape on her mouth streaked with mud, her hair matted with rotted wood and fragments of moss.

But while Kate's eyes were glazed with panic, he knew from the look of her that she was unhurt and gloriously alive.

27

JOYCE COLBY stood with Detective Miles Tebbet and Patrolman Max Prima at the Artists' Gate where Sixth Avenue crosses Fifty-ninth Street and begins its curving northward passage through Central Park.

The night was cold. Many details of detectives and patrolmen had been returned to their precincts and to their normal duties. Traffic was almost normal, the crowds of the morbidly curious drifting off on news that the little girl was back safe with her family.

When Joyce Colby received the phone call telling her that Rusty Boyle had been wounded, she had put on slacks and a sweater, stepped into loafers, and wrapped a polo coat around her slim body before running from her apartment to find a cab.

The wind that whipped across the pond north of Fifty-ninth Street swept through her long red hair and cut like icy whips at her bare ankles.

Miles Tebbet pointed toward the curving extension of Sixth Avenue where he had spotted the revolving red dome light of an ambulance.

"Here's the big guy now," he said.

It had been a chaotic night, Tebbet thought, but

mercifully it was over, and Fifty-ninth Street was practically deserted except for a few policemen and Joyce Colby and the stocky old woman who looked as wide as she was tall with her layers of sweaters under a cloth coat. She had been here most of the night and now stood as patiently as a cow in a field watching the approaching ambulance.

Max Prima walked into the pathway north of Fifty-ninth Street and flagged the ambulance down with his red torchlight.

Miles Tebbet took Joyce's arm, and they walked to the rear of the ambulance, where he pulled open both doors.

The two ambulance attendants flanking Rusty Boyle's stretcher stared at Joyce and Detective Tebbet with the cynical eyes of men who earn their money going to fires and treating bullet and knife wounds.

"What's all this shit?" one of them said to Tebbet.

"One more passenger," Tebbet said, and held Joyce's arm as she climbed into the ambulance.

"That's against regulations," the attendant said, but Joyce had already brushed past him to Rusty Boyle.

She was in his arms, and he was grateful for the clean fragrance of her hair, grateful even for her tears on his cheeks.

Drowsy from the injection the medics had given him, he still had one clear thought: When he was discharged from the hospital, he would go to Epiphany Church at Twenty-second Street and Second Avenue, where he had gone as a youngster. He would go there to say thanks.

Tebbet slammed the rear doors shut, and the

ambulance turned west into Fifty-ninth Street, its dome lights flashing and its siren rising with the winds.

Out of curiosity and simple compassion, Detective Tebbet walked over to the fat, swaddled woman who stared with empty eyes after the ambulance. She stood as if rooted to the ground, and there was something abandoned and lonely in her tired old face.

"Can I be of any help, ma'am?" he asked her.

"No," she said, and turned her vacant eyes toward the trees and traffic in the park.

"Did you know any of the people who were in trouble here tonight?"

She was too frightened and too shrewd to fall into traps. "No, I know nobody," Mrs. Schultz said, and went away from him with her shuffling walk in the direction of Columbus Circle.

She was praying again for the poor strange man she had been told to take care of, but she was praying in her own old language now, not hard like the English they had made her learn, not hard like this country could be to some of its people.

"Gegrusset eist du Maria," she said, whispering the words into the night, *"full der Gnade der ist mit dir du bist Gebenedeit under den weibern und gehendeit ist die frucht deines libes, Gesus.*

"Heilige Maria Mutter Gottes bitt fur uns sinners jetzt und in die stundes unser todes. Amen."

Luther Boyd carried his daughter through clearings that would eventually bring them to pathways flanking the East Drive. Her arms were tight about his neck, and her face was buried against the warmth of his chest and shoulders. He held her in the crook of his left arm, while his right hand gently massaged her back and shoulders.

Words would be of no comfort as yet, Boyd knew from long experience at field hospitals. Soldiers needed letters from home and security foods and the mothering of nurses, but Boyd had never known a wounded soldier to take initial solace from discussing the impact of the bullet, the splintering of bones and the pain and nausea that followed.

Talk might help later, perhaps with doctors. And the two of them might take a long skiing vacation at Tahoe-Donner. Two of them, not three, he thought with bitter resignation.

"Daddy?"

"What, baby?"

She was silent and still in his arms. Then she said so softly that he could barely hear the words, "I told him you'd help."

"Told who, Katie?"

She was silent, pressing her cheek hard against his shoulder.

"You told the man, is that it?"

She nodded slowly.

"I know he killed Harry Lauder," she said. "But I meant it when I said you'd help him. You could, Daddy. . . ."

Her strength and compassion almost brought tears to his eyes. And he realized with pride, but with a sense of loss, that the humanity of this child had been bred into her by her mother, not only by Colonel Luther Boyd.

"He scared me, and he tied me up, but he didn't do

anything else to me," she said. "He wanted to talk to me. I could tell."

This might explain the Juggler's splintered, rambling talk of dates and chocolate and boat rides. Perhaps Kate had seen something in that dreadfully flawed unit of humanity that he, Luther Boyd, could never have seen. In her own terror, she might have had the detachment to feel some sort of compassion for him. Was it that mercy which had allowed her to survive her agonizing ordeal? Kate, with childish wisdom, had been generous to him, had promised him his help. And that might have deflected his monstrous needs, providing the lead time for Luther Boyd to save her life.

"We can talk about it later," he said, and to his relief saw that she had been distracted by the sight of the red dome lights of police squad cars coming toward them through the trees.

"Is Mommy here?" she asked him.

"Yes, baby."

When Kate saw her mother step from one of the cars, she slipped from her father's arms and ran across the meadow, her footsteps stumbling and uncertain, crying for the first time since her father had found her.

Barbara hugged her daughter as tightly as was physically possible and whispered her name over and over again as if this were some guarantee that this warm, living presence in her arms was not a cruel, figmented twist of her imagination.

Other figures stepped from the police squad cars: Detectives Jim Taylor and Ray Karp, Crescent Holloway and Rudi Zahn.

Crescent Holloway slipped her arm through Rudi

Zahn's and hugged it tightly and looked at him with shining eyes. His jaw was swollen and discolored, and there were bandages on his forehead and his cheeks.

"I'm a disaster area," he said.

"No, you look positively gorgeous," she said.

Kate Boyd turned from her mother and looked up at Rudi Zahn.

"Thank you, sir," she said.

"Well, I tried," he said, and while Crescent Holloway hugged his arm even more tightly, he touched Kate Boyd's cheek with the back of his hand. "It turned out all right," he said. "We can be grateful for that."

It was all right, Zahn thought, true and right, and he could say *Auf Wiedersehen* now with poignance but without regret to the name that had haunted him so long and so endlessly, forever, the face that had blazed in his mind through all those weary years: the name and face of Ilana.

And watching the faint smile on his lips and seeing that Kate was holding his hand against her face, Crescent Holloway realized that in some fashion Rudi Zahn was free.

Barbara Boyd stared at her husband. There was a longing question in her eyes, and she desperately needed an answer to it.

28

THE Boyd family was driven home in a police squad car by Detective Carmine Garbalotto, who let them out at the entrance to their apartment building.

Lieutenant Gypsy Tonnelli parked his unmarked sedan on the opposite side of Fifth Avenue and turned off his motor. He intended to wait until the little girl and her parents were safe in their own home before returning to his precinct to begin the massive paperwork that would be generated by this night's events.

Detective Garbalotto waved a good-bye to the Boyds and drove south down Fifth Avenue.

The revolving doors of the building spun and glittered in the darkness, and John Brennan came through them, and Kate was swept with a blend of confusing emotions when she saw the small kitten cradled in his hands. She took it from him and felt it warm and purring against her body. Poor Harry Lauder, she thought, stroking the silky white star on the kitten's forehead. If he hadn't been so jaunty and brave, he'd still be alive. But her little Scottie had to be what he was.

Luther Boyd looked at Barbara. The night's ordeal

had marked her face; shadows like bruises lay beneath her eyes, and her lips, even without makeup, were livid against the masklike pallor of her features.

"When we get Katie to sleep, we can talk about what you want to do, Barbara."

"I'm home, Luther,"she said. Her body trembled as if an electric current had passed through it. There was a sudden, bright shine of tears in her eyes as she asked the question she so desperately needed an answer to. "Is that all right?"

"All right? It's perfect," Boyd said, and put an arm tightly around her shoulders.

They went into the lobby with Kate holding the kitten in her arms and Mr. Brennan leading them to the elevators. Boyd said, "You take Kate up. I won't be a minute."

He walked back the length of the lobby and pushed through the revolving doors and looked across the street at Gypsy Tonnelli.

For what seemed an attenuated interval the two men stared at each other, and then Luther Boyd sighed and said, "Can we agree we both did what we had to do tonight? That we really had no choice in the matter?"

"Let's just agree it's over," Tonnelli said wearily. "No loose ends. They even got a couple of tranquilizer bullets into the lion. Damn cat was sound asleep in a toolshed at Seventy-third Street."

Boyd smiled faintly. "Lieutenant, I've got a bottle of twenty-eight-year-old bourbon upstairs," he said. "How about a drink?"

But the mood was wrong for it, and he wasn't surprised when the lieutenant shook his head with slow finality.

"Thanks, but I've got a ton of paperwork to do,

Colonel," Tonnelli said, raising his voice above the sounds of intermittent traffic.

"Paperwork is for clerks, Lieutenant," Boyd said. "We're field-grade soldiers. And we've got something to celebrate."

Tonnelli turned his face in profile to Boyd and drew a thumbnail slowly down his disfiguring scar, and Luther Boyd, who understood men, guessed at the significance of that gesture and the direction of Lieutenant Tonnelli's thoughts.

Yes, Boyd had something to celebrate. But what of the others?

The white princess was back in her electronically guarded castle, the Gypsy was thinking. That's what they would drink to, that's what they would celebrate.

But who would raise a glass to Manolo and the dead men at the boathouse and the Arsenal? And what did Samantha and Babe Fritzel and Rusty Boyle, with fire in his leg and ribs, what did they have to celebrate?

Could you say that John Ransom had got a break, rotting with cancer and a pair of slugs in his face? That's what he'd bought tonight. And even the human animal killed, he had to matter. The whole city mattered. Or should anyway.

He snapped on his sedan's red dome light and turned and looked at Luther Boyd. The men stared at each other for a long, thoughtful moment.

"Some other time," Tonnelli said.

"I understand, Lieutenant," Luther Boyd said, and gave him a soft salute.

Maybe he does at that, Tonnelli thought, maybe he does, as he shifted into drive, his car rolling smoothly away from the curb.

Luther Boyd stood on the sidewalk and watched the

red dome light of Tonnelli's car as it flowed away from him into the darkness, turning out of sight at last into Fifty-ninth Street, where the mighty equestrian statue of General William Tecumseh Sherman stood in its full arrogant glory on the Grand Army Plaza.

The irony suggested by that statue was a familiar one to Luther Boyd and perhaps to all professional soldiers. The general, an awesome, idealized figure astride a magnificent horse, was being escorted into heaven by a winged angel holding aloft the palm of peace. But while the general's tassled sword was sheathed, his boots were spurred to charge, and he was headed south, forever south toward Georgia.

Standing alone on the sidewalk, Luther Boyd experienced the emptiness that always beset him after battle. Even in victory there was a sense of loss, the dissolution of that inevitable but spurious fraternity generated among combat troops.

He realized then how very much he had wanted to have that drink with Lieutenant Tonnelli.

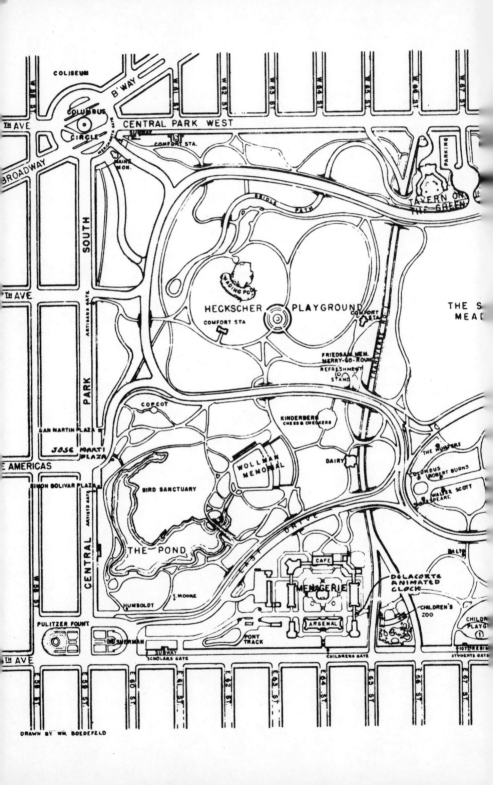